About the Author

Wendy didn't take up writing until she retired. At the age of seventy, Wendy had her first book published. She is the youngest daughter of John and Connie Moxon, and she has a strong bond with both her sisters, Valerie Owen and Carol Wood. Both her son, Spencer Gill, and daughter, Deborah Hotchkiss, encourage her to keep writing.

Photo credit: Masque Photography

HANGMAN'S REST

Wendy Gill

HANGMAN'S REST

Vanguard Press

VANGUARD PAPERBACK

© Copyright 2021
Wendy Gill

The right of Wendy Gill to be identified as author of
this work has been asserted by her in accordance with the
Copyright, Designs and Patents Act 1988.

All Rights Reserved

No reproduction, copy or transmission of this publication
may be made without written permission.
No paragraph of this publication may be reproduced,
copied or transmitted save with the written permission of the
publisher, or in accordance with the provisions
of the Copyright Act 1956 (as amended).

Any person who commits any unauthorised act in relation to
this publication may be liable to criminal
prosecution and civil claims for damages.

A CIP catalogue record for this title is
available from the British Library.

ISBN 978 1 784659 578

*Vanguard Press is an imprint of
Pegasus Elliot MacKenzie Publishers Ltd.*
www.pegasuspublishers.com

First Published in 2021

**Vanguard Press
Sheraton House Castle Park
Cambridge England**

Printed & Bound in Great Britain

Dedication

To my grandson, Scott Jones,
3rd April 1987–17th February 2020
and grandsons, Terry Sanderson, Kris Gill
and Sean Gill.

Acknowledgements

To my husband, Kevin Gill, who supports and encourages me with my writing. To my lovely friend, Elaine Millard, who always knows what to say. To Kerry Stanley and Sarah Heyes, who buy my books, and not forgetting Joan Homer, who gave me my first five star review

A PARK BENCH

Chapter One

Annie hesitated, now the moment had come, should she be doing this or should she abandon her mission? She had come this far, so she took hold of the brass door knocker and gave it three hard raps.

A gentleman in livered uniform appeared in the doorway, a quizzical expression appearing on his face at the sight of a young woman in her early twenties standing upon the doorstep.

The sound of a coach stopping behind her distracted the young woman for a few seconds, and Annie turned to see who had come to a halt behind her.

An elegantly dressed lady emerged from the coach and walked up the five steps to the front door where the young woman stood. Annie stepped aside so the lady could proceed into the house.

"After you, my dear," the elegant lady said.

Annie could think of nothing to say, so she demurely walked inside the house and waited in the hall.

"Thank you, Johnson, that will be all. I take it my son will be in the library?"

The butler nodded in agreement and left the two ladies standing in the hall.

"I presume you have come to see my son?" the elegant lady asked.

"If your son is the owner of this house, yes, I have."

"Come with me then, we shall go and see him together."

Annie was determined to achieve her goal, even though her quest was not her problem and again, she hesitated. This unexpected meeting did somewhat confuse her, but she replied, "Thank you."

The elegant lady held out her hand and said, "Sylvia Belmar."

The young woman shook hands with her. "Annie Summerfield."

"Well, Annie, I am very pleased to make your acquaintance."

Annie followed Sylvia across the hall and into the library where a gentleman in his mid-twenties was standing at the top of a set of library steps reading the titles of the books on the top shelf.

The gentleman was clad in a white, loose-fitting shirt which was open at the neck, tight fitting tan trousers, and white hose stockings.

Looking down to see who had invaded his space, his eye lighted on a very pretty face with brown hair severely tied back into a bun in the nape of her neck. Her gown was long, dark grey and woollen. She held a receptacle in one hand which was covered in a delicate black lace glove.

His eyes lingered on her for a few seconds then travelled to the lady standing next to her. "Good afternoon mother, who is your guest?"

Sylvia looked up at her son. "Good afternoon, Christopher. I met this young woman on your doorstep, I thought she was an acquaintance of yours."

"Is this another of your match making schemes?"

"No, that is why I am here. I have come to tell you I have washed my hands on finding you a suitable wife, I am fighting a losing battle. I have decided I shall not attempt to find you a wife again. I had Linda Wain crying on my shoulder after lunch, at your treatment of her."

"Good, then let that be the last young woman you throw at my feet."

"You wish to see me?" Christopher addressed Annie.

"No, sir, I do not, but needs must," Annie replied.

Silence rained for a few seconds and Christopher was conscious of his leisurely dress. "First, may I apologise for my attire, I was not expecting guests."

"The state of your dress is of no consequence to me, I have not come here for a fashion show, sir."

"That being the case, let us discuss why you have come here," Christopher said as he descended the library steps.

"That poses a problem; I promised I would not tell. I have been trying my best to come up with a solution all the way here on the mail coach."

"You have come to me with a problem you can't discuss?"

"Yes. Well not exactly. I sort of didn't promise not to tell you, for I do not know you."

Mrs Belmar, standing with her back towards the young couple was gazing out of the window with an amused smile on her lips and a mischievous glint in her eye.

"That certainly makes everything clear," Christopher confirmed.

"I do not have time for this, sir. I only have three hours in which to complete my mission for I have spent my last penny on my return coach fare and must be back at the coach station by four o'clock, so I may return home.

"If I miss the coach, I will have to spend the night on a park bench, if I can find one that is, for I do not have a penny to my name. Your house is very unsuitably situated, and it took me ages to find you.

"I was misdirected on more than one occasion and need to settle this matter directly. I do not have time for this small talk, I still have to find my way back to the pickup point of the mail coach."

"Yes, I understand the price of a coach ticket is extremely high. You should have sent me a note and I would have sent my coach to collect you. But do not concern yourself about a park bench, I am sure my mother will provide you with a bed for the night.

"Had I known that the architect that built this house was going to cause you this much trouble I would have taken him to task over it. But alas, he is dead these many years, so I think he got away with it. Don't you?"

"It is easy to put the blame on the architect, sir, but it is your house, you purchased it, so I can see no blame lands at his door. And it is also easy for you to pass the problem over to your mother by saying she will provide me with a bed for the night. I think the blame for that, also lands on your doorstep. Don't you? But have no fear, I will not impose on your mother like that. It is not your mother's problem."

"I think you will find that it is. My mother would never allow you to sleep on a park bench. I personally would have no objection. I think it would be character building."

"Do you indeed. You know nothing about my character, sir."

"Very true, but I would very much like to point out to you that if you intended to catch the four o'clock return coach you should have looked at your fob watch and kept an eye on the time. It is half an hour's ride from here to the mail sorting office, and as it is quarter to four already, and you are on foot, I fear you may have missed it."

"Do I look like someone who could afford a fob watch? Why do you think I am dressed in this drab grey gown, and have tied my hair back like this?"

"I do not know the answer to either question, but I must admit neither enhances your features."

"And that is precisely why I dressed like this, so I did not attract the unwanted attention of any libertine. If I were to sport a fob watch on my gown and wore my hair modish, it would have defeated the object."

"In that case, please feel free to glance at my mantle clock any time you choose." The gentleman nodded in the direction of the fireplace.

Standing in the middle of the mantlepiece stood a large black clock with a round white dial and two ornate black hands pointing at fifteen minutes to four.

Disbelief showed on the young woman's face and she said, "Surely that cannot be right, I haven't had my lunch yet?"

"How very remiss of me, let me order some tea."

"You have no need to do so on my account. I brought some bread and butter with me. A glass of water would be most welcome though."

"There are other people in this room besides you. I was thinking of my mother. I am sure she would welcome a cup of tea and you are more than welcome to join us."

Annie glanced across at the back of the lady standing at the window and she had the grace to blush, and Christopher found it most attractive. He was intrigued by her.

The lady turned, and with a gentle smile on her lips she said to her son, "A cup of tea would be most welcome, my dear."

Christopher stood up, went over to the fireplace and tugged at the bell pull.

The butler opened the door and tea and cake was ordered.

"Now that is out of the way, maybe you could tell me why you have come to see me."

Annie started pacing the room. "I have not come to see you, I have come because I cannot afford a baby."

"You wish me to set up a trust for your baby?"

"Don't be ridiculous, it is not my baby."

"You wish me to set up a trust for somebody else's baby?"

"I don't want you or anybody else to set up a trust. I want the father of the baby to take responsibility for it."

"And you have come to see me, for what purpose? Are you accusing me of being the father of this baby?"

"No, I am not. I have already told you; I am not here to see you."

"Then who have you come to see?"

"Howard Tallow."

"I do not believe I know the gentleman."

"But he lives here."

"I am sorry to disappoint you, but aside from my servants, I am the only occupant of this address. I think this Howard Tallow has been lying to you. I am guessing that he has been tallying with a friend of yours."

"Well, you are guessing wrong, sir. He is married to my sister."

"If he is married to your sister, surely your sister knows where he lives?"

"Yes, of course she does. She has been to reside here with him for their honeymoon."

"I have lived here for the past four years and I can assure you I have not had a newly married couple staying here, honeymoon or not."

"But this is Craven House. I asked directions, and this is where I was directed to, after more than one misdirection I might add. This is Mid-East Mould isn't it?"

"Yes, this is Mid-East Mould, but this badly situated house is called Raven House, not Craven House."

"You mean I am come to the wrong house?"

"I am afraid so."

"This is a disaster. Not only am I to sleep on a park bench tonight, I am at the wrong address. What a pickle I have gotten myself into."

Annie stood up and started pacing the floor and nearly collided with the butler who had come into the room bearing a tray with a teapot and some cups and saucers, followed closely behind by a maid holding a cake stand laden with various pastries.

"Why don't you sit down and have a cup of tea, it might calm your nerves."

"Sit down! I must go this instant."

"Would that be to find your park bench, or the wayward Howard Tallow? It would be remiss of me not to mention that the park to the rear of this house would be a much better choice than the park across the road. One or two odd characters tend to frequent that park after dark."

"You might find this amusing, sir, but I do not. All this is your fault anyway."

"I fail to see what part I have played in this. Indeed, I feel that I have been unjustly accused of more than one misdemeanour. Even the poor dead architect of this house has come under fire."

"You must have known early on in our conversation that I was mistaken in my choice of address. Indeed, our conversation went off on so many tangents that you must have thought I was mad."

"Yes, but very charming with it."

"Well, I will take my leave of you now, and please accept my apology for the intrusion."

Mrs Belmar, who was still standing at the window, turned and came forward and said, "My dear, you would be doing me a great favour if you would sit down, and I will pour us a cup of tea and you can tell us your story, so we may understand it better."

"And how is that going to do you a favour?" Annie wanted to know.

"If you were to leave here and go looking for a bench to sleep on tonight, I would never rest thinking about you. Then I would have to rouse my husband from his sleep to go and look for you.

"The park in the dead of night is not a suitable place for a young woman to sleep. If I were to read in the daily newspaper the next day that the body of a young woman had been found, and that body turned out to be yours, I would never forgive myself. Also, there is the wrath of my husband to consider, for depriving him of his slumber.

"I know it will not concern you if you are lying dead on a park bench, but I think a little consideration for the living is in order. Don't you? It would be much better for all concerned if we indulged in a cup of tea."

Annie thought about this and went and sat on the sofa and straightened her gown around her knees and waited for her tea.

"There, now we are all settled, you may begin," Sylvia said, holding out the cake stand to Annie who gratefully took a delicious-looking slice of cake.

Between bits of cake, Annie began her story. "I live in a cottage, sorry, we live in a cottage, that is my sister, Winnie, and I, on our grandfather's estate in Haverfield. This gives us a moderate amount of independence. Our grandfather also provides us both with a small allowance, so, although we don't have a lot of money to splash around, we are not penniless.

"Not that either Winnie or I are complaining, in fact just the opposite, we are very grateful for our grandfather's protection and generosity.

"Anyway, Winnie and I decided that one of us should come to town and see if we could procure a husband, then we wouldn't be such a burden on our grandfather.

"Because Winnie is by far the prettier, and the younger, of the two of us, we agreed that she should be the one to come to town. We have a friend, well really she was a friend of my mother's, who lives here in Mid-East-Mould, and we kept in touch after my mother passed away. She kindly agreed to put Winnie up for a few months and take her out and about. As it turned out, it was a very good decision. She met a young man called Howard Tallow. They connected at once and fell in love and got married, by special licence.

"My grandfather and I, and Howard's parents, were not invited to the wedding. So, my grandfather and I have not had the pleasure of meeting Howard's family, and vice versa. My grandfather took Winnie to task for doing such a thing, but she insisted it was done out of consideration for him. He asked Winnie what she meant by *'out of consideration for him',* and she said she did not want to put him to any more expense. She added that both of us are not unaware of the expense that he has already laid out for us over the years. There was nothing he could say to that, and the matter was dropped.

"All was well until about three weeks ago. Winnie and Howard came to visit my grandfather and they stayed with me in the cottage where Winnie and I had lived together. This was not ideal, for the cottage is of no great size but Winnie insisted on it. Then, after a few days, Howard wanted to go home. His father owns a tailor's shop here in Mid-East Mould, where he works. He had to get back home, as he was needed at the shop. But Winnie would not remove herself from our cottage, because she said she did not want to leave me on my own.

"I told her not to be so foolish for that was the plan in the first place, but she would not be moved. Howard soon became frustrated with her because he had to get back home, to go work. He had taken Winne to live with his parents in Craven House. This was a temporary arrangement because now they were married, Howard intended to look around for a suitable house for them to live in. Which is a good job because, reading between the lines, I think that is the main reason Winnie insists on staying in Haverfield. I don't think it suits her to be living under the same roof as her in-laws, but she will not admit it.

"Winnie told Howard she could not move away and leave me on my own and they would have to wait until I found myself a husband. Howard said there was no chance of me finding myself a husband, for at the age of two and twenty, I was too old to be of any interest to the opposite sex.

"Well, this did not go down well with Winnie, and Howard said if she wasn't going back home with him, then he was going back by himself, and so he did.

"I told Winnie that Howard was right, and she must go back with him. I intended to find myself a companion for I know of several elderly ladies that would jump at the chance, but still she would not have it.

"She said if her husband had such nasty thoughts in his head then she wanted nothing more to do with him. So, Howard came back to Mid-East Mould and Winnie stayed with me.

"She was totally miserable and unhappy, but would she follow Howard back to Mid-East Mould? No, she would not. Then, three nights ago, she dropped the bombshell. She thinks she is pregnant.

"Early this morning Winnie left home to go and visit a friend for a few days, so I took the opportunity to purchase a return ticket on the mail coach to Mid-East Mould. My intention was to try and talk Howard into coming back to Haverfield with me, and we would try and persuade Winnie to go back to Craven House with him.

"She had made me promise that if I ever saw Howard again, I was not to tell him she was with child because she said he would feel it his duty to go back to her. She did not want to force him to do something he did not want to do. He would feel sorry for her and come back to her for the wrong reason.

"Alas, I have made a complete mess of it, and now I find myself penniless, with nowhere to sleep for the night and I have not accomplished my mission. As you point out, a park bench is not the thing for a young woman to be sleeping on in a strange town. You know the rest. I feel utterly stupid and could kick myself."

"Would your grandfather not have provided you with money to undertake this venture if you had asked him?" Christopher asked.

"Of course he would, he is a wonderful old man; indeed, I do not know what Winnie and I would have done if we did not have Grandfather. He is too old now for all this upset, so I decided to try and work it out by myself and spare him the trauma, for he feels responsible for us."

"Things don't seem to be too bad, my dear. The best thing for us to do is for you to come home with me for the night, and then in the morning you and I will go and seek out Craven House together and see if we can track down Howard.

"My coming with you might help calm the situation down and then if things do not work out, you will not be on your own. I shall accompany you back home," Sylvia told Annie.

"I could not put you to such trouble, Sylvia, but thank you for the offer, I really do appreciate it."

"Not at all, my dear, think nothing of it. I shall look forward to the excitement. Life can get a bit tedious, you know, I love a damsel in distress, you are my kind of woman. I can't stand these flibbertigibbets that frequent the town these days.

"My mind is made up. Drink up your tea and I shall take you home with me. We have plenty of beds and there are no bugs in them, so that need not concern you.

"There are also bolts on the doors on the inside for you to draw across if it makes you feel safer, but there will only be Christopher's father at home besides me, so you will be quite safe."

"Have another slice of cake while you finish off your tea," Christopher told her.

Annie cast him a scathing glance but nevertheless she reached out her hand and took him up on the offer — she hadn't realised how hungry she was.

A look of satisfaction appeared on Christopher's face and delight danced in his eyes as he watched her devour the cake.

Mrs Belmar did not miss the look in her son's eyes and silently thought, *at last, things are looking up*.

Chapter Two

Inside the coach, Sylvia said to Annie, "I think it would be best if we went to call on Howard Tallow before we make our way home and see if he is in. Do you have his address?"

Annie fished in her receptacle and pulled out a piece of paper and handed it to Sylvia, who in turn, handed it to the coachman.

The coach was set in motion and not ten minutes later, Sylvia and Annie, were being shown into the drawing room at Craven House and were being greeted by Mr Tallow senior.

"Welcome to my home, Mrs Belmar, this is an unexpected visit. Please make yourselves comfortable and I will ring for tea."

"Thank you, Mr Tallow, but tea will not be necessary. Annie and I have called on the off-chance that Howard is at home. Annie would like to have a word with him."

"Annie, you say? Is this Annie Summerfield?"

"It is, sir. I am Winnie's sister. I am pleased to make your acquaintance."

"Well, my dear, this is a pleasant surprise indeed. You have a look of Winnie about you. I was just saying to Howard the other day, that it was time he took us to meet Winnie's family. I was not impressed with Howard for taking out a special licence and excluding both Winnie's family and his own from the happy occasion. However, the deed was done and there was nothing we could do about it. Winnie is a very nice young woman and we are happy to have her as a daughter-in-law.

"My wife is out of the house at the moment, but when I tell her you have called, she will be sorry to have missed you both."

"Please do not put all the blame on Howard's shoulders, Mr Tallow, my sister can be very persuasive when she wants to be. My grandfather and I were just as shocked when Winnie came home on the arm of a husband. It all happened so quickly, but I am happy to say they both seem very fond of each other. I was wondering, Mr Tallow, if I might have a word with Howard."

"I am afraid you have missed him. He set off early this morning to go down to Haverfield. I do not know when he will be back."

"Then while I was travelling from Haverfield to Mid-East Mould, Howard was travelling from Mid-East Mould to Haverfield. We must have crossed paths somewhere along the road."

"So it would seem."

"In that case, we will wish you good evening, Mr Tallow, and take up no more of your time. Sorry to have dropped in on you like this, especially as we are not acquainted, it was very kind of you to entertain us at such short notice," Sylvia said holding out her hand.

"Nonsense. Although we are not acquainted, Mrs Belmar, I have heard your name mentioned once or twice at the club. I am a member of the same club as your husband, Stephen, so I am aware of who you are and even your son, Christopher. However, I was not aware that you were acquainted with my new daughter-in-law's family."

"I am not acquainted with the family, Mr Tallow. This was a chance meeting."

Mr Tallow turned to Annie and said, "Although your sister and my son's wedding that took place, caught my wife and I on the hop, it is not an unwelcome alliance. Your grandfather was my old colonel in the army, and what a jolly fine chap he is. He will not know me from his army days for I was a lowly foot soldier, but I saw your grandfather around the camp on more than one occasion.

"You must be very proud of him. You and your grandfather are welcome to call any time you wish, Annie. That invitation extends to you and your husband too, Mrs Belmar, and your son, goodness me, I had better not leave him out."

"Thank you, Mr Tallow, it is nice to meet you too. And I can speak for my grandfather, as well as myself, and extend the invitation to you and your wife and say you would both be made welcome were you to appear on our doorstep." Annie held out her hand to him before they returned to the coach and proceeded on their way.

"What would be the most convenient time for us to leave for Haverfield in the morning? The earlier the better, goodness knows what will be happening there because I did not tell my grandfather I was coming here today. I thought I would be able to get away without anyone knowing that I had come to Mid-East Mould, but I guess that was too much to ask for.

"Not only that, Winnie has gone to stay with a friend for a few days, so there will be no one at home when Howard arrives at the cottage. The first thing he is bound to do is go and see Grandfather who knows nothing about this, he is going to be worried sick."

"That being the case, you and I will travel back to Haverfield this very moment and put your grandfather's mind at rest. What are the directions for the coachman?"

"Fargate Fold, Haverfield," Annie informed her.

These instructions were relayed to the coachman and Annie sat back and watched the town becoming less and less inhabited as the coach left the town behind and set off across country.

Annie asked, once they were clear of the town, "What about your husband, won't he be concerned when you do not return home?"

"Stephen is used to me changing my mind at the last moment. He is aware that I am with Gregory our coachman. He knows Gregory will not let any harm come to me. We will be quite safe, have no fear."

"I was not afraid for myself, Sylvia, I was only thinking of you. It is very kind of you to do this for a stranger, most kind."

"If we women can't help each other out at times like these then there is not much hope for people like you and me. Believe it or not, I too was left on my own at the age of sixteen. I had to throw myself on my mother's brother who took me in. My uncle's wife was not as enthusiastic as he was and so I became an unpaid servant.

"I was left with no money, only the clothes I stood up in and life became very hard for me. I was terribly unhappy and when my uncle's daughter, Letty, became of age, she was sent to town, to come out as they call it. In this year of 1820, a young woman must have a chaperone, or they will lose their reputation.

"Instead of paying for a chaperone for Letty, I was called upon to do the task. I was only one and twenty and Letty, being a spoilt brat, ran rings round me. Free from the restraints of her mother's eye, Letty became wild.

"She would sneak out of her bedroom while I was asleep and go on clandestine meetings with young men behind my back. The mamma of one of the young men found out about it, and a message was sent to my aunt.

"My aunt descended upon us unexpectedly and of course she cast me out. I was left penniless and homeless in a town I did not know. I had a carpet bag with me but there were meagre belongings in it, but they were all I had in the world.

"I was wandering aimlessly along one of the streets when a horse drawn coach came around the corner and caught my carpet bag and sent me to the ground.

"The driver of the coach came to pick me up and he took me to his home until I recovered. When he found out I was destined for a park bench for the night, he took me to his sister's house.

"The man that knocked me to the ground, was called Stephen Belmar, and he is now my husband. Luckily for me, his sister needed a nanny for her two children, so I went to work for her and ended up adoring both her and the two children. Sheila, for that is the name of Stephen's sister, was over the moon at becoming my sister-in-law.

"I have never looked back; Stephen and I have been extremely happy over the past thirty years. So, had it not been for that chance encounter with the coach, I might easily have ended up on a park bench, or even worse, if all the benches were taken. Your story reminded me of my dire straits and I am determined to aid you all I can, or at least make sure you arrive home safely."

"I know I said I was penniless, Sylvia, but my grandfather would have given me some money had I asked for it. We have been very lucky, Winnie and I. Our grandfather loves us and treats us well. It was our choice to live at the cottage. It gave my grandfather space as well as us.

"I know my grandfather will give you any money that you have spent on my behalf, in fact he will insist on it. He is a very proud and honest man."

"If there is one thing I have learnt over the years it is to let the men sort the money out. They provide the money, we women organise it, even if they do not realise it. Best to leave it to them to sort out, that way they think they oversee it, and we will just spend it." Sylvia sent Annie a wicked smile that lit up her eyes.

Annie responded by laughing out loud and settled back to enjoy her trip. The return journey was going to be much more pleasant than the outward journey on the crowded mail coach.

An hour later the coach came to a halt and Gregory appeared at the coach window.

"The light is beginning to fade, Mrs Belmar, and we still have a fair way to go. There is an inn further up the road; I think it would be best if we put up there for the night."

"Very well, Gregory, if you think it best. We shall stop at the inn tonight. I am sure Annie is ready for bed, it must have been a long day for her."

"It has indeed, a nice soft bed sounds very tempting," Annie had to agree.

Chapter Three

Christopher ran up the steps and into his parents' house. He found his father in the library, pouring himself a glass of port.

"Just in time to join me," Mr Belmar told his son.

"Thank you, father, I won't say no."

Christopher watched as his father poured a second glass of port. "What did you think of Annie?"

Mr Belmar paused in his pouring and glanced up at his son. "Annie, I do not believe I know anyone of that name."

"The young woman my mother brought home."

"I have not seen your mother this afternoon. I believe she went to call on Lady Costaby. You know what happens when those two get together."

"Yes, but she called at my house after she had called on Lady Costaby and brought a young woman in with her. She said she had found her on my doorstep."

"Is this another one of your mother's matchmaking schemes?"

"No, those were my very own thoughts when I saw my mother enter the library with Annie on her heels. But Annie found her own way onto my doorstep, she had come to the wrong address. Needless to say, it was my mother who found her."

"That does not surprise me, but as far as I know, your mother has not returned. If she had done so, and bringing a young woman with her too, I would have thought she would have brought her to the library, to introduce her to me."

"But they left my house over two hours ago and they were coming here. Mother had offered to provide Annie with a bed for the night."

"Had she indeed? The young woman must have been in a plight then?" It was a question rather than a statement.

"Yes, she was. It was either a bed here for the night, or a bench in the park."

Mr Belmar looked over at his son and saw the mischief dancing in his eyes. "A park bench was it. That would have done the trick."

"Are you telling me they have not arrived home yet?"

"So, it would seem. I have not seen them if they have."

"Where do you think they have gone?"

"What was the young woman's problem?"

"Annie has a sister who has recently married and has had a fall out with her new husband, so Annie has come to town to try and sort it out."

"And this disagreement could only be sorted out by Annie? Surely it should have been the sister's problem, not Annie's."

"Yes, in a way. Apparently, the husband has said to the sister that, because of Annie's age, she would never get herself a husband, and this stemmed the split."

"And that is the reason why Annie has become involved in this farce. Because he said she would not get a husband because of her age?"

A wicked grin spread across his son's face and he said, "No, the reason Annie became involved in this matter is because she cannot afford a baby."

Mr Belmar looked at his son over the top of his glasses and asked, "What was it about this young woman that caught your eye? What makes Annie different from all the other young women you have met, and cast aside? Lord knows there has been plenty of them, indeed I think your mother has run out of young women to introduce you to. Was it her dress, her poise or her pretty face?"

"There was more than one thing that held my attention. Although she has a pretty face, it was not best displayed. She wore no makeup and her hair was tied severely back. Her dress was of a drab grey and as for her poise she showed no sign of self-confidence. In fact, she went as far as to tell me she was dressed as she was to avoid the unwanted attention from any libertines."

"Well, she certainly got the address wrong for more than one reason." Mr Belmar looked pointedly at his son.

Christopher laughed and continued, "As a matter of fact, it was her air of innocence and the mischief in her eyes that attracted me to her. Our conversation was highly amusing and also intriguing. I had no idea what she was talking about, but it all became clear in the end. Most of all, she reminded me of my mother."

"If that is the case, heaven help us. We have enough on or hands with the scrapes your mother gets into without a stranger encouraging her as well."

"I know you would not change a hair on my mother's head."

"No, I would not. You had better go and find them, heaven knows what they will be up to."

"Aren't you going to come with me?"

"No, I am going to enjoy my port. It is now your turn to have a taste of what my life has been since meeting your mother. The only thing I would say to you is take some money with you. Your mother seems to run up the bills."

"But where am I to start looking, if they have not come home, where can they have gone?"

"Where does Annie's sister's husband live?"

"Craven House, Mid-East Mould."

"Keith Tallow's son is it?"

"It is. Do you know him?"

"I know the father slightly, not the son. Keith Tallow is a member of my club, but we run with a different pack. We are not close friends. I had heard that his son had married old Colonel Summerfield's granddaughter. A bit of a rush job by all accounts."

"Yes, Annie is Colonel Summerfield's granddaughter."

"How interesting."

"Do you know the colonel?"

"No, but I know he has a good reputation. Brilliant army career, very well respected."

"You think I should call at Craven House first?"

"It's as good a place as any to start."

"In that case, Father, I will bid you good evening."

Christopher drank the last of his port and headed back home to pack an overnight bag and get his horse.

Mr Belmar also finished off his port, looked at his empty glass and decided to have a refill. A satisfied smile on his face, at last a member of the opposite sex had caught his son's eye, and his wife must have taken a liking to her too, otherwise she would not be off gallivanting again.

His armchair beckoned and it wasn't long before his glass of port was empty and his newspaper at his feet on the floor. His head resting on the wing of his armchair and slumber enveloping him.

Christopher mounted his horse and made his way across town in his mother's footsteps and waited until the butler opened the door of Craven House. It wasn't long before he too was shaking hands with Mr Tallow.

"My goodness me, I seem to be in demand this evening," Mr Tallow said as they were shaking hands.

"So, my mother has been here earlier today?"

"She has indeed. She had the sister of my son's wife with her, they were seeking Howard, but he had already left for Haverfield. They did not stay long but I got the impression that they too were heading for Haverfield, for that is the direction their coach was taking. Your parent's home lies in the opposite direction."

"That is all I came to find out, sir. Thank you for the information. Now, if you don't mind, I would appreciate it if you could provide me with Colonel Summerfield's address, then I will be on my way as the light is about to fade." Mr Tallow wrote down the address, Christopher held out his hand to Mr Tallow once more, and he was soon heading for open countryside and Haverfield.

After two hours riding, Christopher saw what he took to be a wayside inn so, as the night was closing in fast, he decided that, as he was not sure of his destination, it would be better found in daylight. He decided to put up at the inn for the night.

Gregory pulled up in front of the inn with the not so welcoming name of Hangman's Rest. He opened the coach door and helped Mrs Belmar and Annie alight and told them to go inside and he would join them shortly, after he had handed over the coach and horses to the ostler.

Gregory decided to proceed with caution, it was his understanding that no matter what time of day or night it was, when a coach pulled up at a resting place, an ostler would appear and take charge of the horses. This had not happened, and the wayside inn was in the middle of nowhere with no neighbouring dwellings of any kind.

He knocked on the stable door but got no reply. He cautiously opened the door and waited outside to see if anybody came to the door. They did not, so he decided to continue inside.

His caution was not good enough. After two steps inside the dark stable he felt a blow to the back of his head and he fell to the floor.

The culprit looked down at Gregory then proceeded to pull his victim towards the stalls where he set about making Gregory fast to one of the stalls dividing posts by his wrists, then binding his ankles together. Satisfied that Gregory was safely trussed up, he glanced back towards the silhouettes of the two guards, standing to attention at the windows on either side of the stable door. He nodded his head, pleased with his handy work. Then he turned and left the stable, closing the stable door behind him. He proceeded across the courtyard, and made his way to the rear of the inn and disappeared inside.

Mrs Belmar and Annie entered the inn and found nothing but stale air and silence. There were a few round wooden tables with chairs and four tatty looking armchairs scattered around, but no sign of life. Striding over to a bench at the top of the room, Mrs Belmar found a bell and brought her hand down on it four times. Mrs Belmar presumed this was where the ale was dispensed from. The noise echoed around the inn and when it died down, the silence continued but no one came in answer to the bell chimes.

"This is most unusual, Annie, I think we had better wait for Gregory to return and see what he makes of it." Mrs Belmar looked across at Annie.

"Why don't we go and have a look in the back of the inn, somebody might be in the kitchen and they have not heard us arrive."

"If they did not hear this bell, then they must all be as deaf as a post."

Annie looked across at Mrs Belmar and amusement danced in her eyes.

The first noise they heard came from the top of the stairs that ran from the room they stood in, which they took to be the snug, up to the first floor landing.

Both ladies turned to their right and looked up. They found themselves looking at an elegantly dressed gentleman of around twenty-five years of age. His topcoat fitted him like a second skin, his white cravat boasted the biggest ruby Annie had ever set eyes on, and his top boots were polished to such a high sheen, you could have seen your face in them.

"Good evening, ladies, I am afraid it is of no use ringing the bell, for the innkeeper and his wife are indisposed right now. Would you please come with me?"

"I have no intention of going anywhere with you, and why is the innkeeper indisposed?" Mrs Belmar asked.

"It was not a request; it was an order. It would be wise for you and your companion to come upstairs and follow me."

"We will do no such thing, and Annie is not my companion, she is my friend."

The gentleman standing on the landing fell silent for a few seconds and studied the ladies. "I have to insist on your co-operation either by consent, or, I am afraid, brute force. It will be less distressing for you both if you were to come upstairs and follow me."

"Brute force. If you lay a finger on either Annie or myself, I would not like to be in your shoes."

"It is unfortunate, for I like a woman with spirit and I hate to put you to any distress, but I am afraid I have no choice in the matter. If you would please come this way, I can assure you that neither of you will be harmed."

"And how do you intend to make us comply with your order, sir?"

The gentleman at the top of the stairs nodded in the direction of the door behind them and, turning, Mrs Belmar and Annie saw three more well-dressed gentlemen standing behind them.

Without a word Mrs Belmar took hold of Annie's hand and they headed up the wooden staircase and the sound of creaking wood echoed around the inn.

Before the two ladies had reached the top of the stairs the gentleman turned and walked along the landing and Mrs Belmar and Annie followed.

At the head of the landing the gentleman opened a door and indicated with his head that they should enter.

Both ladies walked straight passed the gentleman and he closed the door behind them. They heard a key being turned. They were locked in.

The room they had entered was in darkness and the only light that caught their eye was a tiny gap in the curtains that gave off a faint glow of the moon shining through.

Annie walked gingerly across the room and pulled back the curtains and the room filled with moonlight. Although not lit up for easy viewing, there was light enough to make out four other occupants in the room.

There was a portly gentleman of undefinable years and a small thin woman around the same age sitting next to him on hardbacked chairs, and she was clutching his hand.

Sitting in an armchair was a young woman around the same age as Annie, and next to her, also in an armchair, was a young man who was also around Annie's age.

"What on earth is going on?" asked Mrs Belmar.

"Please keep your voice down. We have been told that if we keep quiet and cause no trouble we will not be harmed," instructed the elderly man.

"But why?" Annie wanted to know.

"We have no idea," the elderly gentleman whispered back. "I am the innkeeper, and this is my wife. Arthur and Meg Conway. This young woman and gentleman are two guests who are booked in for the night, Mr Sherman and Miss Inksome. We were unexpectedly descended upon by six men.

"They rounded us all up and we were placed in here, in this bedroom, and told to keep quiet and nothing would befall us. I saw they were carrying pistols, all of them, and so here we are, no point in getting anyone killed. Please don't make a fuss or a disturbance, I don't want anything to happen to my wife or our guests.

"So far they have left us alone and we were told that by this time tomorrow they will be on their way and nothing will be stolen or broken. If anything does get broken it will be paid for. The gentleman that let you in here told us that we will be paid for the use of the inn when they leave. None of us know what is going on or what to make of it."

"And neither of you two can give an explanation?" Annie asked the two younger guests.

"No," replied the young man. "I am travelling around the country hoping to find myself a wife. There are no young women living in the little village where I come from and my father says it is about time, I got married so he has sent me off to find a wife."

"N-no," stammered the young woman. "I am, o-on my way to visit an old aunt, s-she is very ill and wants t-to see me. She l-lives some five miles from h-here in a country town called Haverfield."

"I know Haverfield very well, I live on the edge of Haverfield. What is your aunt's name?" Annie wanted to know.

"Miss Jane Inksome," Annie was told.

"Now this is strange because we live next door to Miss Inksome, but we don't know very much about her, apart from knowing she is very old. She does not take very kindly to visitors of any kind. I thought she had a companion living with her who looked after her," the assembled company heard Annie say.

"Yes, she d-did, but my aunt wrote a l-letter to my father, telling him that her c-companion had left her and that she was ill a-and in need of somebody to look after her. Because we do not h-have a lot of money and I have two younger sisters, my f-father said because I s-stammer, I was unlikely to f-find myself a husband. It was decided t-that I should come and be Aunt Jane's companion. I am not looking f-forward to it."

"Well, if we don't find a way out of this predicament, none of us will be going to do what we set out to do this morning," Mrs Belmar said.

"I wonder where Gregory is?" Annie asked.

"I don't know, but something must have happened to him because he should have been knocking on the inn door by now," Mrs Belmar remarked.

"Have you no other staff working here? Where was your ostler when we arrived at the inn?" Annie wanted to know.

"There is only Meg and me. This place is very isolated and we rely on passing trade to make a living. Some days we see nobody, then we get three or four passers-by in one day. To help keep expenses down, I see to the vehicles and horses while Meg sorts out the rooms. It is the only way we can make a living out of the inn," Arthur told her.

"How long have you been held prisoner?" Annie asked the innkeeper.

"Only from tea time today. Meg and I were in the kitchen getting a bit to eat ready for these two guests. As I have already told you, half a dozen young men bearing pistols walked into the inn. We were told that no harm would come to us if we did as they said.

"Meg and I are too old now to be putting up any resistance to a gang of young men with pistols, so we did as we were told. Then Mr Sherman was shown in here and, not long after, Miss Inksome."

"Well, I for one will not tolerate this treatment, I am going to try and find out what it's all about." Annie went and banged on the bedroom door.

After a couple of minutes had passed and no response to her knocking, Annie tried again.

"Do you think it is wise to be upsetting someone who is holding a pistol?" Mr Sherman asked.

"You may be willing to sit and do nothing, sir, but I am not. I intend to find out what is going on. If I am to be held prisoner, then I want to know why."

At Annie's third attempt to get someone's attention, the door to the bedroom was unlocked and the gentleman that had locked them in earlier, stood in the doorway.

"Why are we being kept locked in this room? I demand an explanation," Mrs Belmar jumped in before Annie could respond.

"As I have already told you, if you all keep quiet and stay here until noon tomorrow, then no harm will come to any of you. Causing trouble and making a noise is not advisable. I cannot tell you why you are being kept here but it is for your own safety," the gentleman said.

"You mean we are all to be kept in this one room all night?" Annie asked.

"If any of you need to relieve yourself, two knocks on the door will bring one of my men, and they will escort you to a room across the landing, but then you will have to come back here. Is that understood?"

"Perfectly understood, young man. May we at least know your name?" asked Mrs Belmar.

"No, you may not. You will all be released around noon tomorrow, that is all you need to know. That is all I am prepared to tell you."

"If we are all to sleep in this room overnight then the least you can do is provide us with better sleeping arrangements. As you can see, the innkeeper and his wife are not as young as they used to be. A bit of consideration for our comfort would be in order if you want us to comply with your demands, don't you think?" Annie asked the gentleman.

"I will see what I can do," was all the gentleman said before closing the door and locking them in once again.

"I-I think you are both v-very brave to be talking to that man like that," Miss Inksome said.

"I am too annoyed at finding myself in this predicament to give any thought to my safety. How dare they lock us up like this. But having said that, I, personally, did not find the gentleman threatening." Annie began to pace the floor. "Are there no candles to light the room with, are we going to have to spend the rest of the evening in this semi darkness?" Annie asked.

"If you look on the top shelf in the wardrobe you will find a box containing candles," the innkeeper's wife replied.

Annie made her way over to the wardrobe and, stretching up, she felt for a box and it was soon found. Two candles were taken out of the box and lit, and it made the room feel more welcoming. "That's better," Annie said.

"I agree with you, Annie, I did not find the gentleman threatening either. After all they have not laid a finger on any of us. We are going to have to make the best of it for tonight and see what tomorrow brings," Mrs Belmar said.

Not long after this, the key turning in the door was heard and four young men entered the room. They were in pairs, each pair carrying a put-me-up bed with two straw mattresses on each bed. They placed them on the floor without uttering a word then exited the bedroom, and the familiar sound of a key turning was heard by the occupants of that room.

A few minutes later the turning of the key was heard again and a pile of woollen blankets were tossed on the floor. The key was turned and the door locked.

"At least we will have a modicum of comfort during the night. Thanks to you, Miss," Mr Sherman remarked.

"My name is Annie Summerfield, and this is Sylvia Belmar. If we are to spend the night together at least we should know each other's names."

Mr Sherman held out his hand to Annie. "Alan Sherman."

Miss Inksome gave a small curtsey and said, "Freda Inksome."

"Arthur and Meg Conway, innkeepers of the Hangman's Rest."

"Right, let's see what has been brought for us to lay our heads on tonight, shall we?" Mrs Belmar jumped off the bed and went over to the put-me-up beds.

Alan and Annie joined her and they each pulled one of the spare straw mattresses off the two put-me-ups and placed them on the floor.

"Two put-me-ups, two spare straw mattresses and the double bed. I think Arthur and Meg should have the bed for the night, Annie and Mrs Belmar the put-me-ups, and Freda and I will sleep on the straw mattresses on the floor," Alan suggested.

"No, please, you are guests in our inn, Meg and I will sleep on the floor, two of the ladies must have the double bed," Arthur insisted.

"I think Alan had it right first time, Arthur, you and your wife must have the bed. Meg looks as though she could do with a lay down. You will be doing us a favour by having the double bed, for there are three other women in this room and we will only be fighting between us as to the sleeping arrangements. It is just a question of who is to sleep on the mattresses on the floor," Annie insisted.

"I-I think you and Mrs B-Belmar must have the put-me-ups b-because if it hadn't been for you speaking up, we would have had to sleep in the armchairs, and Mr and Mrs Conway would have had to sit on these hardbacked c-chairs all night," stammered Freda.

"Well said, Freda. That is settled then. We might as well make the best of it for we are destined to be here all night," Alan went over to the pile of woollen blankets thrown on the floor by one of the guards and shared the blankets out between the two put-me-ups, and the two straw mattresses.

All the occupants in the room took to their beds for the night and spread the blankets over themselves and it was not very long before they were all sound asleep.

Gregory opened his eyes to find himself bound at the wrists and ankles and the ropes securing his wrists were tied to a dividing post that separated one stall from another. The throb in his head made it momentarily the only thing that mattered, that and the dizziness that engulfed him.

After a few minutes the dizziness subsided, and he glanced around. At first, he could see nothing out of the ordinary, then he spotted the silhouette of a man, standing at an opening to the side of the stable door. The opening was obviously meant to be a window. Gregory looked at the other side of the door and, sure enough, standing at a second window, stood a second man. Both sporting rifles, and these rifles were pointing out into the courtyard.

Gregory thought it best to close his eyes and pretend to still be unconscious, he might find out what was going on before he let his captors know he was awake. At the moment he was in no condition to play the hero. The light was not good inside the stable, so he decided to rest awhile until daylight appeared and hoped some light would enter the stable through the windows. He needed more light to be able to see the situation better. Gregory felt himself drifting back into oblivion.

Christopher woke and stretched after a good night's sleep. Yesterday had been a long day and the inn had been a welcome sight in the fast fading light.

Breakfast was served in a private room and he seemed to be the only guest in the inn. While the innkeeper's wife was placing some tasty looking rashers of bacon on the plate in front of him, Christopher asked, "How far am I from Haverfield?"

"Haverfield, sir? You have taken the wrong road; you should have gone straight on at the crossroads. Haverfield lies some ten miles west of the crossroad, you are now heading south," the innkeeper's wife told him.

"I must have gone wrong in the dark, I can't remember seeing any crossroads."

"You will have to turn right once outside the inn courtyard and carry on straight ahead until you come to the crossroads. Make a left turn and follow that road for about ten miles and you will come to Haverfield."

"Thank you, I will do that. How far is it back to the crossroads?"

"About a mile. It will not take you long to reach them."

After Christopher had eaten his fill, the innkeeper's wife told him that his horse had been saddled and had been brought round to the front of the inn for him. He paid her for his night's lodging then went outside and mounted his horse. He was soon heading back to the crossroads where he took a left turn and back on the right road for Haverfield.

He passed another wayside inn called Hangman's Rest, and only glanced in its direction and carried on, eager to reach his destination. An hour later Christopher was knocking on the door of Fargate Fold and he waited until the door was opened and he was shown into a library.

"Christopher Belmar at your service, sir. I apologise for the intrusion, but I am looking for my mother," Christopher told the gentleman seated at a desk, as he walked across the carpet holding his hand out.

Standing up and crossing the room to meet his unexpected guest, the gentleman held out his hand and the two shook hands. "Colonel Summerfield's the name. I know I had a bit of a reputation with the ladies in my younger days, but it is some years since I have had a young whippersnapper on my heels. What makes you think I have your mother here?"

Cristopher's smile reached his eyes and he said, "I last saw her in the company of your granddaughter, Annie."

"Oh, in that case, you will know Annie's story, but knowing Annie as I do, they could be in China by now. I have not seen Annie for a couple of days and it is no use going down to the cottage where she lives, because she is not there. Winnie, her sister had been intending to be away for a couple of days, but she decided against it and came back home. When she arrived back at the cottage where she lived with Annie, Annie was nowhere to be seen.

"Winnie came over to see me and told me all. I am assuming you know Winnie's story, the whole of it?"

"I do, sir, Annie told it to my mother and me."

"Good, then I have no need to repeat it. I told Winnie that she was being stupid and childish, and she had to go straight back to her husband and apologise to him. The poor lad must work. What was she thinking about?

"Howard didn't give Winnie the chance to go back to Mid-East Mould, for he came down yesterday to whisk her off. Thank goodness Winnie had come to her senses and she agreed to go back to Mid-East Mould with Howard. There was no sign of Annie when I went to see them off earlier this morning."

"Then they must have stopped off somewhere between the crossroads at Wigstyle and here. They did not reside at the same inn as I did, but that is because I lost my way in the dark and took the wrong road. I had to retrace my steps this morning, back to the crossroads but it was only a matter of a mile and then I was back on the right road.

"The only other inn I passed on my way here was called Hangman's Rest, so I am betting that is where they put up for the night."

After this information was passed on to the colonel, there was silence in the room and Christopher felt uncomfortable and could find nothing more to say.

What the colonel said next, was the last thing that Christopher expected to hear. "Can you use a rifle?"

"A rifle! Why on earth would I need to use a rifle? My mother might be a bit eccentric, sir, but she is not dangerous."

Colonel Summerfield did not reply. He walked over to his desk situated in a deep bay window and fumbled in the top drawer. He found what he was looking for and headed back across the room to a cabinet standing in a recess to the right of the door.

Christopher watched as the colonel unlocked the door to the cabinet and he was amazed to see an armoury of rifles and pistols.

Colonel Summerfield threw a rifle to Christopher who caught it deftly, and then he caught a box of ammunition that was also thrown his way. The colonel hesitated, then threw a second box of ammunition over to Christopher and said, "Better take two boxes, we don't know what we will find when we get there."

"Forgive me, sir, if I appear rather slow on the uptake, but we need these rifles and ammunition for what purpose?"

"You said it yourself, the Hangman's Rest is the only place where your mother and Annie could have put up for the night. Most unsatisfactory."

"I am still at a loss as to why we should need these firearms, sir."

"Well, you will just have to trust me, young man."

"I had a similar experience with your granddaughter, Colonel. I could not follow her conversation either. It must be a family trait."

"Did your conversation with my granddaughter come to a satisfactory conclusion?"

"Eventually the plot became clear, yes."

"Then you will have to wait for a satisfactory solution to this conversation, we have no time to lose." After glancing at the clock on the mantlepiece, Colonel Summerfield went over to the fireplace and tugged the bell pull.

When the library door was opened the colonel said to his old retainer, "Penville, have this young man's horse taken down to the stable and saddle him a fresh horse and bring it to the front door along with a horse for me. As quick as you can."

"Very good, Colonel," the old retainer replied as he closed the door.

"We must make haste if we want to be at the Hangman's Rest before midday, so you will need a fresh horse. You will have to come back here and change the horses back over of course. I do not know what kind of stock you keep in your stable, but mine are the finest, made for speed and not afraid of loud noises."

"Why have we to be at the Hangman's Rest before midday?"

"Don't be insubordinate, boy, orders are orders, so pick up your rifle and stow your ammunition safely in your pockets, just in case we get separated. Time to go."

Chapter Four

Night had turned into day and Gregory had not had anything to eat or drink since lunchtime yesterday. But his raging thirst overrode his hunger.

He half opened his eyes and peered through the slit. Daylight was now visible through the windows over the guard's shoulders and he could see that nothing had changed. There were only the guards and himself inside the stable. He cast his eye around the floor where he was sitting. He saw nothing but straw. He slowly moved his head back for he did not want to make any sudden movement that would alert the two guards standing at the windows, that he was now conscious.

He saw, about a foot above his head, a knife that had obviously seen better days, thrust into the post to which he was tied. If only he could reach it without his captors seeing him do so, he might have a chance of cutting the restraints.

Gregory very slowly pulled his feet up towards his body. His eyes were still barely open but neither of the guards turned to look at him. When his feet were practically under his body, Gregory took hold of the post with both hands and took a deep breath.

'Easy now,' he told himself. *'Don't rush it, gently does it.'*

Hesitating for a few seconds, Gregory pulled himself up by his hands and then took his weight on his bent legs. His hands let go of the post and, as luck would have it, the rope restraining his hands was loose enough for him to inch his hands up the post until he could reach and grip the knife handle, and pull it out of the wood.

This was achieved, but then he had to think how to take hold of the post again, so he could slowly lower himself back onto the floor. He bent his head forward and took the knife in his mouth, then he was able to grab the post with both hands and he was thankful to take the weight off his bent legs.

Once back on the ground, the knife still in his mouth, he pushed the blade down his sleeve as best he could, then he removed the knife from his mouth and left just a hint of the handle poking out of the top of his cuff. *'So far, so good,'* he thought.

No movement came from the two guards stood looking out of the windows. No conversation between them either, so Gregory still had no idea what was going on. Neither of the guards turned to look at Gregory to see if he was dead or alive.

The decision was made, Gregory decided he was going to attempt his escape. He slowly bent his head towards his wrists and taking hold of the knife handle in his mouth once again, he slowly pulled the knife out of his sleeve. He managed to transfer the knife into his right hand and with difficulty, he twisted the blade towards the rope and he began to slowly move the knife up and down.

It was slow going, the blade was very blunt, but he continued to make progress until he felt his bonds slacken. He gently forced his hands outwards until he felt the last of the strands of rope give way.

He sat very still for a few moments but neither of the guards moved or turned in his direction. He decided to continue to make good his escape, so he leaned forward and began to untie the ropes that bound his ankles.

He was now free but he had no idea what time of day it was, or how long he had been unconscious. He only knew he had to escape and go in search of Mrs Belmar and her young companion. If anything had befallen either of them, he would not be able to forgive himself. Gregory thought of his next move. There were two guards and both were holding rifles. Chances were, if he overpowered one, the other would have time to get a shot off at him.

His throat was sore and dry from a lack of fluid, he needed a drink. He decided to jump the guard to his left for he was the nearest to him. Once he had captured him, he would put his body between him and the other guard. If the other guard did fire his rifle at him, with a bit of luck the bullet would hit his friend and not him.

Very slowly Gregory rose from the floor and stood still. No movement from either of his captors. Gregory went in for the kill. He rushed forward and grabbed the guard around the waist, at the same time pushing his opponent into the stable wall with his left shoulder. They both collapsed onto the floor.

To Gregory's amazement, the guard disintegrated and he discovered that it was not a guard at all, just gentlemen's clothing stuffed with straw. He looked across at the other guard, and that face was also made of straw.

"What on earth is going on?" Gregory said out loud. He grabbed a tin mug which hung on to the side of one of the stalls and, going over to a trough, he filled the mug with water and greedily drank the contents. Then he repeated the process and, for now, his thirst was quenched.

To the left of the trough was a net bag hanging from a nail and inside the bag were carrots, obviously food for the horses. *'If the carrots are good enough for the horses, they are good enough for me,'* thought Gregory and he plunged his hand into the bag and grabbed a carrot and started munching away.

The colonel and Christopher made good time and when they were approaching the Hangman's Rest, the colonel turned off to his right and headed for some trees that spread out along the back of the courtyard to the rear of the inn.

"Why have we come in here?" Christopher wanted to know when they had dismounted their horses and went to stand at the edge of the wood.

"We need to get the lie of the land before we go charging in," was the reply.

"Just what is going on here, Colonel?"

"I don't suppose you will stop asking the same question until I tell you. If I do tell you we might be able to work together without you continuously asking questions. I had a couple of government men call at my house three days ago and they told me that there was going to be a gold shipment being taken from Gamster to Rudding Town. The people that will be transporting it are the army and a changeover of guards is to take place here at the Hangman's Rest. It should all be over by noon today.

"They wanted me to keep my ear to the ground and if I heard a whiff of any shenanigans going off, would I let them know. Of course, I said yes, I would, but I have heard nothing. I called at the inn on the other side of my estate because it is the one I frequent most. It is also on the route that the gold shipment is going to take so I thought if anything was going to happen, that might be a good place to attack, the last inn on the way to the Hangman's Rest. There was no mention of a gold shipment, so I thought all was well.

"Then you turn up and tell me my granddaughter has gone missing. It must be something to do with this gold shipment, can't be anything else. She must be mixed up in this somehow. She is not a very restful young woman that granddaughter of mine. She falls into one scrape after another."

"I found your granddaughter very entertaining, Colonel Summerfield."

The colonel looked across at his young companion and said, "So that's the way the land lies, is it? I tell you about a government gold shipment taking place and we could have put ourselves at risk, and all you can find to say is that you find my granddaughter very entertaining. Oh, what it is to be young. You had better not dally with my granddaughter, young man, or you will have me to deal with."

"On the contrary, Colonel, I have not held any other young woman in so high a regard as I do Annie. My intentions are honourable. I think if anyone is to get hurt, it is going to be me. She finds my house very ill situated. I have only met her the once, and I have to admit she seems to have imprinted herself in my head and I am damned if I can shift her."

"In that case, young man, you are a lost cause. Might as well give in and let the girl have her way, for if you do not, you will never have a moments peace. I know, it happened to me. My wife died some ten years ago, and she is still here," said the colonel tapping his head, "and I am damned if I can shift her."

The colonel continued, "Enough about Annie, let's get down to the business in hand now you know what it's all about." Going over to his tethered horse, the colonel put his hand in a carpet bag he had fastened to his saddle and came back with a pair of binoculars. "Here, see if you can see anything through these, your eyes are younger than mine."

Christopher held the binoculars to his eyes and looked towards the inn. Their position in the wood was facing the side of the inn. There were no windows for him to spy through. So he turned his attention to the stable.

Just at that moment the stable door opened slowly, and the familiar face of Gregory peeked out. Handing the binoculars back to the colonel, Christopher put two fingers in his mouth and gave two high pitched whistles.

Gregory's head shot back inside the stable and the door closed. Three sharp whistles were heard by Christopher and the colonel. The colonel's eyebrows rose in a silent question when he looked across at Christopher.

"That is the all clear from Gregory, it must be safe for us to run across to the stable."

"And how do you know this?"

"He is my father's coachman; he has been for as long as I can remember. They are the best of friends as well, and Gregory was my friend and playmate whilst I was growing up. I had no brothers or sisters to play with so Gregory was a substitute. He taught me to fish, he is a brilliant fisherman.

"This is a game I used to play with Gregory when I was growing up. I would hide, and he would go into the wood or into one of the rooms at home and, if the coast was clear, he would give three short whistles. If there was anyone around it would be just the one whistle. My whistle was always two short blasts to let him know I was about. Just a game we played."

"Lucky for us. He is trustworthy?"

"I would trust him with my life, Colonel. Not only me, but my father trusts him to look after my mother's life too. I think the best thing for us to do is run over to the stable and hope no one sees us."

"I will be eighty on the ninth of August, my running days are over. That is why I keep my horses; they do the running for me. You run over and find out what is going on and come back and let me know."

"I don't think that is a very good idea, Colonel. We need to stay together. If I start running backwards and forwards between the stable and the wood, I would be spotted. If there is funny business going on at this inn, then there are bound to be lookouts. I don't want to take a risk on being seen when my mother's life could be at stake, and your granddaughter's too, of course. We will walk across to the stable together and hope we are not detected."

"Very well, no point in putting it off," said the colonel and started for the stable with Christopher at his side.

As they approached the door, they saw it open slightly, and the colonel squeezed through followed by Christopher.

Gregory held his hand out to Christopher. "Am I pleased to see you. What is going on here?"

"There might be a robbery going to take place here, but that is only guess work. Let me introduce you to Colonel Summerfield, he has had a whiff of the transportation of government gold from one place to another and this is where a changeover of guards is going to take place. It could be a good place for a robbery, no nosey neighbours to see what is going on, but all this is only conjecture. What with you, my mother and Annie going missing, it is looking more and more likely that the colonel is right."

Gregory and the colonel shook hands and the colonel asked, "Have you heard or seen anything suspicious whilst you have been here?"

"Have I just. I have been kept prisoner here in this stable from tea time yesterday. I think it was yesterday. I was knocked out, so I am not sure for how long. I became fully conscious about half an hour ago. I dropped Mrs Belmar and Annie off at the front of the inn and brought the coach and horses around to the stables. No ostler came to take the horses from me, so I opened the stable doors and looked inside.

"No sooner had I poked my head through the door than I felt a blow to my head and when I regained consciousness, I was tied to one of the stall posts. There were two guards standing at the windows, but neither of them had spoken, they had not said a word all the time I was awake. Neither had they moved. I managed to cut the ropes to my wrists then untie the ropes that bound my ankles.

"All the time I was watching the two guards but neither turned around to look at me. When I was free, I made a charge at the guard nearest to me, and, damn me, he collapsed onto the floor, and so did I. When I looked at the so-called guard, I saw he was a scarecrow. I checked the other guard and he also turned out to be a scarecrow — men's clothing filled with straw.

"I was none too pleased to find out that I had been kept prisoner all night by two scarecrows. I was just about to work my way into the inn when I heard your whistles, so I ducked back into the stable and waited for you to come."

"Who was it that hit you over the head?" asked the colonel.

"Sorry, I can't answer that. I never saw anybody. The first thing I saw were these two scarecrows. Bloody fool I felt when I found out I had been held captive by two scarecrows."

"My father is going to like that," Christopher told him.

"There is no need for you to tell me that, I am aware of the comments I will receive from your father. I will never live it down. How did you get involved in this mystery?" Gregory asked the colonel.

"Annie is my granddaughter, is she safe?"

Gregory scratched his chin. "Don't know, Colonel, Mrs Belmar and Annie entered the inn whilst I saw to the coach. I sincerely hope so. Your granddaughter seems to have a knack for getting into trouble, if you don't mind me saying so. We seem to have gone from one incident to another since she entered our lives."

"I know the feeling well. We had better go into the inn and find out what is going on in there and let us keep our fingers crossed that the ladies are inside and safe," the colonel told them.

"Do you think that is a good idea, Colonel?" Christopher asked. "Where are all the horses that are needed for the change over? There are no horses in this stable. Where are all the soldiers for the changeover? If what you say is true, they would be soldiers. I would have thought that goes without saying, if it involves government money. Why would anybody put scarecrows at the windows in a stable unless it was to deter anybody who had intention of hiding in there?"

"And where is my coach and two horses?" Gregory wanted to know, noticing for the first time there was no sign of either.

"Come on we are wasting valuable time here. No good asking me all these questions, let's head into the Hangman's Rest and find out the answers." And with that, the colonel marched out of the stable with Christopher and Gregory not far behind.

Chapter Five

A glass of milk had been taken up to the captives in the upstairs bedroom along with slices of toasted bread.

Annie was restless, she walked over to the window and tried pulling at the metal bars across the window. None of them moved.

"Why are there bars on the windows?" Annie asked.

"We put the bars across the window in case any of our guests have children. We had a couple staying here and they had three children, well when I say children, they were child size, but more like monsters. Up to everything, and one of them nearly fell out of the window, that is why I had them put there. Little did I know they would hold me captive in my own home," Arthur told them.

"Is there anything in this room that I could use to loosen these bars with? Then I could tie some sheets together and climb out of the window and go and get help," she asked the innkeeper.

"You can't go climbing out of the window, you'll break your neck," Alan said.

"Well, I have to do something, I am not sitting up here waiting to be released, if we ever are. How do we know they are not going to kill us, for we have all seen their faces, you know?

"Although they have not treated us too harshly so far, we do not know what is going on and, whatever it is, might end in tragedy. And if it does, we will all be witnesses. That is not a good thing. We must try something. We can't just sit on our hands and do nothing. There was not much we could do last night in the dark, but now it is daylight, we need to try to escape.

"Do you have any ideas on the subject? After all, it is your inn and you know what you have in this room that could aid our escape." Annie once more aimed her question at the innkeeper.

The innkeeper and his wife exchanged glances, and this was not missed by Freda who stammered, "S-she is right you k-know. We have to do something. I will h-help you, A-Annie.

"Good for you, Freda, any help would be appreciated."

"Tell them, Arthur, I think it is for the best. Annie is right, we have to do something."

"We are a bit too old in the tooth, Meg, to be playing the hero," her husband said.

"This is our inn, Arthur, we have lived and worked here for too many years now and those men have no right to lock us up in our own home. Tell them, please," Meg pleaded.

After a few seconds hesitation, Arthur looked at Annie and said, "There is a secret stairwell to the left of the fireplace, it takes you down into the kitchen. You had better take a candle to light your way. When you get to the bottom, before you open the door into the kitchen, it would be advisable to use the peephole in the door to see if there is anybody in there.

"You had better blow out the candle before you do this because the light will shine through the peephole and alert anybody who is in the kitchen. There is a latch halfway up the door to the right, just lift it up and the door will open. If the coast is clear, make your escape through the back door, then across the back courtyard and into the wood. Once inside the wood, turn right and follow the edge of the wood until it ends. You will find you are facing a field. Go straight forward across this field, and you come to some crossroads.

"Carry on moving forward, straight across the crossroads, and about a mile further along that road you will come to another inn called, Devil's Dyke. You might be able to get help there."

"How exciting," Annie said.

"Damned dangerous thing to do if you ask me. Nice names for inn's around here, Hangman's Rest and Devil's Dyke," Alan remarked.

"I-I agree with A-Annie. I will c-come with you."

"And I shall be glad of your company, Freda."

"I didn't say I wouldn't come with you, just warning you against it, that's all. I think it would be best if I went alone and you two ladies stayed here," Alan told them.

"No such thing, it is my idea and I am going to try to escape and get help. Meg is right, those men have no right to come into someone else's home and tie them up. And anyway, I want to do it." Annie dug her heels in.

"A-and so do I," agreed Freda.

"I would just like to point out that none of us have been tied up, that at least should count for something," Alan remarked.

"All right, technically we have all been locked up, but we might as well have been tied up for we are all tied to this room. Annie went over to the side of the fireplace and looked for the handle, but she could not see one.

"You have to slide the top overhang at the side of the mantlepiece out, and release the hidden catch then the door will spring open," Arthur told Annie.

Annie did as she was told, and all this added to the excitement as she pulled at the catch and the narrow door sprang open.

"Who is coming, and who is staying?" she asked.

"You will find that the stairwell is not very wide, so it is of no use Meg and me coming with you, I no longer have the lithe figure I used to have. I would only get stuck, so off you go and be careful," Arthur told her.

Whilst Annie was finding the catch for the stairwell door, Freda had made herself busy by lighting a candle then she went to stand at Annie's side.

Alan took the candle from her and said, "Here, give me the candle and I will go first."

Annie looked over at Mrs Belmar. "Are you coming with us?"

"Ten years ago, Annie, I would have been leading the expedition, but now, I will only hold you up. You will make quicker progress without me, please be careful but have fun too, that is what life is all about. Off you go."

Alan made his way down the stairwell and Arthur had been right, there was only enough room for them to squeeze their way down. At the bottom Alan found the latch that Arthur had told them about, and indicated to Annie to take hold of it, so she did. He found the peephole which was covered with a loose piece of wood, so before he moved the peephole cover to one side, he took the innkeeper's advice and blew out the candle before he placed it on the floor.

He pulled the cover back and placed his eye to the door. The kitchen was empty as far as he could see. He waited a few seconds just to make sure then he whispered, "Ok, Annie, open the door."

Very slowly Annie inched the door open until it was wide enough to squeeze through and all three stood in the kitchen listening.

Freda closed the stairwell door behind her and saw the piece of wood sticking out at the side of the door frame, that had sprung up to reveal a hole about the size of a finger so you could place your finger in and lift the latch from the kitchen side of the door if so needed. Freda pulled the piece of wood down and heard it click into place and the panelled door blended into the rest of the panelled wall, so if you didn't know the door existed, you would never be able to detect it. They all silently crossed over to the back door and Alan poked his head out. He saw no sign of life, so he started across the courtyard and headed for the wood. Annie and Freda followed.

The wood was soon reached and they all shot into it where they each found a tree large enough to hide behind.

"So far so good," Alan said.

"Yes, that was easier than I expected," Annie agreed.

They followed the edge of the wood and soon came to the open field that Arthur had described and, at the other side of the field, they could see the crossroads.

Alan thought how exposed it was. Three people making their way across an open field was asking for trouble, but he kept his thoughts to himself and started out.

They had to climb over the fence at the other side of the field, but this was accomplished without mishap and they were heading down the road towards the Devil's Dyke Inn.

As they approached the inn, Annie touched Alan's arm and said, "See that coach at the side of that building, it belongs to Mrs Belmar."

"Are you sure?"

"Of course I am. I travelled down here in it with her."

"Then maybe we should approach with caution."

They approached the building to the rear and found it to be of wooden construction. "I think this is the stable block," Alan whispered.

"I think you are right," agreed Annie.

"I will go around the side of the stable — the coach will hide me if anybody is watching — and see what I can find out," Alan told them.

"We will all go around the side of the stable," Annie replied.

"Y-yes we will, it is our a-adventure as well as yours," said Freda.

"I can see I am not going to win this conversation but keep as close to the side as you possibly can."

Alan started to make his way down the side of the stable and Annie and Freda followed. The coach shielded their presence and it was a good job it did, for in the middle of the courtyard was a sturdy wagon with a large wooden crate fastened to it by chains which were padlocked, holding it secure. The crate also had thick iron bars around it, making it nearly impossible to get inside.

The wagon was tipped to one side. One of the wheels had come off and the weight of the wooden crate had made it tip over, but the chain constraints had held it securely fastened to the broken wagon.

Three men were frantically trying to remove the chains, but the chains stood fast, they would not yield.

Alan moved down the side of the coach and looked through a window into the stable. The stable door must have been open because the inside of the stable was flooded with light and he saw ten men, in soldier's uniforms, sitting on the stable floor with their hands bound behind their back, and their ankles tied together.

Alan's mind was doing overtime. The situation at the Hangman's Rest, and these tied-up soldiers here, had to be connected. The theft of the coach from the Hangman's Rest and the broken wagon here, well, he thought, it doesn't take a genius to work that out, they intended to transfer the contents of the crate to the coach.

He needed help and the best people to give him that were the soldiers. "I am going inside. You two stay here and keep your eye on those three over there and let me know if any of them start making their way over to the stable."

Cautiously, Alan crept into the stable and the first thing he saw was a man sitting on the floor to the left of the door, facing the soldiers and a rifle resting across his knees. His head was bent forward, resting on his chest, and, as luck would have it, he was fast asleep. Alan tiptoed across to the sleeping man, gently picked up the rifle, turned it round and brought the butt end down on the sleeping man's head. The man fell to one side and lay unconscious on the stable floor.

He ran across to the first soldier and untied his hands. He left the soldier to unfasten his own ankles and moved across to the next soldier, and soon all ten were standing on their feet.

Alan pointed outside and held up three fingers. The soldier nearest to him nodded, and, going over to the discarded rifle, picked it up and handed it to one of the other soldiers, pointing to the wooden ladder leading up into the stable loft. The soldier nodded, turned and made his way up the ladder.

The soldier that seemed to be in charge pointed at two of the other soldiers, and then he pointed at the door. Silently one of the two soldiers bent and picked up two lengths of rope that had held them all captive, and went over to the unconscious villain and dragged him out of sight of the open door. He then proceeded to tie the villain up and made sure he was unable to escape. The second soldier made his way to the opposite side of the door and they stood on guard.

"What's the situation outside?" The soldier spoke quietly.

"Three men trying to lift a large wooden crate up. It looks like the wagon it was standing on lost a wheel and the weight of the crate tipped it to one side and the wagon has collapsed."

"Did you see any rifles?"

"No, but I wasn't looking for rifles, so that doesn't signify anything. There might be."

"We have to get that crate back into our possession. We were handed some ale back along the road and it was very welcome, I can tell you, for we had been on the go nearly twelve hours. We all guzzled it down and carried on our way. We were handing that crate you have seen over to another set of soldiers at the next inn we came to, so we thought no more about it until one of the lads said, *'I feel light headed'*.

"But it was too late because we all felt light headed, and the next thing we knew we were tied up here. We had been doped, of course, with the ale. Serves us right, there will be hell on when we get back to camp, but if we can get the shipment back, things might not be as bad as we thought."

"What's in the crate?" Alan asked.

"I am not supposed to tell anyone but if it hadn't been for you, we would still be tied up. Government gold."

"Hell," remarked Alan.

"Exactly my thoughts when we were told we would be overseeing the transportation of it."

"What beats me is how Mrs Belmar's coach came to be stationed outside this inn when Mrs Belmar was dropped off at the Hangman's Rest," Alan remarked.

"I overheard the robbers talking and one told another to go to the Hangman's Rest to see if he could steal a wagon. I didn't know it at the time, but you say a wheel has come off our wagon? This will have created a problem for them, they needed a different form of transport for the gold," the soldier replied.

"That must be it then, he saw the unaccompanied coach with two horses hitched up to it, and took that instead," Alan said.

A movement in the doorway caught the soldier's eye and he placed his hand on Alan's arm and nodded in the direction of the door.

Alan caught the flash of royal blue and he knew it was Freda's skirt. His two companions were sneaking into the stable. He held up a finger to the soldier and walked across to the door, and there, standing behind the door, were two of the prettiest faces you could wish to see. Unfortunately, they were both held by the arm by the soldier on guard who they had not seen when they sneaked into the stable and hid behind the door.

"I told you to stay out there."

"When you didn't come back out we thought you might be in trouble, so we have come to rescue you," Annie told him.

"Because you don't seem to be able to understand orders, it is I who is rescuing you, instead of you rescuing me. It is a good job these gentlemen are on our side or goodness knows what might have befallen you both," chastised Alan.

"It's all right," Alan told the soldier, "they are with me. Come and meet our new friends." Alan led them across the stable to the soldier who seemed to be in charge.

Annie and Freda were released and appeared from behind the door and they followed Alan over to the soldier. "This is Annie, and this is Freda, my name is Alan Sherman. Sorry I can't remember the ladies' surnames, we only met last night for the first time."

"Captain Norman, at your service, ladies." He made a polite bow in their direction.

Both ladies curtsied back, and Annie said, "Pleased to meet you Captain."

"No more than we are pleased to meet you and Alan. Alan has released us from a very embarrassing situation. We need to distract the men on the wagon if we can, then we can rush in and disarm them if they have rifles. The soldier up in the loft has a rifle, and he knows how to use it, so we should be all right. What to distract them with, that's the problem.

"I can distract them for you, if you like," Annie said.

"And s-so can I," Freda offered.

"That is very kind of you, ladies, but I will not allow you to put yourselves in danger," the captain said.

"W-we could take them a drink, I b-bet they will be grateful for a d-drink. They will never suspect us," Freda told him.

"That might not be a bad idea. History repeating itself. You would be getting your own back for drinking the drugged ale," agreed Alan.

"There are some tin mugs hanging on the posts at the side of the stalls, I think they use them to measure out grain for the horses. There is water in the trough over there. It might just work, like you pointed out, it worked on us," Captain Norman agreed.

Three mugs were brought to the trough and filled with water then Annie and Freda made their way out of the stable and started walking across the courtyard towards the three unsuspecting men.

One of the men caught a movement from the corner of his eye and he turned to look, but at the same time he grabbed his rifle and pointed it in Annie and Freda's direction.

Seeing two young women walking towards them carrying mugs, the rifle was lowered then his two partners in crime were nudged in turn and they too turned to see two visions approaching them bearing mugs.

Annie and Freda both worked their way to the side of the broken wagon and the three men had to turn their backs to the stable to reach down for the much-needed mug of water.

They did not get to drink the water because, before they could lift the mugs to their lips, soldiers had surrounded the wagon.

The robbers could see there was no escape so they descended the wagon and allowed their hands to be secured behind their backs.

The captain asked the largest of the three men, "Where are our horses?"

Knowing it would not take the soldiers long to find them he replied, "To the other side of the inn there is a paddock, we put them in there, this barn is no size to fit them all in."

"Where are all the other members of your gang? For I know there must be more than the three of you to be able to move this merchandise," the captain wanted to know.

"We were caught on the hop, the soldiers and the wagon were early, we weren't expecting them until the next morning. The other members of the gang were going to arrive later on this morning, then, if there were other customers at the inn, it wouldn't look as though there was something going off. And anyway, by the time the rest of us arrived, any guest should have been on their way," was the reply.

Chapter Six

The colonel opened the door to the Hangman's Rest and walked in. Just like Mrs Belmar and Annie had done the previous night. They found themselves standing in a small but clean room with a bench to the top of the room, and tables and armchairs scattered around. There was no sign of life.

"Colonel Summerfield?" a voice asked from the top of a staircase to their right.

All three turned to face the sound of the voice, and they saw a well-dressed gentleman standing at the top of the stairs.

"That's me, and to whom am I speaking?" the colonel asked.

"Captain Roger Freeman, at your service, Colonel Summerfield."

"Do I know you?"

"No Colonel, I think not. When I was a young recruit, I saw you once or twice marching around camp, but I don't think we ever met."

"You must be here for the changeover of the gold."

"You know about that?"

"An old army colleague of mine came to visit me, he was doing a reconnaissance of the area prior to moving the gold to a safer place and he asked me to keep my ear to the ground and let him know if I heard a rumour regarding the transportation of the gold. I have not.

"But my granddaughter has gone missing, and as she was on her way home from Mid-East Mould, she would have been travelling the route that the gold was to take. She would have been in the company of this young man's mother. Have you seen them by any chance?"

"Are these two gentlemen in the army, Colonel?"

"No, I don't think so. We have only met these past three or four hours."

"Do you think it wise to be mentioning the gold in their hearing, sir?"

"Too late to be worrying about that, they are both involved in the affair, like it or not. And so far, they have turned out to be honest English gentlemen and I think they are on your side. So let's get on with the business in hand and see about this gold that is being moved. But before that, have you seen my granddaughter?"

The captain turned his head and nodded to one of the soldiers now standing next to him at the top of the staircase.

The soldier turned and vanished around a corner, but it wasn't long before he came hurrying back with Mrs Belmar, Arthur and Meg.

"The other three have escaped, Captain."

"Now, how did they do that?" Captain Freeman asked the innkeeper.

"There is a secret stairwell that runs down by the side of the fireplace in the bedroom you locked us up in, and it leads down to the kitchen. I told the young people to cross the courtyard and go into the wood at the rear of the inn. To go across the field to the crossroads and then onto the Devil's Dyke, which is another inn and the only other dwelling for miles around. They have gone for help," Arthur told him.

"If they made their escape through the back of the inn, that is why we did not see them. We have all been watching the front of the Inn waiting for the arrival of the shipment. What time is it?" the captain asked.

"Nearly one o'clock," replied the soldier.

"Something has gone wrong. The gold should have been here by now. Are you two involved in this incident? Have you been keeping us occupied whilst your friends have been robbing the government?" asked the captain.

"Three hours ago, I had not heard of the gold and when I did hear of it, it was from the colonel's mouth and we have been together ever since," Christopher told him.

"Two hours ago, I had not heard about the gold and when I did learn of it, it was from the colonel's mouth. I have been tied up and kept prisoner by two scarecrows, you think that is something to be proud of?" Gregory asked.

"Two scarecrows, what on earth are you talking about?" asked the captain.

"I went to take the coach to the stables when we arrived here yesterday evening and I was knocked out. When I came to, I was bound hand and foot. There were two figures standing at each window looking out onto the courtyard with rifles also pointing onto the courtyard.

"The light was not great in there, but I managed to cut the ropes that bound my wrists and I charged the nearest figure to me. It collapsed and we both fell onto the floor. It turned out to be a scarecrow, men's clothing filled with straw. On further inspection the other guard was also a scarecrow. I decided to try to find out what was going on and I came across the colonel and Christopher, and here we are."

"There are no horses in the stable and our coach has gone," Christopher told them.

Mrs Belmar came forward and asked, "Are you all right, Gregory?"

"Yes, thank you, Mrs Belmar, it's only my pride that has taken a beating, that is all."

"The horses are safe in the wood, we decided that they could graze in there and be ready for when the gold shipment came. Three of my soldiers are keeping them company. I am sorry I had to lock you upstairs, Mrs Belmar, but because of the high risk of danger whilst we were changing over responsibility for the gold, I thought it would be in the interest of your safety.

"The innkeeper will get paid for housing my soldiers and myself overnight. I did what I did because I thought it would be for the best, to keep you all out of harm's way. Just in case there was any trouble. Where a shipment of gold is concerned, you can't be too careful. Once we were on our way one of the soldiers would remain here for an hour or so, then release you from the bedroom. You would have no idea what had taken place, or which way we had taken when we left, so you would not have been able to inform anybody of our whereabouts, therefore you would not have been at risk.

"It has all been to no avail, the shipment seems to be missing. I bet it has either been waylaid, or the driver has taken the wrong turning at the crossroads. I am going to ride over to the Devil's Dyke and see if there is or has been any sign of the wagon. It should have been here over an hour ago," the captain told them.

"I will come with you. I too took the wrong turning at the crossroads in the dark last night, so I will show you the way," offered Christopher.

"Then get your horse and I will meet you out front."

The captain and Christopher headed out and into the wood. Once inside the wood, the captain turned right, and Christopher turned left. The horses were found, and they met back up in front of the inn. It wasn't long before they were heading down the road towards Devil's Dyke, and on approaching the inn, Christopher put his hand out and touching the captain's arm, he said, "That's our coach."

"Better dismount and go on foot, it will be quieter."

They dismounted their horses and walked them forward, keeping the coach between them and the inn. Like Alan had done, the captain looked slowly around the side of the coach and he saw the soldiers trying to hoist up the large wooden box.

He led his horse forward and came to a halt at the side of the group of soldiers.

"Having problems?" he asked.

The nearest soldier looked up and recognised the captain. He stood up straight and saluted him. "Yes, Captain, a wheel has come off the wagon and we are trying to hoist it up to replace the wheel, but the crate is extremely heavy. We are not making much headway."

"Why are you at this inn, you should have been at the Hangman's Rest, which is back to the crossroads and left for another half mile. We were waiting for you there."

"Yes, Captain, we were heading for the Hangman's Rest, and we were making excellent progress, in fact, if all had gone to plan, we would have been at the Hangman's Rest around midnight, half a day early. But about five miles back we passed another inn and we had been travelling most of the day in the sun and as we approached the inn, a serving wench came out with some tankards of ale and offered it to us.

"Our captain saw no harm in us having a drink of ale and we were all allowed to have a tankard each. We never left the gold, Captain, we drank the ale whilst we were sitting on the wagon or on our horses. Then we went on our way. It was about ten minutes later that we all started to feel drowsy and the next thing we knew, we were tied up over in the stable.

"We were rescued by a young man and two ladies. They have gone back to the Hangman's Rest to inform you of our situation."

"Where are the men that drugged you?"

"They are now tied up in the stables, Captain. Our captain is over there with them, keeping guard, whilst we try to repair the wagon."

"In that case, if you are now back in charge of the gold, I will have a word with your captain and then go back to the Hangman's Rest and send help back to get the wheel back on the wagon, so we can continue on our way."

"That would be much appreciated, Captain."

Alan, Annie and Freda had headed back to the Hangman's Rest and at the crossroads they decided to cut back across the field and through the wood and approach the Hangman's Rest from the rear.

"I w-would just like to s-say, I have enjoyed my little a-adventure. I don't think I w-will be having much f-fun looking after my aunt. It has been n-nice meeting you both and I shall not f-forget this little a-adventure, ever," Freda told them.

"Likewise," said Alan. "When my father said he wanted me to take two months away from our farm and go out and meet new people and try to find myself a wife, I thought he was mad. But I can see he was right. I have spent all my life on our farm and we are miles away from other neighbouring farms, so I have had a very sheltered life.

"This has certainly opened my eyes and, I must admit, I have enjoyed it too. I would not have missed it for the world either. Nor will I forget either of you, I hope we can all become friends and keep in touch."

"I w-would like that very much," Freda told him.

"Good, then that's settled."

Annie smiled and made no comment, but she noticed Alan was in no way expecting a reply from her.

As the three friends were making their way through the wood towards the back of the inn, the captain and Christopher were making their way along the road towards the crossroads missing each other by minutes.

There was no sign of life on the outside of the Hangman's Rest as the three adventurers looked across the courtyard towards the inn. Alan said, "We are just going to have to take the bull by the horns and walk straight in. After all, according to the soldiers back at the Devil's Dyke, the men that locked us up in the bedroom are also soldiers and are waiting for them to deliver the gold, so they can take charge of it.

"I don't think they are in association with the robbers. Like they said, it was for our safety we were locked away. You two wait here and I will go ahead on my own and, if I don't come back, go and bring help from Devil's Dyke."

"No way are we letting you go back in there on your own, we are coming with you. I agree, I think they are soldiers too, I don't think they intend to harm us. I never felt threatened by them, so it is of no use hanging around dithering, let's go." Annie started forward.

"Yes, if you are g-going back in, then s-so are we," Freda told him.

"Very well, but keep behind me," Alan instructed.

The kitchen door was not locked when Alan tried it and all three trapesed into the inn and headed for the sound of voices. They saw Mrs Belmar, the colonel and Gregory seated in the scattered armchairs in the room that they had found themselves in when first entering the inn from the front door.

There was no sign of Arthur and Meg but when the colonel saw his granddaughter he stood up and came towards her. "Annie, my dear, are you all right?"

"Yes, of course I am. We have been on a bit of an adventure, that is all. Freda, Alan and I have had a very entertaining morning."

"Do you know, my dear, you remind me of me when I was your age. I seemed to find myself in situations that young ladies of your age should not find themselves in," Mrs Belmar told Annie. "Christopher and the captain have gone looking for you all. Have you not seen them?"

"No, but we did come back through the wood so, if they were on the road, our paths would not have crossed," Alan replied.

The front door of the inn opened and in walked Christopher and the captain.

"So, you found your way back did you. A merry dance you have led us," Christopher remarked.

"I was looking for a park bench to spend the night on," Annie said innocently.

"A park bench, there are no park benches around here, we are in the middle of nowhere," stated Alan.

"Take no notice of her, if you try to follow a conversation with Annie you are sliding down hill," Christopher advised him.

Alan held out his hand and Christopher shook it. "Alan Sherman."

"Christopher Belmar."

"This is Freda Inksome, and I believe you must have already met Annie."

"Pleased to make your acquaintance Miss Inksome." Christopher smiled down at her."

"Likewise." Freda gave him a small curtsey.

"Where are all my men?" the captain wanted to know.

"Two of them are keeping lookout upstairs. Arthur and Meg took the other four men down to the stable to show them where the potato stack is, they have offered to make us all a meal. We did not complain about that, I am sure you must all be ready for something to eat before you set off on your long journey to wherever it is you are going," said the colonel.

"In that case I shall make my way down to the stable and take some of the men back to Devil's Dyke to help get the wheel back on the wagon. When the wheel has been replaced, I will tell the men to bring the shipment here and then we can all partake of a meal before we leave." And with that the captain made himself scarce.

"I w-was supposed to meet the mail coach at the crossroads at nine o'clock this morning, b-but I guess I have m-missed it," Freda said.

"You may share my park bench, Freda," Annie said.

"You will find out that my granddaughter talks a lot of nonsense sometimes, I should let it pass if I were you. You will, of course, come home with us, and Annie will take you to your aunt's, my dear. Mrs Belmar has been telling us of your plight. Do not distress yourself." The colonel patted Freda's hand.

"Yes, and I will accompany you too, just in case she throws you out then you will not be left on your own," Alan told her.

"You are all s-so v-very k-kind," Freda stammered.

After a very satisfying meal, the captain and his men changed into their uniforms and were soon on their way, the wagon creaking under the weight of its load.

Before they had departed, the captain had sent one of his men back to Devil's Dyke to bring the coach back to the Hangman's Rest. Whilst they waited for the coach's return, Gregory asked, "What do you make of the scarecrows, Colonel? They had to be there for a purpose, somebody is not going to go to the trouble of creating two scarecrows and placing them at the stable windows for nothing."

"Yes, it is a strange one, that. You seem to have your wits about you, what do you make of it, Christopher?"

"I think it was the soldiers that built the scarecrows in case they were set upon by thieves. If by any chance robbers did attack, then seeing rifles pointing out of the stable, any thief would make the same mistake that Gregory did.

"I think the robbers took the right turning and intended to head for the Devil's Dyke to tie the soldiers up in the stable there. They knew soldiers were waiting for the gold shipment at the Hangman's Rest so they intended to change clothes with the soldiers they had drugged then make for the Hangman's Rest and pounce on the unsuspecting soldiers here. They would tie them up and hope to give themselves five or six hours in which to vanish with the gold, before the soldiers either escaped and raised the alarm or someone found them and released them. Either way, they expected to have some time in which to disappear.

"Unfortunately, for the robbers, the soldiers that were transporting the gold were well in front of their schedule, they had made good time. They must also have been observed by the thieves for them to know where they were on the route. So, the three robbers at the Devil's Dyke must have been set in place a day early just to be on the safe side, and that was a lucky twist in the plan for them, they were able to drug the soldiers as planned.

"Unfortunately, for the robbers, only part of their plan worked. It came unstuck when they were trying to turn the wagon round and a wheel came off. They could not lift the wagon up to replace the wheel because of the weight.

"They had to change their plan so one of the robbers made his way to the Hangman's Rest and stole our coach with the intention of taking the gold out of the crate and putting it in the coach. That did not go too well either, because they could not get the crate open. I also think the innkeeper and his wife of the Devil's Dyke, were in on the robbery, because when the captain and I went into the inn to make sure they were all right before we came back here, they were nowhere to be seen. The Devil's Dyke stood empty. He thought that the lady who I thought was the landlady of the Devil's Dyke, was the same lady who drugged the soldiers. The captain said he would set the ball rolling and make enquires once the gold was delivered."

"Sounds reasonable to me. I agree with you, I think those scarecrows were put there by the soldiers, for the purpose you said, to mislead any robbers that might appear. I also think it was a soldier that knocked Gregory out and tied him up for his own safety, as well as theirs.

"The soldiers must have heard the coach arrive. They would not have left Gregory roaming about, it was a loose end that had to be tidied up. After all, the soldiers did not know that you were innocent travellers, you could have been robbers. I don't think the captain is going to admit to it though, he did pretend to know nothing about the scarecrows when Gregory mentioned them.

"Did you not see anything untoward in the courtyard at Devil's Dyke whilst you were there?" the colonel asked.

"I never saw the courtyard. As soon as I dismounted, the landlord appeared and took my horse to the stable while I went inside to sort out a room for the night. This morning, when I opened my bedroom curtains, the bedroom must have been situated at the front of the inn for all I could see was rolling countryside. The landlady told me while she was serving breakfast that my horse had been saddled and was waiting for me out front. And so it was.

"Yes, I think you are right, Colonel, it would make more sense if the soldiers were keeping a lookout at the front of Hangman's Rest, for that is the direction the shipment would take. What with a wood to the rear, no wagon would be able to travel that way. I think that is why they did not see our coach being taken. The rear exit to the courtyard is just around the bend further up the road so the soldiers on guard would not have seen it being taken. I also think that the captain was right about the landlord and landlady of the Devil's Dyke being part of the robbers' gang. They had to know what was going off in their back yard." agreed Christopher.

"Yes, well, all that is behind us now, it's for the soldiers to follow all that up, thank God. We've done our bit and we have all come out of it safe and sound. The only one of us to be pitied is poor Gregory, he is going to have to live with his scarecrows for the rest of his life," ended the colonel.

"I think it was very brave of Gregory to do what he did. All he could see was the back of the two figures and they could have been alive and there were two of them, not just one. That was two against one and Gregory did not think of his own safety when he pounced on that scarecrow. I think he warrants a medal," Annie told them.

"Damn right I deserve a medal," Gregory agreed.

Chapter Seven

Mrs Belmar's coach was brought from the Devil's Dyke Inn and she, Annie and Freda piled in.

Gregory was driving the coach and the colonel, Christopher and Alan were riding their horses. Steady progress was made and soon the coach was drawing to a halt at the impressive canopy covered entrance of Fargate Fold.

A stable boy appeared from around the side of the building and took hold of the reins of the horses pulling the coach, whilst they all alighted.

The colonel, Christopher and Alan, dismounted and tied their horses to the back of the coach and the colonel led the way in.

When they were all sitting comfortably in the morning room, drinking hot chocolate, the colonel said, "I think it would be wise if you all slept here tonight and then we can get things sorted out and organised for your departure in the morning."

"I would appreciate that, Colonel. I have decided to stop falling into these adventures, the thrill seems to have gone out of them now. I will leave it to the young ones. Gregory and I will travel home first thing in the morning," Mrs Belmar said.

"I am most relieved to hear you say that, Mrs Belmar, because I was thinking along those lines myself, especially after the scarecrow incident. That never would have happened in my younger days. My eyesight is not up to scratch these days," Gregory had to admit.

"Damned poor excuse to be giving for being duped by two scarecrows. I have heard many a broad tale whilst in the army, but I think this takes the biscuit. Even so, it is a splendid tale, I shall think of you, Gregory, every time I see a scarecrow and, believe me, come harvest time, there will be one or two scattered about the countryside," the colonel said.

"That settles that then. What about you, Christopher, are you coming home with us?" his mother asked.

"Yes, I just needed to know you were all right and, of course, I can see you are. I also needed to know that Annie found her park bench. It would seem she didn't need to go in search of one after all."

Colonel Summerfield told Annie that Winnie was now back in Mid-East Mould. Annie smiled and said to her grandfather, "Howard's father informed us that he was on his way to Haverfield to take Winnie back with him, I am pleased to hear he succeeded in his task. I had no need to have journeyed to Mid-East Mould, but I am rather glad I did. I have had a very exciting time and I enjoyed it very much."

"I have had a very exciting time t-too. And it delayed me having to go and meet my aunt J-Jane. My father says she is a tyrant and he has not seen her for twenty years. I am very pleased t-to have met you all. I shall always r-remember these past forty-eight hours," Freda told them.

"I shall go with you in the morning when you go to meet your aunt Jane, and if she is as bad as your father says she is, you must come home with me. I will not allow you to go back home if your father is so hard-hearted as to throw you to the wolves," Alan told her.

"That is very k-kind of you, Alan, but I really could not put you to so much t-trouble. What would your m-mother and f-father say if you returned home with me on your arm? I should die of e-embarrassment," Freda told him.

"They sent me away to find myself a wife and I have not met anyone so far on my travels that I have taken to as I have taken to you. So, if things do not work out for you when we meet your aunt, you must come home with me to meet my parents. We might be able to work something out," said Alan.

"But w-what about my s-stammer?" Freda wanted to know.

"What stammer?" Alan asked.

"You c-can't have missed it, it is pronounced."

"It is only lack of confidence, Freda, that makes you stammer. Once your confidence takes a turn for the better, you will soon be rid of it once and for all. But let us sleep on it. Please give it some thought and if you feel you could not bear to come home with me, then there will be no hard feelings. You never know, you might like your aunt Jane."

"You are the kindest person I have met in many a long year. Yes, I will sleep on it and see what tomorrow brings. Thank you for the offer, I might take you up on it," Freda told him.

"Did you notice something?" asked Annie.

"Such as what?" Christopher asked.

"Freda just told Alan she would think about going back home with him and she did not stammer once."

They all looked at Freda and she felt her colour rise. "I believe you were right. I did not stammer. Surely it can't be as simple as that, feeling confident in the company I am in, that has stopped me from stammering. But I do feel relaxed and at ease with you all."

"I, for one, found your stammer charming, and it did not detract any from your gentle nature and plucky attitude when faced with a difficult situation. I am full of admiration at the way you came up to scratch when things got tough," Alan told her.

"I only followed Annie's lead, and, anyway, I was enjoying myself too much to be concerned for my own safety. To which I might add, I think that came down to your presence, Alan, you made me feel safe," Freda had to admit.

"It would seem more than one friendship has materialized out of this encounter," the colonel commented, looking across at Christopher.

"It would indeed, Colonel. May I have your permission to call on Annie in the near future?" Christopher asked.

"No good asking me, lad, it's Annie you need to ask. She never does anything I tell her to do, as I have already said, she is not a very relaxing woman. She has a mind of her own. She thinks I don't know why she went to Mid-East Mould. I didn't become a colonel in the army by hiding my head in the sand. I knew what she was about."

"How did you know?" an indignant Annie asked.

"Winnie told me all about the row she had with Howard, and what it was about. I asked her if she had told you about it and, of course, she said yes, she had. It was not a very hard task to put two and two together and make seven, which is what you will have done, and I knew you would be off to try and make things right.

"No use trying to stop you either, for I know I would not have won that battle, so I let you have your head. Life is much simpler that way. Are you listening, lad?" ended the colonel, looking again in Christopher's direction.

A delighted laugh burst from Alan's lips and he said, "Loud and clear, Colonel, loud and clear."

Chapter Eight

Annie was the first to go down to breakfast and, whilst she was waiting for her grandfather and his guests to join her, she heard footsteps crossing the hall, and when she turned to see who was about to join her, Christopher was walking into the breakfast room.

"Good morning, Annie. You are looking delightful this morning. A curl in your hair and a pretty yellow gown has worked wonders."

"Thank you. Good morning, Christopher, I hope you slept well?"

"Very well, thank you. I am pleased to see you are on your own, there always seems to be crowds of people milling around. Before we are descended upon, may I repeat the request I made to your grandfather last night. May I have the pleasure of calling upon you at the weekend?"

"I would like that very much, Christopher."

"Good, then I shall be down to see you on Saturday. I hope the others aren't too long before they come down because I am devilish hungry."

No sooner had he got the words out of his mouth, voices and footsteps were heard on the other side of the door and soon the breakfast room was full of people and a bountiful breakfast was had by all.

Not long after breakfast was over, Annie watched the coach and the straight back of Christopher upon his horse, make their way down the drive and they were soon out of sight. She had decided not to accompany Freda to her aunt's house when she heard that Alan was to go with her. She would let them have a little time together on their own for she had seen the attraction between them.

Alan and Freda decided it would be best if they walked to her aunt's house. Freda said it would delay the meeting just that little bit longer.

"Remember, Freda, you don't have to stay if you don't want to. You can come home with me and meet my mother and father. My mother was quite upset when my father suggested this trip. I must admit I fought against it because I did not want to find a wife like this.

"Now, I think my father was very wise to send me off for a couple of months. Like you, I would not have missed this for anything, it has been a splendid adventure and with very charming company.

"If I had not done as my father suggested we would never have met and that would have been a tragedy. If you do decide to stay with your aunt and things don't work out for you, I have told Annie that you will call upon her and she will send me word to come and collect you. Is that understood, Freda?"

"Yes, I understand, and it is very kind of you. It is nice to know that I have someone like you looking out for me."

"We are nearly there now. Do you want me to come in with you?"

"If you don't mind, I would very much appreciate it. I do not know what I am going to find once inside."

"Then let us knock upon the door and find out." Alan took hold of the brass door knocker and the noise of the knocker could be heard echoing around the inside of the house.

There was no reply to the knocking, so he tried again but still nobody came to open the door to them.

Taking hold of the door knob, Alan turned it and found that it yielded to his touch. He slowly pushed the door open and shouted, "Hello, is anyone at home?"

There was only silence as they stood just inside the hall.

"What do we do now?" Freda asked.

"I think we should look around. After all, if the old lady is ill, anything could have happened to her if she has been left on her own."

"I agree, we have to see if she is all right. Even if she sends us away, we can't leave without making sure nothing has befallen her."

A search of the house failed to find any living person in any room, the house was deserted.

"Shall we have a look around the back garden? Maybe she is outside in the sunshine," Freda suggested.

"Good idea," said Alan making for the back door.

The kitchen was as deserted as the rest of the house and so was the back garden. The back garden consisted of a huge overgrown lawn, weeds and nettles were in abundance.

"No one has been this way for years by the looks of this," observed Alan.

"No, but if my aunt has decided to take a walk on the lawn and has fallen down, she will never be seen again."

Alan burst out laughing and said, "Good comment, Freda. But if someone had walked through that long grass there would have been indications of it, but no one has walked in that grass for years by the look of it."

Freda nodded. "I think we had better go back inside and do another search of the house just in case we missed a room, because the house is much bigger than I expected it to be. There cannot be any servants living here, the house is as neglected, as the grounds. The furniture has not seen a duster in many a long month."

"If we fail a second time to find anyone, I think we should go back and see the colonel, he may know something," Alan said.

"I agree, we should go and see the colonel if we discover no one, but I doubt he will be able to help us. I think if he knew anything, he would have told us before we set out."

"Yes, I suppose you're right. Let's do one more search then make our way back next door."

They entered the house via the kitchen door and made their way back into the hall. They were stood in the hall, trying to decide which way to go when the front door opened and in walked an elderly lady. Freda and Alan looked across the hall at the lady but said nothing.

She was very tall and very thin and her grey hair was scraped tightly back into a bun in the nape of her neck.

"Can I help you?" the elderly lady asked when she saw Freda and Alan standing in the hall.

"And to whom am I speaking?" retaliated Alan.

"My name is Miss Bluemont, and I own this house. And you two would be?"

"Miss Bluemont! You are the lady that looked after my aunt, she wrote and told us you had left her and that she was ill and needed someone to look after her," Freda replied.

"Yes, I did leave her, but only for two days. I had to come back because I had nowhere else to go. But you still have not answered my question, who are you and what are you doing in my house?"

"This is Miss Freda Inksome, and my name is Alan Sherman. We are here to see Miss Inksome."

"If you want to see Miss Inksome, you will have a long way to travel. She died two weeks ago and she will be down there." She lifted up her skirt slightly and stamped her foot on the floor. "For she was no angel and would not be allowed in up there." Miss Bluemont pointed towards the heavens.

"My aunt is dead?"

"Yes, and I believe you must be the niece that stammers. The old witch told me that she had written to her brother and he was sending his eldest daughter down to stay with her. She was none too pleased about that. She said your father was sending you down here to stay with her because of your stammer. She said she was being used because he wanted you out of the way until he could find husbands for your sisters.

"That is how she was, a nasty piece of work who saw no good in anyone. She made my life a misery but when you have nowhere else to go, no money and have my looks, it was the best I could hope for. The old witch left everything to me, such as it is, but I am glad to have it.

"There is a little money and if I use it wisely it will see me out. But I am under no illusion that she left everything to me out of the goodness of her heart. She left it to me because she did not want her brother getting his hands on her estate. It was done out of spite, not friendship, but I will take it and be thankful for it. I have just come from the solicitors and he has given me the key, so at least I now have a roof over my head.

"You are welcome to stay if you wish, there is plenty of work to do here. You could work for your keep and help get rid of some of the grime that has built up over the years. Then there is the garden that needs attending to. There isn't enough money to be splashing out on a handyman."

"Thank you, no, we have plans of our own. When no one came to answer the door to our knock, we came inside to see if Freda's aunt was all right because we had been told she was very ill. Congratulations on your good fortune. We will be going now. Good luck."

Alan took Freda by the arm and led her outside. An uncomfortable silence rested between them and when Alan looked down at Freda's face, he could see tears running down her cheeks.

Alan stopped and took her in his arms and kissed her, and when he lifted his head, she laid her head on his chest and continued to cry. Alan let her cry herself out then he handed her his handkerchief and she wiped her eyes and blew her nose.

"I am sorry for crying on your shoulder, Alan. It is a mixture of relief, anger and guilt. I am glad my aunt is dead for I do not think I could have looked after someone with such a nasty disposition. I am furious at my father for sending me down here because of my stammer.

"After all, it is not my fault I have a stammer, it is not as if I am a murderer or anything like that. And I feel guilty for being glad my aunt is dead, but she did not sound a very nice person."

Alan put his arm around her waist and started walking down the long drive again. "I am glad she is dead and I don't feel guilty about it. Now you can come home with me and find out what a real home is like, and do you know, Freda, I think your stammer has gone for good, although I had no objection to it, I was becoming quite fond of it."

Freda looked up at Alan and said, "I have a lot to thank our fathers for, for sending us on these missions, because if they had not, we would never have met. And those robbers of course, for entangling us in their plot."

"Me too," he replied.

Annie watched her two friends walking up the drive with arms around each other's waist and laughing. It was a good sight and it brought a smile to her face. Roll on Saturday, it was now her turn to find romance that had so far eluded her.

Her grandfather came into the room and went over to see what had captured her attention. He saw two young people, happy in their own company, walking towards his house. "Not jealous, are you, Annie?"

She turned and looked up at her grandfather. "No, sir, I am not. I was just wondering what it is that makes one person like another far more than is good for them. What do you think it is that attracted Freda to Alan, and vice visa, for they are certainly made for each other, wouldn't you say?"

"What was it that attracted you to Christopher, and vice versa? For you were certainly made for each other."

"Do you think so, sir?"

"I do, don't you?"

"Yes, I do, but I couldn't tell you what it is about him that attracts me."

"It is one of the mysteries that occur in our lives that is never going to be explained."

"Can I ask you, Grandfather; did you take a liking to Christopher?"

"I liked him the moment I laid eyes on him walking across my carpet with a smile on his face and his hand held out in friendship," he told her.

"I am so glad to hear you say that, for if you like him, that is half the battle won."

"I take it he has asked you if he may call upon you?"

"Yes, he is coming at the weekend and I can't wait to see him."

"That being the case, Annie, I want you to leave the cottage and come and live here with me."

"Why would that be, sir?"

"Because I don't want the young man calling on you at the cottage while you are alone. But more than that, it is too lonely down there for you. I have been meaning to mention it since Winnie got married and went to live in East-Mid-Mould. I was hoping that you would find it lonely on your own and ask if you might come up to the house to live, but you haven't. I didn't want to make you feel as though you are being forced into it. Now if you are having a young man calling on you, I want you up here where I can keep an eye on things."

"Truth be told, Grandfather, it is lonely on my own down at the cottage, so, if it is all right with you, I would love to come and live here in the house with you."

"Then let us go down to the cottage and pack your bags, we want to be ready for the weekend."

The End

TWO PAIRS OF STOCKINGS

Chapter One

Isabel walked dejectedly along the dim corridor of The Wayfarers Inn. The funeral had gone as expected and her aunt Dora had looked very peaceful as the coffin was closed. Isabel had glanced at the scenery from the grave side. Rolling hills, valleys and a wide river winding its way to who knows where. Her aunt Dora would have loved the view.

On the one hand Isabel was sad at the loss, they had been the very best of friends and she was going to miss her terribly. But then again, her aunt Dora had suffered for the past eighteen months due to ill health.

Isabel had to admit it was a relief to know that her demise had put an end to her suffering.

The opening of a door to her right brought Isabel back to the present and she glanced casually that way. What she saw was a man of about forty years of age, looking back into the room, and Isabel followed his gaze.

Tied to the bedpost by her wrists, and a dirty looking piece of rag bound across her mouth, was a young girl in her early teens. Isabel and the young girl fleetingly made eye contact, but that glance told Isabel that the young girl was in need of help.

Isabel walked straight on, heading for her own bedroom that she had booked for the night. She unlocked the door and rushed inside, closing the door behind her and turning the key.

She placed her ear to the door but all she could hear at first was the pounding of her own heart. Isabel took a deep breath and held it until she heard a male voice say, "That should keep you from running away before I get back," then the sound of a door closing.

There was no time to think. Isabel unlocked her own door and made her way back along the corridor and tried the handle of the door leading into the room in which she had seen the young girl.

The door was locked. From experience, Isabel knew that in most of the inns, in this year 1821, all keys fitted most of the locks on the doors to the other rooms in the inns.

Isabel put her own key into the lock and, sure enough, when she applied pressure to it, she felt it give and she found herself inside the room where the young girl was still tied to the bedpost. Going straight over to the bed, Isabel untied the young girl's hands and dragged her to her feet, before heading out of the door, pulling the young girl with her.

Once out in the corridor, they heard the sound of footsteps running up the stairs and a voice saying, "You bloody idiot, I told you not to leave her on her own."

"But Hubert, I was hungry, I was only nipping downstairs to get something to eat," wailed Edgar.

"The next time I tell you to do something, you do it. After I had eaten you could have made your way down to get something to eat whilst I kept guard, but no, you have to go and leave that girl on her own. Idiot, you are a bloody idiot, Edgar.

Isabel went to the door straight across from the captive's room, tried the door handle and, thankfully, it gave way. She dragged the young girl in behind her, slammed the door shut, and shot behind it.

Sitting on the edge of a single bed was a portly gentleman dressed in a loose white shirt, tight leggings and wearing one boot. The other boot was in his hand and Isabel did not know whether the gentleman, was taking his boots off, or putting them on.

Angry voices reached the ears of the three people in that room. The door was thrust open once again, and the same gentleman whom Isabel had seen closing his bedroom door as she had passed by, stood in the doorway.

The door hid the two ladies, but the eyes of the gentleman sitting on the bed, moved from his two uninvited guests, to the not so clean looking gentleman standing in his doorway.

The gentleman on the bed was so incensed at this unexpected intrusion into his bedroom that he threw his boot at the intruder, asking, "What the hell do you want? Get out of my bedroom or I shall call the innkeeper, and have you thrown out of the inn."

The intruder glanced around the room and saw nothing except a boot sailing through the air and heading in his direction. He quickly closed the door, and the boot, hitting the door, fell to the ground.

The incensed gentleman's eyes returned to the two ladies, and seeing the plight of the younger of the two, instantly had the feeling of dread.

Isabel put her finger to her mouth indicating to the speechless gentleman to remain silent. She turned to the young girl and did the same to her. Isabel then, with the same finger, pointed down to the floor, directed to the young girl to stay put, and she turned and left the room.

Heading back along the corridor and down the stairs, Isabel went in search of the innkeeper and found him clearing tables in the private little parlour where she had eaten her evening meal.

"I am sorry to disturb you, sir, but I have come to pay what I owe you, for I must be off at the crack of dawn. I need to be away as soon as I am dressed. I have to attend a funeral tomorrow and I still have a fair way to go. Would you be so kind and ask the stable boy to hitch up my wagon for me at first light?"

"I will have it attended to, Miss, have no fear about that. That will be two shillings altogether, and I hope everything goes well for you tomorrow. Uncomfortable business, funerals."

"Thank you, that is very kind of you." After paying her bill, Isabel turned and headed back up the stairs and, taking a right turn, she headed back along the corridor.

She was just in time to see the young girl's captor coming out of her bedroom. "What, may I ask, are you doing in my bedroom?"

"You saw the girl, didn't you?"

"What girl?"

"The one I had in our room. As you passed by, you saw the young girl."

"I have no idea what you are talking about. Did you find a young girl in my bedroom?"

"No, I did not. May I ask why a young woman like you is wandering along the corridor of an inn on her own at this time of night? You are up to no good. What have you done with the young girl?"

Isabel was saved from having to reply to this when they were joined by a second gentleman, equally scruffy looking and he had an angry scowl upon his face.

"Who is this?" the second gentleman wanted to know.

"She was passing our bedroom when I was going out, so she might have seen what was going off inside."

The second gentleman's gaze returned to Isabel and asked, "Where have you been?"

"It is none of your business where I have been. What is going on here? Why are you two wondering around the corridor of this inn and accosting its guests? I have a good mind to go and have a word with the innkeeper, tell him about your weird behaviour," Isabel told them.

"Just tell us where you have been, and we will leave you alone," said the second gentleman.

"Although I have no need to explain my actions to you, I forgot to have a word with the innkeeper about my departure tomorrow. I have a funeral to attend so I must be off early. I went back down to pay the landlord what I owe him. It will save time in the morning."

"I will ask the innkeeper if that is so, and if he says different, you will be seeing us again."

"Please feel free to go now and ask him whilst I wait here with your friend. Although it displeases me to have to stand beside either of you, for you could both do with a bath. If it will satisfy your curiosity, and you will leave me alone, then I will put up with the smell."

Then Hubert said, "Let's go, Edgar," and the two gentlemen headed back along the corridor. She heard their footsteps descending the stairs.

Isabel, satisfied that, for the moment, the two ruffians where no longer above stairs, shot back into the portly gentleman's bedroom.

Isabel was amused to witness the portly gentleman still sitting in the same position as he had been when she had left his room. His eyes never leaving the young girl.

The young girl was still standing behind the door, wearing the gag, and staring back at him.

Isabel went over to the young girl, took the dirty piece of material away from her mouth, tossed it behind an armchair, then led her to the bed and sat her down next to the gentleman.

The gentleman stood up instantly and moved away from the bed. "Who the devil are you?" he demanded.

"My name is Isabel Fenfield, but I have no idea what this young girl's name is." Isabel looked at the young girl expecting her to inform them who she was, but she was disappointed. The young girl did not speak.

"Look, we have to get this young girl out of here and as far away from those two blackguards as soon as we can. I am going to have to go back to my room for the rest of the night in case I have any more visits from those two. They must not find out where this young girl is, they are up to no good. She must stay here with you tonight."

The incensed gentleman said, "Stay here for the night, not likely she isn't. You found her, so you keep her in your room. I don't want another visit from that scoundrel."

"We have no time to be quarrelling. Of course, she must stay here. Before it gets light in the morning, I want you to take this young girl out of the inn and find somewhere to hide along the road heading north towards Confield.

"I have arranged with the innkeeper to have my wagon hitched up and ready for the off at dawn. I will pick you up along the way, so watch out for my approach, but do not let anybody else see you."

"You are taking things too much for granted, young woman. Why should I get involved in your conspiracy? It isn't the done thing."

"It is not my conspiracy. I tumbled into this, just like you have. What is your name?"

"Ralph Leadsmythe."

"Well, Ralph, I wish you both goodnight and will see you at dawn, somewhere along the Confield road. I must go back to my room now. If those two scoundrels come looking in my room again, I must be there, or they will want to know where I have been, and we do not want that, do we?" And with that, Ralph was rendered speechless and left to his own devices.

Isabel made her way to her bedroom, locked herself in and placed a hardbacked chair under the door knob, then got undressed and made ready for bed.

Ralph did not have such luck. He eyed the young girl up and down and was displeased with the situation. He had never been in the petticoat line and he had certainly never been left in charge of a young girl in her teens.

"You had better take the bed. I will keep watch in the chair. Who are you?" he wanted to know.

The young girl did not reply but kept her eyes on Ralph as she stood and pulled the bedclothes back. She sat on the edge of the bed and swung her legs under the covers, her feet still encased in her brown leather ankle boots. Fully clothed, she laid down, and brought the covers up to her chin. She continued to keep her eye on Ralph, who returned the favour by keeping his eye on her. The young girl was the first to feel her eyelids drooping and then they closed altogether, and she was fast asleep.

Ralph went to sit in the tatty old armchair and took off his other boot, his eyes never leaving the young girl. He did not remember closing his eyes, but he must have done, for when he woke up, the crick in his neck told him his head had been laid to one side.

Ralph had no way of knowing how long he had been asleep, but he had no problem in remembering his unasked-for situation. He stood up and walked across to the window. Peeking through the curtains, he found it was pitch black outside, he could see nothing.

He pulled on his boots and then put on his coat. He walked over to the bed and shook the young girl by the shoulder, none too gently, and whispered, "We have to go. We need to get out of the inn before anyone is stirring, I don't know what time it is, but it is still dark, so it should hide our departure.

"We will have to go into the stables and get my horse, but I need something to cover his hooves with. If I don't cover his hooves, the noise on the cobbled courtyard will wake the whole inn."

Ralph went over to his carpetbag and pulled out two pairs of hose stockings. "These are going to have to do. It is just until we get out of earshot of the inn, then they can come off, that is if there is anything left of them after the horse has trampled them into the cobblestones. I am going to have to leave my carpetbag here and come back for it."

The young girl did not speak, but she climbed out of bed and waited until Ralph had put his head around the door to make sure the way was clear, and followed him into the corridor.

Ralph closed his bedroom door and locked it behind him, and then they crept forward, along the corridor onto the top landing, down the wooden staircase, and out of the inn.

Because they had exited through the front door, they had to creep around the side of the inn, and across the courtyard to the stables.

Luckily for them, the stables were deserted and the only sound that echoed around the wooden walls was the snorting of the horses at the unexpected intrusion of the night visitors.

Ralph's horse greeted him with a whinny and allowed him to pull one of his stockings over each hoof. They were very ill fitting and stretched to the limit, but they would serve their purpose.

Quickly saddling his horse and fixing the reins in place, Ralph walked his horse out of the stables, and with his heart pounding in his chest, they made good their escape across the cobbled courtyard, and out onto the Confield road.

After walking for a short distance Ralph took off the four stockings, noting as he did so, the sorry state they were in, so he tossed them to the ground, then jumped up into the saddle. He bent down to give the young girl a hand up so she could sit behind him. This was accomplished and once the young girl was safely sitting behind him with her arms around his girth, he urged his horse forward.

Hoping to find a good hiding place for them to stay until he could relieve himself of his burden, Ralph headed in a straight line until he could see, off to his left, a dark patch against the dark skyline.

He guessed that this was a wood, so he headed straight for it. A good place to hide, he decided. Daybreak was approaching fast.

Chapter Two

Isabel woke early and saw that it was beginning to get light, so she dressed and crept along the corridor, onto the top landing, down the wooden staircase and out of the front door.

She crept around the side of the inn, across the courtyard and into the stables. There she was met by a stable boy who was busy hitching up her wagon.

Not long after that, she was heading along the Confield road. She had met nobody as she negotiated the tricky exit to the inn courtyard. Slowly at first to cut down the noise, but as she got further away from the inn, she racked up the pace. She was a crack whip, for she had been taught by her father and she had no fear of overturning the wagon.

Light was rapidly showing her the way. She had passed nothing along the road where anyone could possibly hide, and she hoped and prayed that Ralph and the young girl had managed to achieve their goal.

She saw to her left the rooftop of a building surrounded by a high boundary wall and high trees to the rear. She could see the huge wooden gates were firmly shut, so she dismissed it as a hiding place.

She carried on for another mile or two but all she came across was open countryside, nowhere for anyone to hide. Isabel turned the wagon around and headed back the way she had come.

Ralph found, to his dismay, that what he had thought to be a wood, turned out to be a secluded, high boundary walled dwelling.

'There's nothing for it,' he thought, *'I will try to get help from the people who live here.'*

He turned and held out his hand to assist the young girl down from the back of the horse. After the young girl was safely on the ground, Ralph dismounted and handed the reins to her.

He tried lifting the latch that secured the huge wooden double gates closed and found, to his delight, they were not locked. He pushed one of the gates open, and the girl led the horse through. She waited while Ralph closed the gates on the outside world.

Mr Leggett, with his black Labrador bounding in front of him and his shotgun folded over his left arm, pulled at his high-necked collar. The morning was beginning to warm up. He unbuttoned his overcoat, which boasted three capes hanging from his shoulders, to reveal tan leggings encasing a fine pair of muscular legs. His feet were clad in shining black top boots. He came to an abrupt halt.

His dog had stopped on the edge of a little copse and was giving off a low growl. He silently raised the barrel of his shotgun and, pointing his finger and giving it a flick, the dog followed the command to go forward. Mr Leggett followed.

What met his eyes when his dog came to another abrupt halt was a portly gentleman closing his gates, and a young girl standing at the head of a horse.

"May I help you?" Mr Leggett asked.

Ralph spun round, and he saw a shotgun pointed in his direction.

Mr Leggett instantly recognised the portly gentleman and said, "Ralph, this is an unexpected pleasure. What the devil brings you here?"

Ralph looked from the shotgun to the face of the man holding the gun, and saw the friendly face of Lester Leggett staring at him.

"My God, Lester, can you help me, you say? I'll say you can. Look what I have here." Ralph pointed to the young girl.

"She is a bit young for you isn't she, Ralph? I didn't know you went in for that sort of thing."

"She isn't mine."

"I assumed she was with you."

"Well, you assumed wrong."

"Who is she with then?"

"Me."

"I think the best thing to do is go up to the house and try to sort this out."

"What are you doing here?" Ralph asked as they walked up the drive towards the house.

"This is my country home. The house I reside in, in Pencroft, is our town house."

"Damned lucky fellow to have two houses, I don't have one. Lost my job and now I am roaming around looking for work. Bad business I can tell you."

"I thought you worked for old Mrs Freeman."

"So I did, but she has gone to live with her daughter, too old to be living on her own. That is what the daughter said anyway. But all she was after was the money they got from the sale of her mother's house. They didn't give a damn about me."

"Sorry to hear that, it must be uncomfortable for you."

They had reached the house now and the door was opened by a butler and Mr Leggett said, "Canberry, have Mr Leadsmythe's horse taken care of and ask for tea and toast to be sent to the morning room."

"Very good, sir," the butler replied.

Once they were all comfortably settled in the morning room, Mr Leggett said to Ralph, "I would like to hear your story from the beginning. I was slightly confused with it at the gate."

"You are confused! Just you wait until I have told you how I came to have this young chit of a girl on my hands, then you will know what confused means. I had rented a room at The Wayfarers Inn, about a couple of miles to the north of here. I was on my way to Confield to see if I could procure myself another position, for I had heard Confield is a large town and there might be jobs going there.

"I had eaten my evening meal and was in the process of taking off my boots for bed, when this raving lunatic came into my room dragging this young girl with her. Not only that, the young girl had a dirty piece of cloth tied around her mouth. Made me gip, I can tell you. Why anyone should be barging into a fellow's room wearing a dirty piece of cloth around their mouth, is beyond reason.

"They hid behind my door, and, blast me, if the door didn't fly open again and there stood a scallywag. I had never seen him before, and I don't want to see him again, so I threw my boot at him, told him to be off or I would set the innkeeper on him."

Mr Leggett's eyes sparkled and there was only the tiniest shaking of the shoulders as he waited for Ralph to continue.

"Well, you know me from The Boxers Club, so you will know I do not go in for all that dancing around in that boxing ring. I like a quiet life, don't mind watching, but I never join in. Anyway, who wants to get their face bashed in for the sport of others? Not me.

"Then, this lunatic just walked out of my bedroom leaving me with this young girl. I have asked her who she is, but she isn't talking. The lunatic told me to set off early, take the Confield road and hide somewhere along the road and she would pick us up. Not that I needed picking up, for I have my own horse

"In the dark I mistook this place for a wood. I intended to hide here until the lunatic came to take this girl off my hands. What she didn't say was what I had to do with this chit if she didn't come and pick her up. You can't get a word out of this one, so it's no good asking her where she lives, if she had told me, I would have taken her back home. Now I'm lumbered with her.

"It all happened so quickly I didn't have time to think. There I was minding my own business and the next thing I know I have this young girl in my bed. The lunatic was bossy, very bossy, wouldn't take no for an answer. Bad business, very bad business.

"There were two of those scallywags roaming all over the inn. Don't know for sure but I think they were looking for this young girl, and, blow me, I had her. I had to put my stockings on my horse's hooves, so we could sneak out of the cobbled courtyard without being heard. Some damn funny business is going on if you ask me." Ralph finished and took a bite of his toast.

"Bad business indeed, Ralph. I wouldn't go around telling many people that last night you had a teenage girl in your bed, it might be taken the wrong way," Mr Leggett advised.

Ralph cast an enquiring eye at Lester. "Too young, Ralph, much too young, to have in your bed."

Ralph considered this, turned white, then red, and stammered, "I wasn't in bed with her. I had to sleep in a damned uncomfortable tatty old armchair. Don't you go around telling everybody I've had a chit of a thing in bed with me, because I have not, she had the bed, I had the armchair." Once more Ralph attacked his toast, he needed comfort.

"If you say so, Ralph, I believe you," Mr Leggett couldn't help replying.

The two scallywags woke and went in search of the innkeeper. They found him outside in the backyard, stacking barrels.

"Have any of your guests left this morning?" asked Hubert.

"I don't see what that has to do with you," replied the innkeeper.

"We found a guinea on the floor of the corridor, we want to return it to them," Hubert told him.

"Leave it with me and I will see that she gets it," the innkeeper said.

"How do you know where to send it on to?" Hubert wanted to know.

"That young woman in the room two doors away from yours left at dawn. She had a funeral to go to," was the reply.

"Oh yes, she did say something of that nature when we met on the corridor. We are heading in the same direction as she will be travelling. We will try and catch up with her and hand it over to her. Has anybody else beside the young woman left the inn?"

"No, they have not," confirmed the innkeeper.

"Then the money must belong to the young woman. Come on Edgar, let's go."

"Where are we going?"

"Anywhere away from here, we must get away, the game is up. If that woman made off in the middle of the night, then I am guessing she took the girl with her. It will not be long before the constabulary comes knocking," Hubert said.

"But what about the ransom money we were going to demand?" Edgar wanted to know.

"You can forget that. We should never have attempted this kidnapping in the first place. We will head in the opposite direction to home, Confield is no place for us now. We need to get as far away from home as we can. There is nothing there for us now anyway. The gull-catchers are after us, and you know what will happen if they do catch up with us, so we cannot go back home."

"But what are we going to live on, and where are we going to sleep?"

"Can't you use your own brain for once and stop asking questions. We are going to live off whatever turns up, nip in and out of people's houses. Pick up anything that they leave lying about. Sleep in barns or anything else we come across. It's that, behind bars or worse — we could find ourselves six feet under. Take your pick, I am heading out."

"Well, at least we will have the guinea to keep us going," Edgar said.

"What guinea?" Hubert asked.

"That guinea you told the innkeeper about, the one you found on the corridor floor."

"Sometimes, Edgar, I want to knock that stupid head off your shoulders. I did not find a guinea, you idiot, I made it up. I had to tell the innkeeper something so I could find out if the story the girl told us was true, that she was going to a funeral. I needed to try and find out if anyone else had left the inn, and it worked. Because nobody else has left the inn, that woman must have taken the girl with her. We have searched the inn from top to bottom and the girl has vanished."

"That is disappointing," Edgar said. "Now we are left with nothing."

"Seeing as that is how we started out, we had better disappear before the innkeeper is asking us for his dues."

Isabel saw the high wall she had passed earlier come into view, so she made straight for it, but before she reached her destination, coming in the opposite direction was a coach that also made for the huge double gates.

The two vehicles reached the gates at the same time and out of the window of the coach the pretty face of a young woman appeared. "Hello, may I help you?"

"Good morning, I am seeking a kidnapped young girl and a man called Ralph, I think they may have taken shelter here," Isabel told her.

"Now that is what I call an entrance, a kidnapped girl. Did you do the kidnapping?" the pretty face wanted to know.

"I did I'm afraid, and I have two not so pleasant gentlemen on my trail," Isabel admitted.

"What makes you think she will be here?"

"I told Ralph to hide somewhere along the road to Confield and this is the only place I have passed that someone could hide in, so I have returned to make enquires."

"You had better follow me and we will make enquiries together."

Arriving at the door of the impressive building, the young woman told her coachman to see to Isabel's horse, then she took her inside.

The door to the morning room opened and three pairs of eyes looked in the direction of the door and what they saw was a young woman and Isabel entering the room.

Ralph looked up from his toast and spluttered, "There she is, that's her, that's the lunatic." He pointed to Isabel.

Mr Leggett stood up and, walking over to the pretty young woman, he kissed her on the cheek and said, "Good to have you back, Minnie. Did you enjoy your little visit to see your friend?"

"Thank you, Lester, it is good to be back. Yes, I had a pleasant two days visiting Brenda, it was nice to see her again."

Mr Leggett moved over to address Isabel. He held out his hand to her, and as they shook hands, his comment was, "You are the loveliest lunatic I could ever wish to come across."

"Why thank you, I will take that as a compliment."

"She ain't you know, watch your step, Lester, or you will be dragged into her scheming," Ralph warned.

Lester's eyes sparkled down at Isabel and he said, "Lester Leggett, at your service, and my sister, Minnie,"

Isabel smiled back and said, "Isabel Fenfield."

"Well, Isabel, you seem to have made a good impression on Ralph, he has done nothing but talk about you since he has been here," Mr Leggett informed her.

Her eyes sparkled up at Mr Leggett and he was lost, his heart missed a beat then quickened up most alarmingly, a new experience for him, and one he decided he liked.

"What have you been saying about me?" Isabel asked Ralph.

"I told him you dumped this young girl on me then left me to take care of her. It is not the thing to do, damn it. She is all yours now. I wash my hands of the whole affair."

"Have you had breakfast?" Lester asked the two ladies.

"No, I set off very early because Brenda's father said it looked like rain," his sister told him.

"Nor I. I too set off early, but for an entirely different reason," Isabel said.

"Yes, tell us more," Minnie exclaimed. "I have never met a kidnapper before."

"Come and sit down and I will pour you both a cup of tea and I will ring for more toast, Ralph has demolished the last lot," Lester said amicably.

"Well, no one else was eating it. It is a shame to let good food go to waste and, besides, I was devilish hungry. You haven't been sneaking around in the middle of the night, dragging a young girl with you," Ralph said in his defence.

Isabel went across the room and sat beside the young girl. "How are you, my dear? Has Ralph been looking after you?"

"I shouldn't bother asking her anything, she has not uttered a word since you dumped her on me. She will not even tell me her name. Who the devil is she?" Ralph asked Isabel.

Isabel replied, "I have no idea who she is, but being tied to a bedpost by those two ruffians is enough to scare the bravest of us. I was heading along the corridor towards my room at The Wayfarers Inn, and as I passed one of the other rooms, the door opened and out stepped this shabbily dressed man.

"He turned to say something to someone in the room and I followed his eyes, and, for a split second, I saw this young girl, tied to the bedpost and she looked terrified. Our eyes met and she was pleading for help. I couldn't ignore the fact that I had seen her tied to a bedpost and gagged by a filthy piece of rag, now could I?

"When I heard the man close and lock the door to the room, and his footsteps receding along the corridor and heading for the stairs, I peeked out of my bedroom door. The man was no longer in sight. I left my room and headed for the door to the room that I had seen the young girl in. I tried the door but of course it was locked, so I used the key to my room to enter his room. I untied the young girl, pulled her to her feet and dragged her out of the bedroom with me.

"Unfortunately, just as we had escaped out of their room, I heard angry voices approaching from the direction of the stairs. We did not have time to make it to my room, so I opened the nearest door, and it just happened to be the room Ralph was in.

"I must say it was a bit of good luck for us. Ralph threw his boot at the scoundrel when he burst into his room looking for this young girl. You were magnificent, Ralph, pity your boot missed the mark, but good try all the same."

All eyes looked at Ralph and he was pushed into saying, "I told you she is a lunatic."

Laughter echoed around the room and Ralph was the only one not to share in the merriment. Instead, he buttered himself the last piece of toast.

When the second round of toast arrived, Isabel buttered two slices and took the plate over to the young girl who accepted it gratefully and began to eat the offering.

"I might know who she is," Minnie told them.

"And how would you know that?" her brother asked.

"Brenda told me, whilst I was there, she had heard that Milton Burns' granddaughter had been kidnapped."

"Milton Burns, isn't he the money lender from Sunwest?" Ralph asked.

"You know money lenders, Ralph?" Isabel asked with a raised eyebrow.

"No, of course I don't know him, but I have heard of him. Everybody has heard of him. You do not want to get on the wrong side of Milton Burns," Ralph told them.

Mr Leggett stood up and went out of the morning room and into his study. Picking up his quill, he dipped it into the ink and wrote a short note, folded it over and sealed it with some sealing wax, then tugged at the bell pull.

His butler appeared at the door. "Go to the stables and ask Tom to have a ride into Sunwest and deliver this letter straight away. The address is on the front. Please stress to Tom that it is very urgent."

Mr Leggett went and re-joined his guests and asked Ralph, "Did you pay your dues at The Wayfarers Inn before you left?"

Ralph looked aghast at Lester. "Damn me, I didn't. Never gave it a thought, had too much on my mind."

"In that case," said Mr Leggett, "we will await a visit from the constabulary."

Ralph looked at Isabel and asked, "Did you pay for your room before you left?"

"Of course. I didn't want to be arrested for avoiding paying my dues. But I hold up my hand and confess I told a little white lie. I told the innkeeper that I was leaving at dawn because I had a funeral to go to, and that was not true. I had been to a funeral earlier that day, but it sounded an excellent excuse for me to give to be leaving at such an hour. I am sure my aunt Dora, whose funeral it was, would not have been offended at my using her funeral as an excuse. She would have found the situation very amusing."

"Found the situation very amusing? I would have you know that since you pushed your way into my life, in less than twenty-four hours, I have had the threat of scallywags on my heels, I have had a young girl left in my care, and now I find out that you have kidnapped her. But to beat it all, I have the police on my heels, and, even worse, Milton Burns. I hope to God he asks how his granddaughter came to be in my care before he takes out his shotgun.

"I had to give up my bed for the night to this young girl who has not uttered a word of thanks, and that reminds me, I woke up with a stiff neck after sitting all night in a tatty old armchair. I had forgotten about my stiff neck with all this hullabaloo nonsense going on. And then there are my stockings, what about them? The horse ruined them, and now I have no spare pair of stockings. Why didn't you choose somebody else's door to barge through? I suppose you find all that very amusing too?"

"Just a word of advice, Ralph, just in case you have forgotten, don't mention to Milton Burns if you see him, that you had his granddaughter in your bed. Or he might indeed use the shotgun and ask questions later," Mr Leggett couldn't help remarking.

Ralph cast a furious glance at Mr Leggett, then he looked in Minnie's direction and his face became bright red.

"I think under the circumstances you acted very wisely. But I do not see why you should be complaining about having to give up your bed for the night. After all you have not paid for it," Isabel told Ralph with an innocent look on her face.

Ralph was once more bereft of speech and could only manage to say, "And this is all the thanks I get for putting my head in a noose."

"You had been to a funeral, had you? Were you close to your aunt Dora?" Lester asked Isabel, after all the laughter had died down.

"Yes, very close. She was my mother's sister and when my mother died, we became even closer. She was two years older than my mother so when my grandfather died, aunt Dora inherited the family estate. My grandfather made sure my mother was well provided for after he died, so she bought the little cottage I now live in on the outskirts of Confield. Aunt Dora never married, so she had no one but me. Now my aunt Dora has passed on I have no other relatives, only my old nanny, Flossy. The solicitor who attended the funeral tells me aunt Dora has left everything to me and he is coming to see me the day after tomorrow to sort things out.

"Aunt Dora has rather a large house in Teesman, and I have no idea how to go on with it, so I shall have to find out quickly and learn even quicker. As I have already told you, I live in the cottage that belonged to my mother, on the edge of Confield, with my old nanny. Looking after a little cottage is far different to looking after a house the size of aunt Dora's.

"Flossie, my nanny, would have accompanied me to the funeral, but I considered the journey too exacting for her at her age, she will be seventy-one next month."

"Teesman, I have just left Teesman. Who was your aunt?" Ralph asked.

"She was known as Miss Greenman."

"A large house you say? More like a huge estate."

"Did you know my aunt Dora?" Isabel asked.

"She occasionally called on my employer and, on the odd occasion, I would drive my employer over to visit her. But enough about your aunt Dora, what am I going to do about the constabulary? The innkeeper at The Wayfarers Inn is bound to send them after me."

"Have no fear, Ralph, I know the innkeeper, and I will sort things out with him. And if the constabulary do come looking for you, that will be sorted out too. Under the circumstances, I think they will understand," Lester said, trying to calm the agitated Ralph down.

"I think it would be a good thing if the constabulary were to come, then we could get this business sorted out," Minnie said.

"You sound just like she does," Ralph said, nodding in Isabel's direction. "Don't give a damn if a fellow is arrested for kidnapping."

"Don't tell me you would have preferred it if Isabel had not seen this young girl tied up to the bedpost, and left her to her fate with your two scallywags?" Minnie asked.

Ralph had the grace to blush and said, "No, I would have preferred it if she had barged into somebody else's bedroom rather than mine."

"Well, what is done now is done, we are going to have to make the best of it. I have sent a note to Milton Burns, informing him that we might have his granddaughter here. Let us hope he gets here before the constabulary or we might find ourselves in a sticky position. With Milton Burns reputation I don't think he will be keen to make contact with the constabulary, do you?" Lester asked them.

Chapter Three

Whilst they were eating their toast, it was decided that they should all stay the night, in order to see what turn of events took place later that day. Not knowing what time to expect Mr Burns, or even if he would appear at all, it could be too late in the day to be setting off for Confield. If Milton Burns did arrive, and he was the young girl's grandfather, then the problem of what to do with her was solved. If he was not, then they still had the problem. The constabulary would have to be brought in.

After everyone had eaten their fill, Minnie showed them to their rooms to enable them to have a short rest and refresh themselves before lunch.

Ralph said he was most grateful because he was dead on his feet. Having to rise at an ungodly hour, and go sneaking about the inn with rogues and scallywags roaming about, had been no mean task. He was most grateful to be able to pass his burden back to Isabel, he was washing his hands of the whole affair.

Minnie tucked her hand through his arm and led them all upstairs. She opened the first bedroom door she came to, and slipped inside, indicating with a nod of her head, that Ralph was to follow her. This was to be his room.

Ralph made no complaint, but was shocked beyond belief when she winked at him and whispered, *"Next door to mine."*

He rushed in, pushed Minnie out and slammed the door closed behind her. He stood with his back pressed to the door and thought, *'It must be something I ate. It can't be anything else. Any minute now I am going to wake up, this is not happening to me, it is too ridiculous for words.'* He turned and looked for a key. No key. But there was a bolt, so the bolt was drawn across. Happy that the door was securely bolted shut, he made for the bed.

Isabel looked at Minnie when they heard the bolt being set in place and they both started giggling as they walked further along the landing.

"I like Ralph," Minnie told Isabel. "He makes me laugh. Poor man doesn't know what to expect next."

"I know, I like him as well and if this young lady here could talk, I think she would tell us she likes him too." Isabel put her arm across the young girl's shoulder and said, "I think your grandfather will be here to collect you as soon as he receives Mr Leggett's letter, so you may as well share my room. It should only be for a few hours."

After leaving Isabel and the young girl in the comfort of a second bedroom, Minnie made her way back downstairs to join her brother in the morning room.

"Well, kidnappers, scallywags and money lenders. It has certainly been an entertaining morning."

Her brother smiled. "Very entertaining indeed. I think all our lonely days and nights might be over Minnie, don't you?"

"What do you mean by that?"

"I saw the way you looked at Ralph. I have never seen you look like that at any man before. And I saw him keep glancing in your direction, and each time he did so, his colour heightened, so I think the feeling is mutual."

"I must admit he roused my curiosity somewhat. In fact, I went as far as to tease him when we parted at one of the spare bedrooms. I whispered in his ear that, it was the bedroom next to mine to see what his reaction would be. He physically pushed me out of the bedroom, and slammed the door shut on me, then drew the bolt across.

"It was so funny, and a totally different reaction to that of any other man I have ever come across. If I had whispered in another man's ear that my bedroom was next to theirs, well, I will leave the rest to your imagination. He is a breath of fresh air and I find him extremely amusing."

"Yes, I could tell you did. I must admit he had my shoulders shaking. I think he is enjoying himself immensely too, but he isn't going to admit it."

"I guess Isabel had the same effect on you. She seemed to fit in perfectly well, as though she has been a regular visitor here. Funny how things turn around from one moment to the next, isn't it?

"I left Brenda's this morning feeling very deflated, for she is very happily married and content. I have never met a man that I think I could spend the rest of my life with. Then out of the blue, Ralph appeared, and for some odd reason, I took to him straight away."

"When Isabel said she had been left everything by her aunt Dora and she had no idea how to go on, my first instinct was to protect her, to tell her I would help her sort everything out. When this kidnapping business is concluded, that is what I am going to do. Accompany her home and leave Ralph here to help you run this place, tell him we need a bookkeeper and see if he is willing to be employed by us.

"He will never suspect what's in store for him, so you had better take it easy with him. I don't think he will say no to coming to work for us, do you? After all, he is looking for a job and whilst he is working here you can work your magic on him. The poor man will never know what's hit him."

Minnie thought about what he had just said and pictured her life having Ralph around all the time, and she liked the vision. "I hope he will accept the offer, Lester, I hope he is willing to stay, the thing is, I might have scared him off. I will have to put him on a diet of course. Once he has lost that puppy fat, I think he will look most handsome. Don't you?"

Lester laughed and remarked, "Poor Ralph,"

She chose to ignore him, turning on her heels she said, "I will go and see cook and tell her that there will be three more mouths to feed at lunch time."

"Don't forget to tell her, a low-fat menu," Lester said to her retreating back.

He heard her laughter echoing around the hall as she headed for the kitchen. It was good to hear.

It was a pleasant lunch, and Ralph kept them all entertained with tales of deception and lechery by his last employer. She was seventy years of age and the things she got up to made him blush. She had the money to pay for anything she wanted. And pay she did.

They had all retired into the morning room once lunch was over and, around two thirty that afternoon, the butler appeared in the doorway. Following close behind him was a tall but slim and imposing figure of a gentleman in his late fifties, early sixties. He was flanked on either side by two burly looking men who you would not want to mess with or meet on a dark night.

The young girl, on seeing the three gentlemen, jumped up from her seat and ran across the room, throwing herself at the tall gentleman saying, "Grandpapa, Grandpapa. I am so pleased to see you, Grandpapa, thank you for coming for me."

"Eliza, are you all right? You know very well if I had known where you were, I would have come for you. I came as soon as I received the letter from Mr Leggett. Are you sure you are all right?"

"I am now. Oh, Grandpapa, I am so glad to see you, you have no idea how glad. I have been having a very unpleasant time of it."

"Have you now, and who has been making your life unpleasant?"

The look that the elderly gentleman cast around the occupants of the room, and the two burly men taking a step forward, made Ralph's face turn a deathly white. A look of guilt was so clear on his face that Milton Burns took it to be Ralph.

Their eyes locked and Ralph was so scared, he could not remove his eyes away from the stare of Milton Burns, or utter a word in his own defence.

"None of these people here in this room, Grandpapa, they have been looking after me." She ran to Isabel's side and added, "this is Isabel; she is the one that kidnapped me from my kidnappers."

Mr Burns came forward and held out his hand. "I am in your debt, young woman. It is no use saying thank you, for returning my granddaughter back to me. Thank you, does not express the gratitude I feel. If there is ever anything you need, you must come and see me or get word to me. I will be forever at your service. Whatever it is, if you are in need of help or in any kind of trouble, you must let me know. Is that understood?"

"Yes, sir, I understand and thank you. It is a comfort to know that I have someone to turn to if I am in need of help."

Eliza then went across to Ralph and said, "And this is Ralph, you owe him two pairs of stockings, please Grandpapa."

"Two pairs of stockings. Why do I owe him two pairs of stockings?"

"Because he put his spare stockings on his horse and they were ruined, and now he does not have a spare pair."

Mr Burns looked at Ralph and said, "You have a horse that wears your stockings? I am not surprised you don't have a spare pair. In my line of work, I meet many people who have odd fantasies, but a man that likes to dress his horse up in his stocking, now that I have not heard before. Doesn't the horse object to it? After all, it is not normal for a horse to wear stockings."

Ralph looked at Eliza and said, "You could have given a clearer explanation than that."

Eliza laughed, stood on tiptoe and kissed Ralph on his cheek. "I prefer my version of events, it lets the imagination run riot. Anyway, my grandpapa will not mind if you have a tendency for dressing up your horse, like he says, he has heard them all, or he thought he had."

"Everyone to their own. If my granddaughter wants me to buy you two pairs of stockings, so be it. It is not often that Eliza puts her trust in a stranger, especially a man, but she seems to be at ease with you. Although I must say you are the most unlikely hero I have come across. Alan, make sure Ralph gets his stockings, we don't want him to miss out on dressing up his horse. Better make it a dozen pairs of stockings, he's going to need them."

"Very good, sir. Where do you want the stockings sending to?" one of the burly men asked Ralph.

Ralph was once again rendered speechless; his nightmare was back.

Lester came to Ralph's rescue by looking across at Alan and telling him, "Send them here, we will see that Ralph gets his stockings."

Mr Burns did not miss the sparkle in Lester's eyes and smiled. "You must be Mr Leggett, the one who sent me the letter."

Lester came forward with outstretched hand. "I am, sir, Lester Leggett."

"I am very pleased to make your acquaintance, Mr Leggett. The same applies to you, and anyone involved in helping Eliza out of her plight. Anytime you need help, just come and see me. Alan is my right-hand man. He will sort your names out and make a note for me before we leave. I cannot thank you all enough.

"Especially you, Ralph, how did you come to be involved with the rescue of my granddaughter?"

"I had lost my job and was on my way to Confield to try and find employment. I booked into The Wayfarer's Inn for the night. It just happened to be the room that Isobel charged into. I was in the wrong room at the wrong time, how's that for bad luck? Getting mixed up in this mad adventure, and being chased all over the countryside by kidnappers, is not my idea of fun at all."

"You are looking for a job, are you? I am always looking for reliable men to come and work for me. You may come and work for me if you so wish. I am sure Alan here could sort something out for you."

It was Isabel who came to Ralph's rescue this time for she said, "I am sure none of us need your thanks, Mr Burns. Eliza is a charming young girl. We have all been happy to help,"

Ralph had the urge to say he had not been happy to help, but the presence of Alan and his pal, made him keep his tongue between his lips.

"Tell me, Mr Leggett, how did you know that Eliza was my granddaughter? And how did you know where to send your note to? Not many people know where I live and I am not aware that we are acquainted," Mr Burns asked.

"My sister, Minnie, had been to visit a friend for a few days, and she lives in Sunwest. Her friend told her that, rumour had it, someone had kidnapped your granddaughter. Upon hearing the story of how Isabel and Ralph came to be in possession of a young girl, by kidnapping her from her kidnappers, and they were all on the run, she put two and two together.

"Minnie told us that it is not often you hear about a kidnapping so hearing about two kidnapping tales in the same vicinity, it was easy enough for us all to agree that she had to be your granddaughter. Isabel saw Eliza tied to a bedpost in an inn that both she and Ralph were guests in. Had it not been for her quick thinking, Eliza might very well still be tied to the bedpost.

"As for knowing where you live, I am a member of The Boxers Club and gossip is rife there, it spreads like wild fire. So your name has been mentioned on more than one occasion. Various aspects of your dealings are quite renowned, including where you live. The tattlers love to spread the gossip I'm afraid. There is no hiding place for anybody, the truth will out along with untruths. The knack is to sort out which story is true and which is not.

"Some people will believe the lies before the truth. I think many more people than you realise are aware of what you do, and where you reside. No doubt a lot of things I have heard about you are far from the truth."

"I see. Well on this occasion, I am very pleased the tattlers have been at work, it has given me my granddaughter back. Who was it that kidnapped you, Eliza?" Mr Burns asked.

"Two men. One called Edgar, and the other Hubert. That is all I can tell you. That is what they called each other anyway. I had never met them before, and I hope I never see them again," Eliza told him.

"How did they capture you?"

"I had gone to Edna's. We were playing hide and seek in the wood at the side of her house and I was pounced on. I did not see who had pounced on me because they put a sack over my head. I screamed and screamed and kicked and kicked until they laid me on the floor, took the sack off my head, then they put a filthy piece of rag across my mouth to stop me screaming.

"Edgar said it was no use putting the sack back over my head for I had seen what their faces looked like now. They took me to that inn where Isabel saw me tied to the bedpost. One kept the innkeeper busy, and the other one forced me up the stairs and onto the landing where we waited until the one talking to the innkeeper, came up with a key and let us in the room."

"Those two scoundrels. They owe me a lot of money. I suppose they thought of blackmailing me to get you back. Well it has backfired on them. Did you get that, Alan?"

"Got it and noted, sir."

"Good, let me know the outcome, or even better, bring them to me, I will deal with them."

"Very good, sir."

"What are you going to do to them, Grandpapa?"

"There is no need for you to know that, Eliza, but I guarantee they will not lay a finger on you again. It will be an excellent opportunity for me to let it be known that if anybody touches you in future, there will be no mercy shown when I catch up with them. And catch up with them I will. Let the tattlers do their best work with that."

"Why didn't you speak to any of us and tell us of your situation?" Isabel asked Eliza.

"Grandpapa told me that if I ever found myself in an awkward position, not to speak. Best not to let anybody know my grandpapa was Milton Burns. So that is what I did."

"Precisely the point I tried to get over to Eliza, do not speak, because of the gossips that Mr Leggett has just been speaking of. The kidnappers might not have known she was my granddaughter and it is better that they did not. As it turned out they did know, but no harm has been done and I have my Eliza back and Alan will make sure Hubert and Edgar are brought to me to be dealt with.

"I would just like to say that not everything you hear about me will be true, ninety percent of the time the gossips have exaggerated, as you have already pointed out. If you do not cross me, you have nothing to fear from me. I hope you will all regard me as your friend from now on. Do I make myself clear?"

"I think we all understand, sir," Mr Leggett replied. "So, as a friend, if you don't mind me mentioning it, Mr Burns, I think it would be advisable if you made yourself scarce. I am expecting a visit from the constabulary because Ralph, in making good his escape with your granddaughter, left The Wayfarers Inn without paying his dues.

"The innkeeper might have informed the constabulary and they might be on the lookout for him. The first place they are going to call at is here, as we are the first house from The Wayfarers Inn on the way to

Confield. I am guessing you would not like to be here if they do come knocking on my door," Lester informed Mr Burns.

"In that case, we shall be on our way. I will always be in your debt."

Lester escorted them out and returned to join the others. "Now that is settled, what about you and I returning to The Wayfarers and sorting things out, Ralph, then we can all be comfortable."

"Yes, and I also want my carpetbag. I had to leave it behind in my room, so the only clothes I have at the moment, are what I am stood in," Ralph informed them.

"But before we go, Milton Burns offered you a job, Ralph, you didn't reply when he said he would find you a position working for him. Is it something you would consider doing?" Lester asked.

"I might be desperate to get a job, but I am not suicidal. Can you imagine what it would be like working for him? No thank you. I will carry on my way to Confield to try and find employment there. Like I was doing before all this happened."

"There is a job going here. What do you think about staying here and working for Minnie and me?"

Ralph glanced over at Minnie and, once more, his face became bright red, and he lost his tongue.

"I will take that as a *'yes'* then, shall I?"

Ralph dragged his eyes away from Minnie and asked, "Doing what?"

"Keeping our books in order, of course. That is what you do, isn't it?"

"There's a job going here? Who is doing the books now?"

"Minnie is."

"Then why are you asking me to come and work for you if Minnie is doing the books?"

"Because in eighteen months, Minnie will be married and having a baby, with a fair wind and a bit of luck. That is why we need someone to do the books."

"You are getting married?" asked a disappointed Ralph.

"I certainly hope so," Minnie replied.

"Whoever he is, he is a lucky man," Ralph stated.

"Why thank you, Ralph. I will let you know who he is when I have caught him. I might add that you will be the first to know," Minnie replied.

"Well, if there is a job going here, I will snatch your hand off. That would be splendid, I accept. I must admit, I didn't like the idea of going to work in a busy town. I much prefer the countryside. This has turned out to be most advantageous for me. Blow me, I never thought having a kidnapped chit of a thing left on my hands would work out like this. Thought I was going to end up behind bars or left to the tender mercies of Milton Burns." Ralph held out his hand to Lester, looked over at Minnie and his colour instantly heightened.

"As for you, Isabel, thank you for bringing Ralph here, now we have a much-needed bookkeeper," Lester told her.

"It must have been fate taking a hand for I just tumbled into this like Ralph did. There is no need to thank me because I have enjoyed this little interlude. It has been a pleasure meeting you all and to add to that, I now have a money lender as an ally." Isabel's eyes sparkled with mischief.

"Would you care to take a stroll in the garden before Ralph and I make our way to The Wayfarers to settle his bill?" Lester asked Isabel.

"Very much, it will help me sleep," was her reply.

"I don't think you will need your coat, it is a pleasant evening, so we can use the French window instead of going out of the front door." He pointed to the glass doors revealing a splendid view across a lush green lawn.

Lester held the door open for her to pass through and indicated to his right so Isabel started walking that way.

"You mentioned your aunt's estate and that a solicitor was coming to see you to go through all the legal minefield. I would be more than willing to accompany you home and be by your side whilst the solicitor is taking you through it. I had to go through the same procedure when my father died, he had left everything to my mother of course, which was an unusual thing to do.

"Normally, the father passes his estate onto his eldest son, but my mother and father doted on each other and he was making sure if anything happened to him, she was taken care of. Not that my father was in any doubt that Minnie and I would take care of our mother because we also doted on her. My father knew that when my mother passed away, she would leave the estate to me and Minnie.

"Again, it is unusual for the daughter to be included in the will, but it is her home as well as mine. When our mother died, I had to go through all the legal stuff again, so I am becoming a dab hand at it.

"I think that is the reason Minnie and I have never found anybody that took our fancy, because our mother and father were so happily married, we never seemed to meet the right person. Then out of the blue you and Ralph turn up at our door. Minnie has taken to Ralph, she tells me he is unlike any other man she has met. That is why we have offered him the job as bookkeeper. Minnie wants to get to know him better."

"I must admit he is comical. He moans and complains about everything but knuckles down and gets on with the job. I think he has secretly enjoyed himself the past couple of days, but he is not going to admit it. Have you seen how he blushes when he meets Minnie's eye?" Isabel's delighted laughter was infectious.

"I have, he gets tongue tied too. Enough about Ralph, let's go back to your problem. Ralph said that your aunt Dora's estate is a large one, and if it is, it will not be an easy job to learn all the administration it takes. You could always sell it or you could take the task on and try to make a go of it. You are a young woman and a highly intelligent one at that. If your aunt Dora could run the estate, I don't see why you should not be able to.

"There is another option you could take if you so wanted to. As I have already said, I would be more than willing to accompany you home and give you support if you needed it. It would give me something to do and it would give Minnie space to work on Ralph. Poor old fellow doesn't know what he's in for. Minnie is already talking about putting him on a diet, but I don't think he will object too strongly, do you?"

"No, I don't. If you are sure you don't mind, I would appreciate your expertise, but I don't want to put you out of your way. No doubt I will eventually find my way around it all, but I would be an idiot to refuse your help if you are willing to provide it."

"In that case it is settled, we journey north tomorrow. Let's hope the weather is on our side too. Shall we go back and inform the others and arrange for our transport to be ready for first thing tomorrow morning? I told Ralph I would go back to The Wayfarers Inn with him, and make things right with the innkeeper, and pick up his precious carpetbag. So, when we get back, he and I will head out to The Wayfarers, then we can be comfortable for the rest of the evening."

Their amusement showed on their faces as they looked at each other and a friendship was born, no need for words. They walked back towards the house and Lester lazily pointed things of interest out to Isabel.

Although it was a very distressing time for Isabel, she felt as though a great weight had been lifted off her shoulders, she no longer felt alone in the world.

As for Lester, his search for a life partner had come to an end. His father had been lucky enough to meet his mother, and he had never looked back. Lester knew he would never have course to look back either, there was nothing for him to see. His future on the other hand was shining so bright, it was blinding.

When they reach the French doors and entered the drawing room, Minnie and Ralph were sat in companionable silence.

"Minnie, I am having to go away for a few days. I have offered my help to Isabel and she has accepted it. I know you are capable of running our estate and, now you have Ralph to help you, my conscience is clear."

"Very well, Lester, as you wish. I hope everything goes well for you, Isabel, I'm sure it will. And there is always Ralph if you need him." Minnie smiled over at Ralph.

"I would just like to point out that I already have a job, thank you. One man, one job. Can't take too much on, not good for my health," Ralph complained.

"Are you refusing to help Isabel after all she has done for you?" Minnie asked him.

Ralph's face became bright red once more and he stammered, "I didn't say I wouldn't do it, did I? Just pointing out that I do have a job now and I am not looking for other work."

"Well, that's settled then, Ralph is willing to give you a hand if you need it, Isabel. Isn't that good of him?" Minnie gave them all a beautiful innocent smile.

Ralph was rendered speechless.

Lester and Ralph made their way to the stables to collect their horses and Lester said to Ralph whilst they were fixing the reins in place, "Would you like to borrow a couple of pairs of my stockings for your horse, Ralph? I don't want you to feel you are riding a naked horse around the countryside."

Ralph gave Lester a scathing look and replied, "Very funny."

Lester burst out laughing. "You are never going to live this down, Ralph."

"You don't have to tell me that. This is what you get when you put yourself in danger by interfering in someone else's business."

"But there is always a plus and minus to everything. Are you saying that you wish you had not had a hand in helping Eliza escape from your scallywags? Because if you are, you would never have landed up at my door and you would still be looking for a job. To say nothing of meeting my sister, Minnie."

"They aren't my scallywags, don't want them," Ralph grumbled.

"And Minnie?"

Ralph had the grace to blush and he turned away. Giving his saddle one last tug, he mounted his horse and left Lester laughing as he also mounted his horse and set off after the retreating Ralph.

At the Wayfarer's, Lester had a word with the innkeeper. As it turned out, the innkeeper had no idea that Ralph had left the inn. He had seen Ralph's carpetbag in his room and he had thought he had gone for a ride and would be coming back. Ralph paid his dues and went to collect his belongings and they were soon heading back home.

Chapter Four

Ralph had been shown into a comfortable room in the servants' quarters and he sat on his bed looking round. He couldn't believe his luck. He had found a job without even trying. It was out in the countryside and this was the nicest room he had been given as his own in the past ten years of making his way in the world.

He was much relieved to be installed in the servants' quarters, for it made him feel very uncomfortable when he thought he might have had to sleep in the bedroom next to Minnie.

Minnie was another thing that made him feel uncomfortable, but in a different way. He liked the way he felt when he caught her looking at him. Even though he felt ridiculous when his cheeks became infused with colour and he knew she knew what was going through his mind. Damned embarrassing. Life was complicated, but he would work it out, with Minnie's help, God willing.

Lester had asked him if he wished he had never met Isabel, Eliza or the scallywags, well he had to admit to himself, he had had a great time and he had met Minnie. A slight smile appeared on his lips, he swung his legs onto the bed, placed his hands behind his head and he lay on the bed, let his mind wonder, and his smile got bigger.

The following morning, Lester had stowed Isabel's luggage onto the back of her wagon, along with his own. He tied his horse to the back and took his place at her side. Taking the reins from her, he set the horse in motion and they were on their way down the drive heading towards Confield.

Once clear of the gates, Lester said, "Well, Isabel, it was a very interesting day yesterday, I must say."

Isabel laughed. "You can say that again. Goodness knows what Flossie will say about all this."

"Flossie being your nanny?"

"Yes. When my mother died, I inherited the little cottage on the edge of Confield from her along with some money and Flossie. The will stated that I had to look after Flossie and not turn her out of the cottage. I know why my mother put this clause in the will, it was not to keep a roof over Flossie's head, for she knew I would not turn her out. She did it so Flossie could keep an eye on me. There wasn't a fortune, but if I was careful, Flossie and I would be all right. Now there is the family estate in Teesman. I was not expecting it. Aunt Dora also has a nephew called Samuel Bergun.

"He is the son of my mother's brother who, had he not been killed in the war, would have inherited the estate even though he was younger than my aunt Dora. That was because of him being a man of course. I expected the estate to be left to Samuel, it came as quite a shock when the solicitor told me aunt Dora had left everything to me.

"I had never met Samuel before the funeral, and when I did, I wished I hadn't. When he heard I had inherited the family estate, he caused a very unpleasant scene. He said I had bullied aunt Dora into leaving the estate to me and by rights it should have gone to him. The solicitor told him that aunt Dora said in no uncertain terms that Samuel was not to get a penny.

"It was written in the will, that if aunt Dora outlived me, then the estate was to go to a children's orphanage she visited and helped support. I didn't know anything about the orphanage, she had never mentioned it to me. The solicitors say that aunt Dora said she knew that when I find out about the orphanage, I would continue to support it, whereas Samuel would not.

"I must admit I did not like the man and I felt threatened. When Milton Burns told me that if ever I was in need of his services, Samuel's face flashed before my eyes. It is a relief to know that Mr Burns has my back."

"Mr Burns is not the only one who has your back. If Samuel should come seeking you out, he will have me to deal with."

Isabel glanced up at Lester and Lester, feeling her eyes on him, looked down at her and he was pleased to see colour flood her cheeks and he smiled gently at her. Isabel averted her eyes and tried to control her breathing.

It was a pleasant journey to Confield and Lester was soon pulling the horse to a halt and, as Isabel jumped down, the cottage door opened and a spritely lady of undefinable years appeared at the door.

Isabel ran up to her and gave her a warm embrace. "Flossie, I would like to introduce you to Lester Leggett, he will be staying with us for a while. I am expecting a visit from a solicitor and he is here to help me out."

The old lady eyed the gentleman who stood before her, and it was a few seconds before she held out her hand to shake the one he had extended to her. "What have you been up to Isabel?" she asked keeping her eye on Lester.

"Nothing, only a bit of kidnapping, it detained me from returning home yesterday. Oh, yes, I also have a money lender as a protector if ever I need one. And I collected this gentleman on the way. He will be our guest for a few days."

"I don't believe a word of it, but come on in, young man and we will have some refreshments. You must be parched travelling in this heat," Flossie said.

"There is a spare room at the back of the cottage, I will put clean bedding on for you, you will be quite comfortable in there. Not much room but the bed is built for comfort," Flossie informed him as she poured him a cup of tea.

"That is very kind of you, Flossie, but I had intended to stay at the nearest inn until the solicitor has been. I don't want to put you to any trouble or stain Isabel's reputation."

"It will be no trouble, and as for Isabel's reputation, she can look after that herself. I shall be here to chaperone her, and anyway there is nobody to care about her reputation other than me, for she does not care a fig for it herself. Very independent is our Isabel. Look at her bringing you here. She must have a good reason to trust you, so that is good enough for me. Drink your tea whilst I go and see to your room."

"Are you all right with that arrangement, Isabel?" Lester asked when the old lady had vanished behind the closed door.

"Yes, of course I am. Don't let Flossie fool you, she is all for a woman having her own independence, she has lived on her wits for as long as I have known her. She and my mother were the very best of friends and she is part of my family, in fact, now aunt Dora has departed, she is the only family I have. I have known about Samuel for a long time of course, but I do not class him as part of my family. If half of the things aunt Dora told me about him are true, then I want nothing to do with him.

"I don't regard Flossie as a servant, she is a wonderful old lady and I don't know what I would do without her. I don't know how she is going to react when I tell her that aunt Dora has left me the family estate, she is not one for big houses, or so she tells me. She says most of them take a vast amount of money to run and, in the winter, the cost of heating them does not bear thinking about."

"She has that right," Lester stated, "the winter months do tend to run away with the money."

"I hope you will be comfortable in the spare room, it is much, much smaller than the one you are used to, but it should only be for a couple of days. The solicitor said he would call on Friday and that is tomorrow so things should be sorted out by the weekend," Isabel told him.

"I am sure I will. If the bed is comfortable that is all that matters, the size of the room is irrelevant. I must say this cottage has a good feel to it and the garden is charming, I shall look forward to you showing me round."

Flossie returned to the sitting room and said, "Right, now things are sorted out, I want to hear how things went at the funeral."

"It looks like you will have to postpone your trip around the garden until tomorrow, Lester, we have a story to tell." Isabel smiled over at Lester.

"I shall be content to sit and listen to the story again, it holds my future in its hands, fire away."

Milton Burns was sitting at his expensive mahogany desk in his study with a large ledger open in front of him. He was not best pleased when a knock at the door broke his concentration.

"Come," he growled.

Alan turned the handle and entered the study, he knew better than to interrupt his employer when he was working unless it was urgent. "Begging your pardon, Mr Burns, but a piece of news has reached my ears that I think you should hear about."

"I'm listening,"

"Freddie came to see me and said it is on the grapevine that someone called Samuel Bergun has been asking around if anybody knows of anyone who is willing to knock a bit of sense into a young woman."

"And that should be of interest to me because?"

"The young lady that Samuel wants knocking about is called Isabel Fenfield."

"Is it now. Thank you for the information, Alan. I think we had better have a word with Samuel Bergun. Bring him to the club tonight and let's see what he has to say for himself."

"Very well, Mr Burns, I will see to it."

Samuel was sitting on a wooden chair in the shabby little flat he lived in, in Teesman. He had kept a close eye on the health of his aunt Dora when he had heard she had been taken ill. He was the only male relative that Dora had and he was sure he was going to inherit the family estate. He had recently taken to visiting her, and at the same time he had made a mental note of all the fittings and fixtures in the house, they must be worth a fortune, and they would soon be his.

Aunt Dora, on the other hand, had no illusions as to why Samuel had been visiting her, he had never done so before she was taken ill. It gave her much pleasure to see his gracious concern for her, knowing full well that the estate was going to Isabel and not him. She had heard rumours about him being involved with a gang of ruffians that robbed unsuspecting farmers. He would take the stolen items and sell them on, taking a cut of the proceeds. When she had found out where he lived, and what he got up to, she had not been impressed.

Dora had given the solicitor instructions that if Samuel tried to have the will contested, he should not be allowed to do so. The estate was going to Isabel and those were her wishes.

As soon as Samuel stepped out of his flat, he was surprised to be greeted by two of Milton Burns minders. "What do you two want?" he asked, not knowing who they were.

"We would like you to come with us," one of the men said.

"What you want and what you get are two different things. Why should I come with you? Shove off."

"We are not asking you. We are telling you."

"I have dealt with tougher men than you, so you had better shove off and leave me alone."

One of the two men went and stood in front of Samuel to block his progress.

Samuel drew his arm back and aimed a blow at the man's head. The man in front of him ducked to one side and placed his fist in Samuel's chest. Samuel's aim had missed its target, but the strangers had not, and his chest felt as if it had exploded. He found himself gasping for breath at the unexpected force that had landed in his ribcage.

"Better come with us, Samuel," said the man who had punched him.

"Like hell I will." And without further ado, Samuel launched another attack on the same young man but once again he was out of his league. The young man brought his fist up and Samuel ran straight into it, catching his left eye.

"Better come with us, Samuel," repeated his assailant.

"I'll have the runners on you for this. What the hell do you want? You have no bone to pick with me, get the hell out of my way."

"You might think you are a tough guy, Samuel, but you have no idea what tough is. You had better come with us and be done with it. There are two of us, you are not going to overcome us both. You will come with us, one way or another. The choice is yours."

"Where are you taking me?" Samuel asked.

"You will know when we get there."

"Don't have much choice, do I?"

"No, you don't," agreed the young man.

Samuel followed the two young men into town and into the club known as The Spendthrift. He had never frequented this club, his finances had never been what one could call flush in the pocket, and he knew that the gaming tables required more money than he would ever have.

"Why are you bringing me here? I have never been inside this place before, are you sure you have the right man?" he asked.

"You are Samuel Bergun, aren't you?"

"Yes, I am."

"Then we have the right man." They had arrived at a door along a corridor which was located through the club. Whilst making their way through the club, Samuel had taken in all the gambling tables and all the beautiful young ladies that spun the wheels and dealt the cards to the cream of society.

The door was opened and Samuel was told to enter by a nod of the head from one of the two men and the door was closed behind him.

Samuel was astonished to find himself in the most opulent room he had ever seen, and he had seen a lot of well fitted out rooms in his career as a burglar. His eyes wandered over the Chinese porcelain jugs and vases, Indian rugs and wall cabinet stuffed with trinkets of all shapes and sizes.

"I would advise you to get any thought of entering these premises out of you head, Samuel. I have it well protected, and if by any chance you were to find yourself confronted by any of my loyal men, I would not like to be responsible for your safety. Is that clear?"

the gentleman seated at a large desk asked after noticing Samuel's roving eye.

Samuel, realising that Mr Burns had read his mind, could only stand and nod his head. Although Samuel did not know Milton Burns, he knew of him and of his reputation and he knew him by sight. What on earth Milton Burns should want with him, he was at a loss to know.

"I will not ask you to sit down, for this will not take long. I believe you have put the word out that you want somebody who is willing to use violence against a young woman by the name of Isabel Fenfield. Is that correct?" Milton asked Samuel.

"Isabel! What on earth can Isabel mean to you?" asked Samuel.

"That is none of your business. I am telling you that if one hair on Isabel's head is touched, I know where to find you. She is under my protection so you had better forget all about her. Is that understood?"

"Isabel is under your protection, what the hell has she done to deserve that?"

"Again, none of your business. What has she done to deserve you putting her at risk of being assaulted?"

"She has stolen my inheritance."

"How so?"

"Isabel is my cousin and our aunt has left the family estate to her when it should have come to me. I am the only surviving male member in the family. Isabel has no right to it. I was just going to frighten her into transferring the estate to me. After all, it is mine by rights."

"I don't think so. If your aunt left her estate to Isabel, then she has a legal right to it. Your aunt must have had good reason to leave everything to Isabel and not you. Were you close to your aunt?"

"Well, we became close these past few months. I visited her once or twice whilst she was bedridden. If I had known she had left the estate to Isabel I wouldn't have put myself to so much trouble. It wasn't much fun visiting her. She kept asking me questions about myself, none of her damn business."

"That being the case, I think your aunt left the estate to the right person. Have I made myself clear when I say nothing had better happen to Isabel? I can assure you I would have no conscience in dealing with you if you do not heed my words."

"You don't leave me much choice, do you?"

"Oh yes, you have a choice. Your choice is, live or die. The decision is yours, Samuel. We all have to make choices in this life, some are right and some are wrong, and we all have to live or die by them. Now get out of my club and this had better be the last time I lay eyes on you." And with that, Milton went back to his bookkeeping and Samuel was escorted out.

As he walked back home, Samuel tried to piece together how Isabel had come into the world of Milton Burns. He was in no doubt that Milton would keep his word if he had Isabel beaten up. He would have to concede for the moment. Milton Burns would not live forever and when the time came, things would be different. He would attend to Isabel himself, he was not about to give up altogether.

Only Samuel did not know about Lester Leggett, so his plan was doomed before it had started. Nor did he know that Mr Burns had every intention of living forever, well, as long as he could possibly achieve, anyway. Mr Burns was not ready yet for a wooden overcoat, it was not on his agenda.

Samuel had lived a very selfish life. He had lived off his mother until he was one and twenty. His mother took in washing and was also the cleaner for the local inn. Mrs Bergun had gone out to work early one morning and never returned. She was found lying on the path that she walked on her daily route from their home to the inn at 5 o'clock in the morning.

His concern was not for his mother, but for himself. He would now have to fend for himself and he didn't like the thought of that. Because he now had money problems, he took to stealing, breaking into people's homes and taking whatever he could lay his hands on. But the last time he had entered somebody's home, he had nearly been caught, so he decided to pack it in.

What he was going to do for money he had no idea, he lived in a little village on the edge of Teesman called Polepack. He had rented a one room flat over the top of a cobbler's shop, and his rent was now due, but he had no money. He felt in his pocket and produced three pennies, and he placed them on the table in front of him. He decided to go to the ale house and try his hand at gambling, he was good at cards, he had made a bob or two playing cards in the past, so he was going to see if his luck was in.

It turned out his luck was not in. He was now penniless. He had drunk the last of his ale and was just about to go home when he picked up on a conversation at the next table.

"Have you heard about Len?" he heard one of the two men say.

"No, I haven't been to the inn for a couple of nights, what about Len?" came the reply.

"He's been arrested,"

"The devil he has. When was this?"

"Three nights ago. He was up to his usual tricks and he got caught. You do know he was a highwayman, don't you?"

"I had heard the rumour, but I didn't know if it was true or not."

"It was true, right enough. He made a good living at it. He would hide up in Cramcrack woods and hold up any unsuspecting traveller. But his luck ran out three nights ago, when he held up a traveller. The traveller just happened to be a soldier on his way home to see his family. Well, needless to say, the soldier was more than able to protect himself and he overcame Len, and took him to the police, and Bob's your uncle, no more Len."

Samuel's mind was working full belt. That's it, he would try his hand at being a highwayman. It was risky according to the conversation he had just overheard, but also lucrative. He decided to take the chance. He would need a horse of course, but he didn't have one. Mr Franklin had a horse, he wondered if Mr Franklin would lend him his horse, after all, he had been a good friend of his father's and he had once been engaged to his aunt Dora.

Dora and Mr Franklin were engaged to be married before he went to war and that was the last time Dora had seen Mr Franklin. Dora had never formed an attachment to any other man, and it was said she was waiting for Mr Franklin to come home from the war. His mother had asked Mr Franklin once why he had not married and he had told her that Dora had been his only love. But being in the army, and seeing the things that no man should have to see, had affected his head.

It had been years before he was able to get back to being somewhat normal again, but the nightmares still plagued him sometimes, and he didn't think it was fair on Dora to expose her to his nightmare.

Samuel stood up and set off on his five-mile trek to go and see Mr Franklin. It was around seven o'clock in the evening when he had arrived at the farm. It wasn't a very big farm and things were beginning to look neglected but that did not concern Samuel, he continued up to the farmhouse and knocked on the door. Mr

Franklin was pleased to see Samuel standing on his doorstep and he was invited in.

Samuel asked Mr Franklin if he could borrow his horse for the night and he would bring it back in the morning. Mr Franklin said yes of course he could if it would help him. And so Samuel began his journey as a highwayman.

Unfortunately, it was a short-lived career. Samuel had stood in Cramcrack woods on four occasions in the last two days, and not a single traveller had passed that way. He had no money and no flat, he had been turned out of his flat because he didn't have any money to pay the rent.

This was no life, he had nearly been caught robbing people's houses, he had been threatened by Milton Burns, and he had no roof over his head. He would have to look for employment. It was a dejected Samuel that returned the horse back to Mr Franklin and it showed on his face.

"What's the matter, lad?" Mr Franklin asked.

"I've gotten myself into a bit of a fix, sir. I have no money, I have lost my flat, and I am going to have to seek employment. I have no idea where to start looking, because I can't do anything, so I am at a loss as to where to go from here."

"You need look no further, as you can see for yourself my farm is rundown because I can no longer work it like I could. If you would like to come and live here with me, I will show you how to maintain the land, get the farm going again. I have no children and no one to leave the farm to so when I die it could be yours. You are Dora's nephew, at least I could do that for her. You will have to work for it though, you will have to prove to me that this is what you want, and let me see an improvement to the farm before I die," Mr Franklin told Samuel.

"It would certainly solve all my problems, sir, and give me something to work for."

"It would also solve all my problems too," Mr Franklin had to admit.

Chapter Five

The solicitor arrived at the cottage in Confield around ten o'clock on Friday morning. Isabel had asked Lester to stay with her whilst the solicitor went through the will with her.

There was not much to go through, the will stated that Isabel inherited everything with her aunt's blessing and her aunt hoped she would be happy there, back in the family estate where she belonged.

Papers were signed and the keys were handed over and Isabel found herself the owner of a large estate in Teesman. She was thankful that Lester was with her and he was going to go with her and see what he could do to help get her settled in.

When Flossie came into the room after seeing the solicitor out, Lester said to her, "Better pack a few things, Flossie, and get your hat on, you are going for a ride and you might not be coming back."

"Taking up residence in Teesman, are we? In that case I will go and pack my bags, I am all for taking whatever opportunity arises. Never thought at my age I would be looking forward to a new start in life but I was never one to let the grass grow under my feet. When do you want me to be ready for?"

"Isabel is already up in her room packing, better get a move on."

Flossie needed no more encouragement and walked as quickly as she could across the room and out of the door. Lester smiled at the open outlook on life Flossie showed and he knew that Flossie and he would get on like a house on fire. He already had a soft spot for the old lady and he had only known her two days.

There wasn't much room on the driver's seat with the three of them sitting there, but did they mind, no they did not. Flossie was as excited as a five-year-old waiting for Father Christmas, to see what sort of a house she was to live in. Isabel had told her that there were servants in residence at the estate and from now on she was in retirement, she could do as she wanted with her time, there were people to look after her instead of her looking after others, which she had done all her working life.

Flossie had to admit that she was finding it harder and harder to keep doing the washing, cleaning, dusting and cooking. She was more than willing to allow someone else to do the chores. By the time Teesman was reached, Flossie also had to admit she was ready to climb down from the wagon and stretch her aching limbs.

Both she and Lester were impressed with the entrance to the estate, tall wooden double gates kept people out, and the drive up to the house must have been at least two miles long.

The house was a sprawling three storey building, neat lawns to the front dropping down to a lake at the bottom of the hill. Sheep grazed in a field to the left of the property and, to the rear, a herd of cows could be seen in the distance. To the right a dense wood stood proud and deep. It must have covered at least three acres of land.

"Goodness me," said Flossie as she took it all in.

"Exactly my thoughts, Flossie. This is going to take some looking after, Isabel," remarked Lester.

"There are people that looked after it for my aunt, I am hoping that they will all stay and look after it for me," Isabel told him.

"Your aunt had years of practice looking after the estate and the staff, it came natural to her. You are starting from the beginning but I am going to be around to help if that is what you want," Lester told her.

"I would love that above all things, Lester, thank you."

"No need for thanks, just being selfish. You are the only woman I have met that I feel I can spend the rest of my life with. I knew it the first time I laid eyes on you."

"I feel the same, I have had one or two proposals in the past but I have declined because there was something missing, I just couldn't bring myself to say '*yes*' but with you, I feel comfortable and at ease. I would miss you if you went away."

"In that case, I shall stay, and in a few months, if we are both of the same frame of mind, I will go and see the vicar and make us a couple. Is that all right by you?"

"It is perfectly all right by me. Let us see what the future holds for us. But what about your home and Minnie?"

"It is Minnie's home as well as mine, we have run it together since our parents died. There is nothing Minnie doesn't know about running our estate and now Ralph is there to help her, I have the opportunity to make a life for myself and I think I have found it. I will love showing you how to manage the estate and we will keep it running, just like your aunt Dora did. Time for change for both of us, Isabel, life is looking pretty good at this moment in time, don't you think?"

"Yes, I do," agreed Isabel.

"Well, now that's all settled, can we go in? I am ready for my tea," Flossie told them.

Isabel laughed, "Flossie, I am sorry. I had forgotten you were here with all this excitement going on."

"Yes, I know you had. But I am pleased to have heard it all the same. I can enjoy my retirement now and let Lester take care of you. You had better look after her, young man or you will have me to contend with," Flossie told him.

"I will bear that in mind," replied Lester.

Three months later Minnie and Ralph were married in a quiet little ceremony in a chapel in Pencroft. Lester, Isabel and Flossie travelled down the day before the wedding day. Only a few close friends were invited and they all stayed at Pencroft, the Leggett estate.

To Isabel's surprise, two of the other guests were Milton Burns and his granddaughter, Eliza. When Eliza saw Isabel alighting from their coach, she ran to greet her. "Isabel, how lovely to see you again," she chirped.

"And it's good to see you too. I must say you are looking very well, have you recovered from our little adventure?"

"Yes, I have. I was so thrilled to get the invitation from Minnie to her wedding, I wanted to see you all again and say thank you for what you did for me. I didn't get the chance before, everything happened so quickly."

They had entered the drawing room and were greeted by Minnie and Ralph's other wedding guests and drinks were handed round.

Isabel was surprised to see Ralph sporting tight leggings and tailcoat. His waistcoat, buttoned up at the front, showed off his new slimline figure and he had grown in confidence.

"My, you are looking very dapper if you don't mind me saying so. What happened to your rounded figure?" Isabel asked him innocently.

"You may say what you like, you usually do. If you must know, I have been having a bit of a rough time of it. Minnie has put me on a diet and she has been making me take her for an evening walk every night, even if it is raining. She wanted me to be very much the gent when we got married. Said she wanted all her friends to see what a good catch she has made."

"I must say she has done a brilliant job. You look very smart and handsome in that get-up."

Out of the corner of her eye, Isabel could see Lester and Milton Burns deep in conversation and she wanted to know what they were talking about. She excused herself from Ralph and made her way across the room.

On approaching the two gentlemen, she caught Milton's eye and she smiled at him, held out her hand as she approached and said, "Mr Burns, this is a pleasant surprise."

"For me, too. It is not often I am invited into polite society and I particularly wanted to see you both. I have been telling Lester that I have met your cousin, Samuel Bergun. He is not a very pleasant chap."

"I have to agree with you on that, Mr Burns, he is a very dodgy character. My aunt Dora was very mistrustful of him and when I had met him, I could see why."

"Word got around that he was looking for somebody to make you see sense and transfer your aunt's estate over to him. I have told him that it is not a good idea to threaten you and if a hair on your head it harmed, he will feel the force of my hand. I think he got the message, but just in case he comes around or sends somebody in his stead, all you have to do is let me know, and I will deal with him."

"That is a comfort, Mr Burns, thank you. But Lester is going to stay with me and show me how to go on. I am quite safe whilst Lester is around."

"Good. Eliza seems to be getting on pretty well with Ralph. He seems to have grown in stature since last we met." Mr Burns smiled.

This made Isabel laugh. "He tells me he has been having a bit of a rough time of it. Minnie had put him on a diet and is making him take exercise every day, hence his loss of weight. I think he is secretly proud of his new look, but there is no way he is going to admit it."

"A lot of good has come out of your little adventure, Isabel, I am pleased to have been part of it," Milton told her.

"And so am I, Mr Burns, it has been a pleasure making your acquaintance, and also Eliza, she is turning into a lovely young woman," agreed Isabel.

"Please, call me Milton."

The End

May And Lucy

Chapter One

May was sitting at the breakfast table by herself. It had been a good party the evening before and Lucy had been in good spirits when she had retired to bed at two o'clock in the morning. May did not expect to see Lucy until at least midday.

She wiped her lips with the white linen napkin then placed it beside her empty plate. May and Lucy had been residing in a house in Tarrington Square, Frankly, for just short of four months. The property had been rented by Lucy's father for the sole purpose of attaining Lucy a suitable husband. They were to return home at the end of the coming week.

May's father had been a lifelong friend of Lucy's father and May and Lucy had grown up together and looked on each other as sisters. When May's father passed away their friendship continued. May was a self-confident young woman of considerable means and, as yet, had formed no attachment to any young man that had entered her circle of friends.

Not that May was in any way concerned by this matter. She enjoyed her freedom and had many friends, but her friendship with Lucy was special. When Lucy's father approached May, and asked her if she would chaperone his daughter to Tarrington Square for four months, to see how she took, she jumped at the chance.

As expected, Lucy was an instant success. With jet black hair, dark brown eyes that held a mischievous twinkle, and a peaches and cream complexion, she had all the young men dallying after her. Not that Lucy was in any way desperate for a husband, she too, like May, liked her freedom.

Lucy had known what her father's intentions had been when he had told her he wanted her to go to Frankly for four months. He wanted grandchildren to carry on the family estate, and as his only child, Lucy was going to have to be the one to provide them for him.

When her father told her she was to go with May, on a four-month jaunt, Lucy had put up no resistance. Four months on her own with May in a big town with lots of shops, balls and goodness knows what else, she couldn't believe her luck.

May had an alternative motive to be spending a few months in Frankly, for it was where her mother's father, Colonel Walker lived.

Colonel Walker had a long and distinguished career in the army and he had not had much to do with the bringing up of May's mother. He was away most of the time, building up his reputation in the army. But all the same he had loved his wife very much and he adored May, and he had spoilt her terribly on the few occasions he was at home.

May in turn had a special soft spot for the old man and she had offered him a place in her home when he had finally retired from the army. He had refused of course, he said he was used to being his own boss and he had no intentions of allowing a woman to run his life for him and he had settled in his family home in Frankly. His loyal batman, Hatten, retired with him and he went to look after Colonel Walker and act as his valet, and so May was happy to allow the old man to have his own way, knowing he was well cared for.

May was a poor chaperone, she left Lucy to enjoy herself knowing full well that she had a sensible head on her shoulders and was more than capable of looking after herself, and would not bring any scandal upon her house. So May had made the most of her spare time visiting her grandpapa whilst she was residing in Frankly. She was pleased to see that he was in surprisingly good health for someone of his age.

The door to the breakfast room opened and in walked Lucy, fresh as a daisy and raring to go. "Good morning May," Lucy chirped as she sat down to partake of breakfast.

"Good morning to you too, Lucy, I didn't expect you down this early. What are you scheming this morning?" May asked.

"Scheming, well I like that," said an indignant Lucy. "Why would I be scheming anything?"

"Because you look particularly radiant, and after the exhausting partying you did last night, I thought you would still be abed until midday."

"Yes, it was a good night wasn't it? If you must know, I am being taken for a drive in the park this morning by a very handsome young man, so I am pleased you think I am looking radiant. I hope he thinks so too."

"Are you indeed? I should, by rights, be accompanying you if you are going out with a young man. After all, that is what your father asked me to do. I am not doing a very good job of being a chaperone, am I? Do you need me to accompany you?" May asked.

Lucy looked across the table at her friend. She loved May with all her heart and she said, "No, my dear friend, I do not. I will in no way soil my reputation, or yours, and you may rest assured on that."

"In that case, enjoy your drive. May I enquire who the young man that has captured your interest is?"

"Can you remember me tripping up the front steps the very first day we arrived and a young man, who was passing by, took my hand and led me safely to the front door, well it is he," Lucy told her.

"No, I do not recall the incident," admitted May.

"Oh! I remember now, you were already inside the house when the incident occurred, so I don't think you did meet him."

"He just reappeared did he, and asked you to take a turn around the park with him this morning?"

"No, I have seen him nearly every day since we have been here. He seems to turn up when I am on my own. He was at the party last night. Didn't you see me dancing with him?"

"I saw you dancing with more than one young man. Indeed, it went through my mind that you must have been exhausted. You were tripping around the dance floor so many times, you made my head spin."

A delighted laugh came from two perfectly formed lips and Lucy said, "Yes, it was a very good night. Richard was one of the partners I had, in fact I think, no, I know, I danced three dances with him. That is when he asked me to take a turn around the park with him this morning. He is picking me up at ten o'clock."

"In that case I shall make myself scarce. You had better gobble some breakfast down if you intend to eat, it is nearly ten o'clock now. You don't want to keep him hanging about outside our front door, think of the tittle tattlers. Have a good time, and I trust you to behave with propriety."

"You have my word, May; I will not let you down."

"Good, then I shall have a morning window shopping with nobody to distract me."

Up in her room, May waited until she heard the front door close and ran to the window to peek out at Lucy's admirer. But she was only able to see the straight back and splendid shoulders of the driver, as he expertly manoeuvred the curricle into the busy road along

Tarrington Square, heading for the park gates where members of the ton liked to be seen.

May grabbed her cape and bonnet from off the bed where she had left them, quickly donned them, and headed down the wide curving staircase. She was about halfway down when Jarvis, the butler, walked across the hallway and opened the front door.

On the doorstep stood a gentleman of fashion, hat in hand. He wore a black tail coat; fawn leggings covered his long legs and highly polished knee-high top boots on his feet.

He looked up and saw a young woman standing midway on the stairs, looking with interest in his direction. Their eyes met and a look of distain appeared on his handsome face and without a second glance, the gentleman turned his attention back to the butler. "I wish to see a Miss Embrey."

"Miss Embrey is just going out, sir. Maybe you could call back this afternoon. Do you have a card to leave? I will see that Miss Embrey receives it," the butler told him.

"Miss Embrey will just have to wait until I have had a word with her, then she may do as she wishes," the fashionable gentleman said.

"Miss Embrey is not available, sir. A card will enable her to say whether or not she wishes to see you. This afternoon will be more convenient for her," the butler insisted.

"I don't give a damn whether it is more convenient for her to receive me this afternoon. I will not move from this doorstep, so if Miss Embrey is on her way out, she will have to get passed me first. She may not want the people passing along Tarrington Square, to be privy to our conversation," the gentleman insisted, glancing up at the young woman still midway on the staircase, dressed for outdoors.

"It's all right, Jarvis. I will see the gentleman in the living room, for if he insists on seeing me to such a degree, then I am curious as to know why." May continued on her way down the staircase, and across the hall.

Jarvis turned and travelled at a greater speed than she, and reached the living room door seconds before her. He opened the door and May was able to enter the room without having to adjust her step.

Jarvis was about to turn back to the entrance door to escort the irate gentleman in, but he was too late. The gentleman had not waited to be asked in, he was behind Jarvis and followed May into the room.

May stood with her back to the large Adam-style fireplace, her hands demurely crossed in front of her.

"Please take a seat." May indicated to a dark brown leather two-seater sofa.

"Thank you, but I will stand, this will not take long. I desire a word with Miss Embrey," May was informed.

"I am Miss Embrey, May to my friends."

"Impossible," the gentleman blurted out.

"I assure you my friends do call me May, for that is my name."

"I was not referring to what your friends call you, I find it impossible that someone of your young age should be classed as a chaperone," the gentleman rallied.

"Maybe if you were to sit down you might feel less irritated," May suggested.

"I damn well don't want to sit down. What I have to say to you can be said standing. It has been brought to my attention that my young cousin is making a cake of himself with your ward."

"First of all, Lucy is not my ward, she is my friend. Lucy does not feel that your cousin is making a cake of himself, in actual fact, Lucy is quite taken with him. That is if your cousin is the same young man in question, who has taken Lucy for a drive in the park," May said innocently.

"I bet she is. No doubt she has heard of Richard's vast fortune, and it is his fortune that has taken her fancy, and she has set about luring him into her neatly woven web. There can be no other reason for her to be so taken with him. Money speaks volumes," came the reply.

May's sense of humour got the better of her and she said with a hint of amusement in her voice, "I think you are the one making a cake of himself, sir, your cousin seems to be doing all right for himself. Lucy is a very charming young woman and I can assure you she does not weave webs. She is not a spider. Many a man has fallen for Lucy's innocent personality, but none so far has taken her fancy. Your cousin, again if indeed we are talking about the same young man, seems to have achieved what other men have failed to do.

"I think you do your cousin a great injustice to presume Lucy only finds his money attractive. I might point out to you that quite a few of these other young men that have been dancing attendance on Lucy, also have considerable means to their name and have substantial fortunes in the bank. Your cousin is not the only man in the world to have money, but then again, I only have your word on that. I do not know your cousin personally so I have not had the opportunity to grill him as to his means of support, were he to marry Lucy.

"You should be proud of him, not ridiculing him to a perfect stranger. It does not stand him in a good light if he has to have someone of your standing going around wiping up after him. Are you jealous, sir? Is this the reason you are so adamant with regard to their friendship. Have you taken a fancy for Lucy yourself?"

"Who the devil made you this chit's chaperone?"

"Her father did."

"Then the man's a raving lunatic," said the rattled gentleman.

May's eyes danced, she was enjoying herself very much, and it pleased her to see such an elegantly dressed gentleman, who obviously oozed confidence, struggling to keep his composure.

The gentleman did not miss the twinkle in her eye and this rattled him even further.

"I have not met the lady in question, so how can I be jealous of my cousin, you are reading things into it that do not exist. My aunt, Richards's mother, has asked me to sort this matter out. She will not have a fortune hunter targeting her son, and having seen her chaperone, I have to comply with her. I shall have to have words with Richard, so tell your friend not to expect to see him again."

"Again, if your cousin allows himself to be the target of a fortune hunter, you are not painting him in a good light. How old is your cousin? Please don't tell me he is still in nappies. And how ungentlemanly is it of you to judge Lucy, because you have taken a dislike to me."

"My cousin is quite capable of looking after himself, this is an unfortunate incident and sometimes we all need helping out by someone who has more experience in these matters than they have. And I might add I have not taken a dislike of you. The title of chaperone does not sit prettily upon your shoulders."

"Oh, so you are experienced in such matters, are you? That explains a lot. Tell me sir, are you married?"

"What the devil is it to you? And yes, I have experience in such matters, but I have had the good sense to know when to cut the cord, and not be lured into something I will regret later in life."

"You must be around thirty years of age yourself and I just wondered if you were married or single. Obviously you are single, with an attitude such as yours, I doubt you will attract anybody except fortune hunters, for the lure of your money is more appealing than your personality.

"You are a very handsome man but please do not let that remark go to your head, sir, for you only have to glance in the mirror to see that for yourself, it was not a statement intended to flatter you. As you are still single, the young ladies of Tarrington Square must be very ugly for you not to be enticed by one of them. What a shame. I bet more than one young lady is holding a torch for you. Shame on you." May's eyes danced as she studied the outrage on her visitors face.

"Because I choose not to marry, is nobody's business but mine. I am not the object of topic here; I am simply here to ask you to ask your friend to leave my cousin alone. He is a very naïve young man and your friend is obviously very adept at allurement. I, on the other hand, have more understanding than to let a glittering statement, like you just made about my appearance, go to my head. I have heard it from better women than you who think they have a talent for flattery."

May's delight at the situation was too openly shown for the gentleman not to notice, and, to his own annoyance, it only made matters worse.

"Are you or are you not going to tell your friend to leave my cousin alone?"

"Certainly not, if my friend wishes to meet with your cousin and your cousin has no objection, I do not see why you or I should have any objection."

"You have no idea what you are talking about. You are far too young to know what harm your friend will be doing to her reputation if she is seen alone with my cousin, cavorting around the town with a single gentleman. The whole idea of a chaperone is that the chaperone accompanies the person she is supposed to be chaperoning."

"And how old do you think I am, sir? You come into my house, no, you insist on entering my house, you push yourself forward before the butler could show you in, and demand an interview with me without an appointment.

"You have not yet introduced yourself to me, and you have no consideration for my reputation, sir. For here you are, closeted in this room with me and it has not entered your head that I have no chaperone to protect my reputation. You must be a man with a great reputation with the ladies, your dress boasts money and your manner indicates that you are used to having your own way. The tattlers will have a field day at my expense if you have been seen entering this establishment.

"Your father should have put you over his knee more when you were in short trousers. Then it might occur to you once in a while that you are not the only man in this world, and not all men think in such a selfish way as you do.

"You should leave your cousin to make his own choices. I am sure you would not tolerate any interference from a third party if you chose to dance attendance upon a young lady. That way he will find out for himself if the young lady in question is worthy of his presence. The same way women should be allowed to make the acquaintance of more than one young man. Then there might be more happy marriages than there are.

"It is my observation, sir, that there are more contented married men than there are contented married women. Men are allowed to have as many dalliances as they choose and the more they have, the better other men admire them for it, and the greater their reputation.

"Take you for instance, you are a very handsome man and as I have already stated your dress boasts money. I am sure all your male followers admire your prowess, and all the men that have heard about you, wish the same for themselves.

"I have more faith in my friend, Lucy, to act with propriety than you have in your cousin to respect Lucy's reputation. We are in the year 1813, sir, and we are not living in caves anymore. You should try moving with the times.

"Maybe not everyone is of the same nature as you, sir, and can enjoy a lady's company without grabbing her behind the nearest bush, which is obviously what you think your cousin intends to do to Lucy.

"I will not insult your cousin by warning Lucy not to see him again because, in your opinion, he soils young ladies' reputations, and nor will I insult Lucy's intelligence, or instincts, by interfering in her choice of friend, male or female.

"Then hopefully when she marries, she will be content in her marriage and have no regrets and harbour no ill feeling towards a husband she was forced to marry against her will."

"You are twisting my words; my cousin does not grab young women behind bushes and neither do I. I will, however, grant you the fact that I have acted improperly by coming here unannounced and not introducing myself. But in my defence, I did not know you would be still in the nursery yourself. When the word chaperone was mentioned, it did not conjure up the vision of a young lady of your breeding. My name is Lawrence Wedman, and I can only apologize for my behaviour.

"My aunt came to me and asked for my help with Richard and I fought against it, for it is not in my nature to interfere in other people's affairs and it put me out of joint.

"I was angry with my aunt and I was angry with Richard. I was angry with your friend. I agree with you, they have the right to make their own choice in this matter.

"It would seem I have made more than one blunder this morning. You seem to be more than capable of acting as a chaperone. I have not yet met your friend, Lucy, but I have done her an injustice by categorising her as a scheming woman without prior knowledge of her. I can only apologize and take my leave of you." Lawrence gave May a low bow and walked out of the room closing the door behind him.

May's eyes danced with devilment as she watched Lawrence's retreating back. It had been an interesting meeting and an even more satisfying end to the encounter. It is always nice to win a battle over the opposite sex, and she had sent the gentleman off with a flea in his ear, most satisfactory.

Chapter Two

May decided not to go into town to window shop, instead she went into the library and picked up the book she had begun to read, and got comfortable in the big black leather winged armchair and waited for Lucy to return home.

The noise of voices from the hall told May that Lucy had returned and she was about to put down her book and join her when the library door was thrust open and in rushed her rosy cheeked friend, followed by a handsome, fresh-faced young man in his early twenties.

"May, I have been telling Richard all about you and he insisted on meeting you, so here we are. We have had a very pleasant drive around the park, twice. Richard has introduced me to some of his friends and acquaintances and we have been invited to a ball tonight and of course I asked if it was all right for me to ask you to attend, and it was agreed. So, we are all going to a ball tonight and Richard is to pick us up at seven o'clock." Lucy paused for breath.

The young man came forward holding out his hand and shook hands with May. "I have heard so much about you, Miss Embrey. I insisted on meeting you, I hope you don't mind the intrusion."

"On the contrary, sir, I am very happy to make your acquaintance. I, in turn, have heard a lot about you, and thank you for offering to take us to this ball tonight. It is unexpected but nonetheless, a very pleasant invitation." They exchanged a handshake.

May could see why Lucy was taken with this young man and she also knew why Richard was taken with Lucy. Lucy was in fine form, her joy of life shone out of her mischievous eyes, and her energy was infectious.

'Good choice Lucy. Now it's my turn,' May thought, *'exciting times ahead for both of us. Not much time left to set the ball rolling, but at least now the ball is in my hand. I am going to toss it in the air and see where it lands. Lucy's good fortune in meeting Richard has done me a good turn too. At last I have met a man that takes my fancy.'*

After Richard had left, Lucy asked of May, "How was your morning, did you buy anything at the shops?"

"I did not get to the shops. Just after you left for your drive around the park, I had a visitor," May informed her.

"Did you indeed, and who was that?"

"His name is Lawrence Wedman."

"Who is Lawrence Wedman? I have not heard you speak of him before."

"I have not told you about him before because I have not met him before. He turned up on our doorstep demanding an audience with me, so I obliged."

"What did he want with you?"

"He came to tell me, to tell you, to stop seeing Richard."

"What is it to him if I do see Richard? Why would he want me to stop seeing him?"

"Lawrence Wedman is Richard's cousin. It was Richard's mother who sent him here to demand you stop seeing Richard. But I sent him away with a flea in his ear."

"Why would Richards's mother want me to stop seeing him?"

"I think she is under the impression that you are a fortune hunter. She knows nothing about you, and I think she thinks every young woman of marriageable age is out to set a trap to capture her son. When she finds out you are flush to the gills, all will be forgiven, for once she has met you, she will fall in love with you, just like everyone else who meets you does. You are a very pretty and likeable young woman."

"It is strange that Richard has not mentioned his cousin to me."

"That could be because Richard's cousin is a very handsome man and he might be afraid that your fancy would change and you might like his cousin more than you do him."

"But that is ridiculous."

"Yes, I know that and you know that, but Richard does not. Lawrence is very much the ladies' man and I think there might be a trail of broken hearts a mile long behind him."

"What was he like? Should I be on my guard against him?" Lucy wanted to know.

"He was gorgeous. In fact, I was very attracted to him and I intend to set my cap at him."

"Really?" asked Lucy with her eyes sparkling.

"Yes, really," replied May.

"You have never set your cap at anybody before."

"That is because nobody has ever grabbed my interest like this before."

"I cannot wait to see him," Lucy laughed.

"You will see him tonight at the ball," May told her.

"How do you know he will be at the ball?"

"If the host of the ball is an acquaintance of Richard's then you can bet Lawrence will have had an invitation too. If he knows that Richard is going, he will guess that he has asked you to accompany him. Lawrence will not be able to keep away. He will be out to see you for himself, so be warned."

"I thought you said you had sent him away with a flea in his ear?"

"Yes, I did. Now you mention it, he did say he was washing his hands of the whole affair so he might not turn up."

"Well, I can't wait to see what he looks like now I know he has stirred your interest. This is going to be fun. What do you intend to do to make sure he attends the ball this evening?"

"I had better get the big guns out I suppose," May replied.

Lucy glanced at May's chest and May burst out laughing. "No Lucy, I am not going to bare my breasts to him. I am going to see Grandpapa."

"You are going to see your grandpapa! What on earth for?"

"To ask him to go and see Lawrence and tell him to keep away from me, of course. I shall ask Grandpapa to inform him that we will be at the ball tonight and that he had better keep away from me. That should put the cat amongst the pigeons."

"Why would you do that? I thought you wanted him to come."

"It will rattle Lawrence's cage, that is why. He will not be able to keep away, just you watch. I think it is a long time since somebody told him not to do something, and he will do it, just to make the point. There is good sport ahead, Lucy, and only another week left for us to bag ourselves a husband, and finally, I have mine in sight."

"I also have mine in sight. I hope you know what you are doing," Lucy told her.

"Me too," May had to admit.

May held up the hem of her skirt to stop herself from tripping up as she ran up the five steps to the front door of her grandfather's house. She entered without ceremony, calling, "Grandpapa, Grandpapa," as she closed the door behind her.

A door to her right was opened and a gentleman appeared who must once have stood erect, but was now slightly stooped, and resting heavily upon a silver handled walking cane. He was of undefinable years and his eyes lit up at the sight of his granddaughter standing in his hall.

"May, my darling girl, come on through. I will ring for hot chocolate," the old man said.

May went over, kissed the old gentleman on his grey bearded cheek and tucked her hand through his arm. They walked into the library together each equally pleased to see the other.

After Hatten, the colonel's valet, had delivered the hot chocolate, and pleasantries were passed between him and May, the colonel and May went to sit upon a brown leather sofa, large enough to hold four people. The old man asked, "Now, May, what brings you here?"

"I have come to ask for your help in securing me a husband," May told him candidly.

"You should have saved yourself the trouble. I never get involved in the affairs of the heart. You should know that by now."

"Yes, dear, I do. But I think you will enjoy this. It is going to be great sport."

"It is going to be great sport for whom?"

"Why, for all of us, of course. The chased as well as the chaser."

"Not for me it isn't, never was in the petticoat line. Once your grandmother passed away, I never looked at another woman."

"I know that Grandpapa, and it is a great shame, for you should have remarried and made some other woman as happy as you made Grandmamma."

"Never met anyone I liked as much as your grandmother, May. Anyway, I doubt if any other woman would have stood for me being away for long periods of time like I was because of the army. She was special, your grandmother, no other woman like her."

"I know that too. This is why I have come to ask for your help. I have met someone this morning for the very first time and I have never met anybody before that attracted me so much. He put on a front of being totally in control and used to having his own way and I was able to twist him round my little finger, and I liked him very, very much."

"Who is this wonderful young man?" her grandpapa wanted to know.

"His name is Lawrence Wedman."

"Lawrence Wedman! Lawrence Wedman! You want me to help you trap Lawrence Wedman into marrying you? It ain't going to happen, May."

"You know him then?"

"Everybody in Frankly knows Lawrence Wedman. All the fathers of marriageable young ladies steer them away from that man. He is a libertine, a seducer of women. He is a rake."

"Yes, dear, I could tell that the instant I laid eyes on him, but he is also very vulnerable, and I liked him Grandpapa."

"No, no, a thousand times no, I will not help you hang yourself. What kind of grandfather do you think I am? If I were to get involved with your love life, Lawrence Wedman, would be the last man on earth I would introduce you to."

"I am not asking you to introduce me to him, Grandpapa, for we have already met. I want you to go to see him and tell him to keep away from me."

"Damn it, May, I may be old but my mind is still my own. I thought you wanted me to help you catch him for a husband?"

"That is exactly what I want you to do. If you go and tell him to keep away from me, his nature will not allow him to do so. He will come and search me out, just to make a point, and I will do all the rest. I have already set the ball rolling and I am imprinted on his mind now, and it is going to irk him that I won our little battle, and he lost. He will be out to get his revenge."

"You are playing a dangerous game, May, I do not like it and I refuse to be part of it," her grandpapa told her.

"All I am asking you to do is go and see Lawrence, and tell him to keep away from me and if you just happen to mention that I will be going to Mrs Markham's ball tonight, that would be the icing on the cake," insisted his granddaughter.

Her grandpapa remained silent for a few seconds then said, "Very well. If that is what you want me to do, then I will go and see Lawrence, and tell him to watch what he is about where you are concerned, if he knows what is good for him. Off you go now. I have to get changed if I am paying a call on one of the best dressed men in Frankly. Be off with you and behave yourself tonight, my girl, or there will be trouble ahead for you from this direction. Never mind the trouble you will be bringing down around your ears from Lawrence Wedman, for that is what you are in danger of doing. Do you understand?" asked her grandpapa.

"Yes, dear, I understand. Have no fear I will not bring shame upon you. But I like him so very much, Grandpapa, and if I let this opportunity pass me by, I might never meet anybody I like as much. All he needs is a good woman to keep him occupied and you will see what a fine fellow he is."

"And you are that good woman, are you?"

"Oh yes, I am that woman."

"Then my sympathy lies with him, the poor sod."

May gave a delighted laugh, kissed her grandpapa on the check and, satisfied that she had accomplished what she had set out to do, stood up and said a cheery goodbye. Then she hurried out of the room before her grandpapa could change his mind.

May and Lucy chatted excitedly while they were being dressed by their maids and Lucy said to May, "I can't wait to see Richard tonight and dance with him in front of all his friends and family. It turns out that Mrs Markham, the lady who is throwing the ball, is Richard's aunt on his mother's side."

"Is she indeed? In that case, get ready to meet the opposition," smiled May.

"You think your Lawrence will be there too?"

"He is not my Lawrence yet, but oh yes, I think he might. But I was referring to Richard's mother, not Lawrence. If Mrs Markham is Richards's aunt then logically Richards's mother will have been invited too. I can't see Mrs Markham inviting her nephew and not her sister. Can you?"

"No, I don't suppose she will, unless she has had a fall out with her sister and they are not talking. Families do fall out you know. But that being the case, I am looking forward to seeing what Richard's mother is like. I think it is the first time I have been called a fortune hunter. I can't wait to meet her, how exciting is this?"

"I think you had better get ready to be snubbed by his mother, she has taken a dislike to you even though she has not met you or knows anything about you. She is only protecting her son, you know. After all, if you are lucky enough to have a son and you are told he is making a cake of himself with a fortune hunter, you do not know how you would react."

"If his mother wants to snub me, then so be it. I have more courage in me than to allow myself to flounder at the first hurdle. If his mother wants to do battle with me, then let her put her best foot forward. It will show Richard in his true light at any event. Is he a mummy's boy or his own man? It will be interesting to find out before things become too entangled between us."

"Yes, I know you have a determined nature and that is why I hand out this warning. Just preparing you to be ready for a snub. But at the same time, remember it is Richard's mother whom you are dealing with, and if things go as you are planning, she will be your mother-in-law once you are married. Try not to set off on the wrong foot with her, and let us see where this takes us."

"Very well, if you say so, I shall bite my tongue on the subject. I must admit I am a little disappointed at Richard. Why has he not told his mother about me. Maybe if he had told her about me, she would not have heard about me through the tittle tattlers. Maybe that's why she thinks I am a fortune hunter, maybe Richard is ashamed of me, and that is why he has not told her."

"Good girl. Nice thinking, you could be right about any of these theories, but don't let us make the same mistake as Richard's mother by jumping to the wrong conclusion. Richard might have a perfectly good reason to hide you from her. He certainly isn't ashamed of you, why, he has been parading you all over town, tripping with you on the dance floor and driving you around the park. That is not the actions of a man who is ashamed of someone. And anyway, you are in exactly the same position as Richard is in. Have you told your father about Richard? No, you have not. There is no difference, you know. Until everything is made clear, let us forget this little hiccup and go and enjoy our invitation to the ball and see what unfolds."

The ball was being held in a large, stone fronted, three storey detached house, at the other side of Frankly to Tarrington Square. Lucy, May and Richard found they were three of the early guests to arrive.

Richard escorted them in and waited until they had shed their bonnets and capes, then he walked them, one on each arm, into the ballroom to seek out their hostess. Richard introduced them to his aunt, and she made them feel welcome and lost no time in introducing them to the other guests who had already arrived. Within half an hour the spacious ball room was bursting at the seams.

Richard oozed attendance on Lucy, and May was very much left to entertain herself, which she did by engaging in conversation with some of the other guests with whom she was acquainted. An hour later she spotted a tall elegantly dressed gentleman talking to their hostess.

May's heart skipped a beat and for a few seconds her cheeks were flushed and she was grateful to be on her own at that precise moment in time. May watched as Mrs Markham looked around the room and finally spotted Richard and Lucy, deep in conversation with some of her other guests.

Mrs Markham led Lawrence across the room and interrupted the conversation Lucy and Richard were having with another couple of about the same age as Lucy.

May watched the little party with interest as the introductions were made, and once that was over, Mrs Markham moved on to her other guests.

Lawrence, feeling May's eyes on him, looked across the room and their eyes met. Without breaking eye contact and without excusing himself to the little group he was standing with, Lawrence made his way over to May, who stood her ground solidly.

"Your grandfather came to see me this afternoon, to warn me off from furthering our acquaintance. Well it did not work. I do not like being told what to do, I am three and twenty, I will do as I wish. I was not aware that Colonel Walker was your grandfather," Lawrence told her.

"You are only three and twenty? I thought you were older. You now know how Richard would feel if he found out that you had been to see me to ask me to warn Lucy off from seeing him. His reaction would more than likely be like yours, and he would be determined to see Lucy all the more. And why would it matter to you who my grandfather is?" May asked.

"I have known Colonel Walker these past ten years, and I respect him very much. It was an uncomfortable interview I had with him. He said I had to keep away from you for he did not want your reputation marred by our association. I must admit it rubbed me up the wrong way. How did your grandfather know about our meeting, for I have not spread it around?"

"I was curious about you. You can't blame me for that. When someone barges his way into your house and starts berating you for no apparent reason, it is bound to cause curiosity. I went to call on my grandpapa and I asked him if he knew you and he said of course he did. He said everyone in Frankly knows you, or of you. You have only yourself to blame for your reputation. Reputations are gained from our past behaviour and the wagging tongues they leave behind. He also said you were a rake and a libertine and I was to have nothing to do with you. You cannot blame me for your reputation, sir, surely?"

"Your grandfather has been misled. Most of the things that are said about me are grossly exaggerated."

"You are mistaken, sir. You do not have to defend yourself to me for, as you know, I am a lowly chaperone and a very poor one at that. Why would you care a fig what my thoughts about you are? I also told my grandfather that I already knew you were a rake, for as soon as I laid eyes on you, I knew you were a man about town, and your self-assurance spoke volumes. You are used to having your own way, it was as plain as the nose on your face by the way you insisted on seeing me. When my butler told you I was on my way out that did not deter you. You were determined to have your way, no matter what."

"Don't talk ridiculous, you are no more a chaperone than I am. I will not be told what to do, I am not a baby. If I wish to attend my aunt's ball, then attend it I will, whoever her other guests might be. If you are under the impression I am here because I knew you would be here, you are labouring under a false illusion. The hostess just happens to be my aunt."

"So I have been told. She is also Richard's aunt and the sister of his mother, is she not? No doubt there will be a family gathering later on. It will be an interesting meeting. Do not underestimate Lucy, Mr Wedman, just because she is extremely pretty, her head is not easily turned, she is a very intelligent young woman. As for thinking that you would be here because of me, sir, you have a vivid imagination. The thought never entered my head. You left me with no high expectation of any future alliance between us. If I thought anything about you at all, it was to expect you to be here to cause mischief for Lucy. I saw you being introduced to her, what, pray, are your thoughts now on that subject?"

"I have no thoughts on the subject. I have cast it out of my mind and I have told Richard's mother so too. If Richard is to make a fool of himself over a chit of a thing, then it is up to him. It will be a lesson well learnt for him. I have washed my hands of the whole affair."

"Is Lucy the type of young lady you have made a fool of yourself over?" asked May.

"Lucy is the type of young lady that all men make a fool of themselves over," Lawrence replied.

The sparkle was back in May's eyes as their eyes met, and, to Lawrence's annoyance, he found himself helplessly drawn to them. The same sparkle had lingered in his mind long after he had departed from Tarrington Square, so much so that he had taken his displeasure out on a leather footstool by giving it a few hefty kicks accompanied by, *'Damn the woman!'*

"It is a good job there is no footstool present," Lawrence remarked more to himself than to anyone else.

"Footstool?" questioned May.

"Good for kicking," replied Lawrence.

May raised her eyebrows in question but Lawrence chose to ignore it and asked instead, "How long are you to stay in Frankly?"

An amused smile crossed May's lips and she remarked, "I am afraid that your cousin and Lucy will still keep in touch, even when we have left Tarrington Square, and gone back home, so I do not think it relevant, Mr Wedman."

"My friends call me Lawrence, and I was not enquiring on behalf of Richard. I have already told you I have washed my hands of the whole affair."

"Then what may I ask is the purpose of your question?"

"I was merely being polite. Is it too hard a question for you to reply to?"

"It is not the question, but the reason behind the question that I enquire about," May told him.

"You are a very frustrating young woman," May was told.

"How so, sir?" she enquired.

"You answer all questions with more questions," Lawrence responded.

"If you have washed your hands of the whole affair, sir, I wonder what you are doing attending this ball, for I am reliably informed that you do not attend parties or balls any more. Therefore, I thought it would be safe to accompany Lucy here without having to defend her, Richard or myself. It would seem I was mistaken," May told him.

"I apologise if I have given you cause to think you have to defend your friend or yourself to me, you have not. As for Richard, he is big enough to defend himself. If you must know, I came to see what attracted Richard so much. He is not usually easily distracted by the petticoat line. She must be someone special for him to think so highly of her. Also, I was at a loss as to why he had not mentioned her to his mother. She is forever on to him to settle down and give her grandchildren. If it were me, I would be heartily sick of it."

"That is a remarkable coincidence, for Lucy's father is forever on at her to settle down and give him grandchildren. But it would seem you have timed it well, for here is Lucy now with your cousin dangling after her." May gave him a beautiful innocent smile.

Lawrence's irritation was directed more towards the appearance of Lucy and Richard, which intruded into his privacy with May. He was furious with himself even further when he realised he wanted to have May all to himself. He had had more than his fair share of romance and each one had turned out to be far short of his expectations. Instead of him being the chaser, it had always been the case of him ending up being chased. He did not like it. The thought of living the rest of his life with a woman fawning over him all the time had made him very cynical and mistrusting of women.

Now here she was, May Embrey, installed in his brain and he was angry about it. His peace and quiet shot to ribbons with this intriguing and annoying young woman. He wanted to take her by the shoulders and shake some sense into her and tell her to leave him alone. That is what he told himself, what he really wanted was to take her in his arms and smother her face with kisses, but he pushed the thought to the back of his mind.

Lucy came up to May with both hands outstretched and asked, "May, Richard has asked me to attend a regatta with him tomorrow and I have said yes, but only if you agree to come. Please come, May, please can we go, I have never been to a regatta before and I would dearly love to see one before we go home.

"Richard tells me that Mr Wedman disapproves of him taking me out and about without you being there to chaperon me, so please say you will come."

"Our hostess has already introduced you to Mr Wedman, I believe, Lucy." May inclined her head in Mr Wedman's direction.

"Yes, she has, and you don't look half as scary as Richard paints you. As you have heard, Mr Wedman, I am heeding your words and if May refuses to accompany me to the regatta, then I will not go. If she refuses to come with me, then I will never speak to her again, and Richard will refuse to have anything more to do with me and it will all lay at your door for breaking up our friendship," Lucy told Lawrence.

Mr Wedman cast a scathing look at Richard over Lucy's pretty head and replied, "And you are much prettier than he would have me believe. Your anger with me is misplaced. If you were to use that pretty head of yours, you should realise I am trying to protect your reputation."

"Really, Mr Wedman, I am delighted that you think I am pretty, coming from a gentleman with your reputation with the ladies, is an honour indeed. But I am disappointed in you because that is an enormous lie. You think nothing of my reputation, sir. You are out to stop my friendship with Richard, well you will not do so. What right have you to interfere with our friendship. If our friendship does not last, it will not be because of something you have said or done, it will be because either one of us has decided it will not work. It will be our decision not yours."

Lucy turned her attention towards Richard and continued, "There is no need to be jealous of your cousin, Richard, he's much too old and fusty for my taste. Neither is he much fun, I bet he won't be going to the regatta tomorrow."

Lucy then turned and spoke again to May. "Please can we go to the regatta, May?"

"Weather permitting, I don't see why not, we have nothing better to do." May smiled at her.

"I knew you would come. You are the very best of friends, May."

Lawrence, not used to being ignored, was becoming frustrated in the way things were going. He had not been chastised like that since he was in short trousers. Nor had he been invited to join them at the regatta either, and once again he was peeved.

There was a commotion behind them and, turning, May saw a plump, middle aged woman dressed in dark blue and sporting a diamond necklace around her neck approaching them. Her heart sank.

Anybody observing this woman's stride, and the size of the diamonds at her throat, was in no doubt about her status.

"Richard, I want to go home," the woman said none too quietly.

"Then, by all means, do so," Richard replied.

"I sent the carriage home when we arrived. Jack is too old to be hanging around outside for hours on end. So you are going to have to take me," Richard was informed.

"Mother, I brought Lucy and her friend, I cannot just abandon them and take you home. Where are your manners? And keep your voice down."

"Who is more important, your mother or your floozy?"

"You are treading on very thin ice, Mother. Lucy is not a floozy and I will not have you speaking of her in that way. You are showing yourself up, Mother, in front of all these guests."

"I am showing myself up, and what are you doing, parading around with this fortune hunter? Who is she? She has not been in town very long and she has captivated you with her alluring ways. I bet you have not been formally introduced and here she is, strutting around on your arm as though she belongs there. I will not have it."

Lucy stepped forward before Richard could make any reply and said, "You are correct, madam. Richard and I have not been formally introduced. But it has been my observation since I have been in town, that people who live in town, and those that reside in the rural countryside, have two different codes of conduct.

"It would seem that the town dwellers' manners have a lot to be desired. If a family problem occurred in the country, it would have been spoken of in private and not bandied around the dancefloor. Of course, your son must take you home, if you have been so foolish as to leave yourself without transport.

"May and I will wait here until Richard drops you off at home and returns for us. That way Richard will be spared any more embarrassment in front of his friends."

Lawrence came to Richard's rescue by offering to escort the ladies back home and this offer was gratefully received by Richard.

Taking hold of Lucy's hand, Richard brought it to his lips and kissed the back of it. "My sincere apologies for this scene Lucy. I will take my mother away now, but I will call for you tomorrow at ten o'clock as arranged and take you and May to the regatta."

Silence had fallen in the ballroom as the spectators listened to this exchange, then watched Richard escort his mother out of the ballroom.

Mr Wedman held out one arm to Lucy and the other arm to May, and he and the two ladies followed Richard out of the ballroom.

Mr Wedman went to bring his carriage to the front door and by the time May and Lucy had donned their capes, their transport home awaited.

Arriving at Tarrington Square, May and Lucy alighted and Lucy ran straight up the steps and into the house whilst it was left to May to wish Mr Wedman a goodnight. She thanked him for his understanding of their situation and followed Lucy indoors, thankful that Mr Wedman had made no comment, but set the horses forward once his passengers had alighted from his carriage.

Chapter Three

Lucy marched across the hall with May following, and into the sitting room. "I can't breathe," she gasped.

"Lucy, you were magnificent. I am so proud of you."

"Floozy, that woman called me a floozy, loud enough for the entire ballroom to hear. How dare she?"

"Yes dear, she did, but you outmanoeuvred her with your reply. I think it was Richard's mother that disgraced herself, don't you?"

"She did not do herself any favours, that's for sure, but I still think all the other guests would have been on her side and not mine. After all, they do not know me, and if that woman has been going around telling everybody that I am a floozy, a fortune hunter and goodness knows what else, they will all think I got my comeuppance."

"I don't think that it will damage your reputation long term, Lucy. I think Richard will have something to say on the subject and, anyway, when it is made known that you are a wealthy woman in your own right, that will be proof enough that you are not a fortune hunter, and it will be Mrs Mellor that is made to look the fool. I don't know how you are going to deal with the floozy part of it though. You are a very beautiful young woman and I can see the top of your breast, you know, in that very fetching gown you are wearing."

Lucy glanced down at her breast and she could see her cleavage proudly displayed for all to see. Shocked, she looked up to see her friend's eyes twinkling with mischief, "Lord, May, for a moment I thought you were serious."

"I was just teasing you to try and make light of the unfortunate incident. There was more than one young woman at that ball that was showing much more cleavage than you were, and having a lot less success with the opposite sex. You looked and behaved just as you ought to. If I had thought your dress was indecent, I would have told you so. I thought that would go without saying."

"Yes, I know you would, and I would have been pleased to hear it, my dear friend. Well, I am going to bed. We shall see what unfolds tomorrow at the regatta, and heaven help that woman if she is there also. I will not bite my tongue this time, I am ready for battle. Goodnight, May."

"Goodnight, Lucy, sweet dreams. Let's hope tomorrow brings an end to this upset, then we can settle down and enjoy our last few days here before we have to go home."

"I don't think my dreams will be very sweet for the next fifty years, I am so mad I am furious, at least in my dreams I can commit murder and get away with it."

May watched the retreating back of Lucy, with her head held high and a purposeful gait as she mounted the stairs. May waited a few minutes and with a smile on her lips she started forward and followed her friend to bed. Lucy would be all right, just a little set back, nothing she couldn't handle.

After dropping the two ladies off in Tarrington Square, Lawrence headed for his aunt's house. He had been too angry and ashamed of his aunt's behaviour to utter any comforting words to May and Lucy, in case he said too much. He marched up the steps and into the house without ceremony. He met the butler halfway across the hall.

"Are my aunt and cousin still below stairs?"

"They are, sir, in the morning room."

"Thank you." Lawrence nodded to the butler and marched into the morning room.

He found his cousin pacing the floor and his aunt sitting on the sofa, crying and holding a handkerchief to her eyes.

"What were you about, Aunt Flo? Showing Richard and yourself up like that in front of the young lady he had escorted to the ball. To say nothing of all the other guests that were in attendance. I am shocked at your behaviour. To say the things you said in the privacy of your own home with people you can trust is one thing. But to go tittle tattling it in a crowded ballroom was totally uncalled for. It was very ill performed."

"Enough, Lawrence. I have already taken her to task over it, let it rest now. But you don't know the whole of this mess yet. Unbeknown to me, my mother has arranged for me to escort Colin Boxton's daughter to the regatta tomorrow."

"Colin Boxton the industrialist?"

"Yes, that's the one."

"But his daughter must be forty at least."

"Yes, that's the one."

"Aunt Flo, surely you can't want Colin Boxton's daughter for a daughter-in-law. What has Richard done to deserve such harsh treatment?"

"I am thinking of his future, when I am gone at least he will be well heeled." Aunt Flo dabbed at her eyes.

"Having now met Lucy, I think Richard could do a lot worse for himself, I thought they made a charming couple. What is your opinion on the young lady now you have seen her?" Lawrence looked down at his aunt.

"I must admit she was a nice surprise. She wasn't what I expected and she put me in my place which I admire her for. Most people fawn over me when we first meet, she was a refreshing change."

"I am going to have to cancel my plans to take Lucy and May to the regatta, for you don't snub Colin Boxton and get away with it.

"I shall have to write Lucy a note, to cancel our plans, and have it delivered at dawn with the instructions that she must receive it at once. It is too late now to be sending notes, if the young ladies have any sense, they will be away to their beds by now."

"Would you like me to take them to the regatta, in your stead? I am totally at your service. It might alleviate some of the trouble you may be in with Lucy," Lawrence told his cousin.

"No, I would much rather you accompanied me to the regatta and gave me your support. The very thought of having to entertain Colin Boxton's daughter scares the living daylights out of me. I have heard she is a man eater. You are much more capable of fending off the likes of her than I am.

"I will write and tell Lucy that I will call on her tomorrow night and explain things to her and hope she understands the position I was in. You can also accompany me tomorrow evening when I call at Tarrington Square, and keep May amused whilst I try to smooth things over with Lucy."

"Very well, we will do it your way if that is what you want. But I have heard differently to you, I have heard that Colin Boxton's daughter is just the opposite. The tales relayed to me, say she will have nothing to do with all the eligible men her father throws her way. Time will tell. I am away to bed now if I am to get my beauty sleep for tomorrow, I think I am going to need it. Best get my aunt to her bed too, she looks like she would benefit from it."

The letter arrived whilst May and Lucy were having breakfast. Jarvis entered the breakfast room and presented the letter on a silver tray.

"Thank you, Jarvis, when did this arrive?" Lucy asked.

"Just now, Miss Lingard, I brought it in directly. It was hand delivered and the young man said you had to receive it immediately, it was important."

Lucy opened the letter with shaking fingers.

"The letter is from Richard. Here read it for yourself. Lucy watched as May read:

Lucy, forgive me for I cannot take you to the regatta today, something unforeseen has arisen. I will call to see you tonight, and keep my fingers crossed you will understand the predicament I was in.

Yours, Richard.

"What do we do now?" May asked.

"I think I would like to go home."

"You don't want to go to the regatta? There is nothing to stop us from going you know. I am willing to drive the carriage."

"Yes, I know you would, May, but all the fun has gone out of it now. I don't much care for the people we have met these past couple of days. I bet his mother has forbidden him to take me. I had thought better of Richard than that."

"I think it is wrong of you to jump to conclusions, Lucy, after all, he says in the letter he will call on you tonight and explain everything. Don't you think you should give him the chance to explain? After all, it is not every day that you form an attachment to a young man. You cannot deny that you liked him for even the most naïve of us could read the signs."

"Yes, I do like him, and to be truthful, May, I also liked your Mr Wedman. I thought you and he were made for each other. Unfortunately, I saw the disapproval on his face when he dropped us off home last night."

"I noticed the same, in fact when I wished him goodnight, he didn't even have the curtesy to reply, he just drove off."

"Then let us go home before we both get hurt."

"I think Richard will come after you."

"Well, he won't find me. We never told each other where we lived. I don't know where he lives and he doesn't know where I live, apart from here and we were leaving here in a few days anyway. My father told me not to tell anybody about my fortune then he would not feel that I was being courted for my wealth, so I haven't.

"Richard never talked about his home or his overbearing mother. But then again, I did not ask him. It is a good job too, for if I had known he had such a mother I would rather have fallen up the steps."

May burst out laughing. "Lucy, I am so pleased you are my best friend."

"And I am so pleased you are my best friend too. We have had a good time of it, though whilst we have been here, have we not?"

"That we have, and as you say, we are only going to be here for the next few days before going home, so I don't suppose it signifies. We can't get up to too much in the days we have left, can we?"

"No, we can't and now I have said the word home, I want to go home so let's pack our bags and head in that direction."

"Home it is. But while our bags are being packed, I will call and see my grandpapa before we go, to let him know we are leaving Tarrington Square." May told her.

Chapter Four

Colonel Walker was still in his dressing gown, sitting at the breakfast table finishing off his bacon and eggs. He looked over the top of his glasses as the door opened, and saw his granddaughter bearing down on him. "What now?" he asked.

"Good morning, Grandpapa, I am pleased to see you still have your appetite."

"Good job I ate before you arrived or I might have been put off eating anything."

"Now what makes you think I have come to make trouble?"

"It's that look in your eye and the tone of your voice, it's much too nice and much too chirpy for this time in the morning. Something is afoot and you intend to involve me."

"Yes, dear, I am, but it will not be very taxing for you.

"No, don't bother telling me, I don't want to know."

"I have just come to inform you that Lucy and I will be leaving Tarrington Square, and as soon as I get back to the house, we are going home."

The colonel, still looking over the top of his glasses at her, made no comment.

"Aren't you surprised?"

"I am waiting for the rest."

May jumped up, gave a laugh and went and kissed the old man on his cheek. "If Lawrence calls to ask where I live, I want you to tell him. He might have another young man with him called Richard, and he will be trying to find out where Lucy lives. I would appreciate it if you would tell them what they want to know. No, I insist that you tell them," May told him.

"You may insist all you like, but that does not mean I will comply with your demand. What's your game, May?"

"Grandpapa, you of all people should know it is very difficult to find someone whom you think you can live with for the rest of your life. Neither Lucy or I have come across anybody, until now, who we like as much as we like Lawrence and Richard. You don't have to do anything. I am sure they will come and see you and all you have to do is tell them what they want to know."

"How do you know they will come?"

"I don't, I can only keep my fingers crossed that Lucy, if not me, has made such an impression on Richard that he wants to further their relationship. I think he was very taken with her. I am not so sure about Lawrence though, he said something about kicking a stool, whatever that meant. But I hope he does try to find out where I live, Grandpapa, I hope so very much."

"That being the case, if either one of them come knocking on my door asking directions, I will tell them."

"I knew you would, thank you, Grandpapa. I will leave you to get dressed and I will go and see how things are progressing for our departure."

"I only hope all this scheming does not backfire on you, May, dangerous game you are playing."

"I know, Grandpapa, but it is the best shot I am going to get at happiness, so I have to take the chance. Haven't I?"

"I suppose so, I would have done the same at your age, I'll play your game and see it through, now I am involved in it."

May arrived back at Tarrington Square to see their coach being loaded with trunks and boxes and she went inside to find Lucy. "How are things going?" she asked when she burst into Lucy's bedroom.

"The last of the boxes are being loaded right now. We should be on our way within the hour. Now the decision has been made I am looking forward to going back home. We have had a good time, but now I don't look on this town with as much delight as I did when we first came here. I am ready for home."

"As am I. It is only because you have been let down by Richard that it is making you feel this way. When he comes in search of you and he explains what occurred to make him cancel taking you to the regatta, you will think better of him again."

"What if he doesn't come? How is he going to find out where I live for, as far as I know, I have given no one this information here in Frankly?"

"He is a resourceful young man. He will find you. I sincerely hope so anyway, for if he doesn't, my hopes for Lawrence will be washed down the river along with yours for Richard. It had started to rain as I walked back from Grandpapa's, so I don't think it will be much of a regatta in the rain."

"Come on then, let's go home and if they don't come and find us, we will have to think of another plan. There are bound to be alternatives. I am sure that between us we will hit on something, I am not going to give up that easily."

"That's my girl," May approved.

Chapter Five

The day of the regatta had arrived and Richard opened his bedroom curtains to be greeted by a grey, wet day. He moaned inwardly, it looked like they would have to be closeted in one of the private boxes that littered the river bank. Not an exciting thought. He had not met Colin Boxton or his daughter but he had heard of them. He had made his money manufacturing farming implements, and he had opened a string of shops in which to sell them. He had quite an empire to his name but Richard knew you don't acquire the amount of money resting in Colin Boxton's bank by being a pussy cat.

Richard made his way dejectedly down the stairs and into the breakfast room where he found himself facing his mother, her face haggard from lack of sleep.

"Bad night, Mother?" he asked.

"I am so sorry, Richard; I don't know what made me do it. We know nothing about this girl you are dancing attendance on, I was only trying to protect you."

"Because you know nothing about Lucy is the very reason you should not have jumped to the conclusion you did. Now I am having to go to the regatta with a plump forty-year-old because she has money. I don't know how I am going to get out of this one. Thank God, Lawrence will be there to support me."

His mother burst into tears again and Richard went and put his arm around her shoulders. "Sorry, Mother, don't take on so, it will turn out all right in the end. Let's have some breakfast and see what the day holds for us, shall we?"

"Why didn't you tell me about her, if you had I would never have done what I did. I thought you had taken up with a loose woman and were afraid to tell me."

"I didn't want to get your hopes up. I know how much you want me to get married and Lucy is very special. I knew that once you met Lucy you would take to her instantly, I didn't want to disappoint you in case things didn't work out between us."

"And now I have spoiled everything for you. I am so sorry, Richard."

"I will work it out, don't worry yourself over it, all is not lost yet."

Lawrence picked Richard up in his carriage, he had intended to drive himself but after looking out of his window and seeing the rain running down the window panes, he decided it was better for his coachman to get wet than him. The rain hammered down on top of the carriage and Lawrence said, "I am looking forward to meeting Colin Boxton, I have heard a lot about him. He is a well-respected business man."

"I am glad one of us is looking forward to this meeting."

Lawrence glanced over at his friend's face and burst out laughing. "Don't look so glum, after all, you are not going to church to wed the lass. We will have a pleasant day, apart from the weather that is, then go and call on Lucy and May and tell them they missed nothing. I must say, the weather is on our side, if it was glorious sunshine, there would be an uncomfortable crush. But in this weather, there will not be many people milling around, and with Colin Boxton's money, he is bound to have rented a box."

"They were my thoughts exactly, closeted in a box with him and his daughter, not an appealing thought."

"Where has your sense of humour gone? I am looking forward to seeing what transpires."

"That is because it is not you that is expected to pay court to his daughter. I don't even know her name."

"Brenda is her name."

"How do you know that?"

"Remember Herman Bammber?"

"Yes, Lord, I haven't heard anything about him for months."

"I saw him last week at the club. He had a face as long as a poker. I asked him what the matter was, and guess what?" Lawrence asked.

"I am in no mood for guessing," grumbled Richard.

"Well you should be. He is going to be your saviour."

Richard looked across at Lawrence and asked, "Herman Bammber, why has he anything to do with this mess?"

"It turns out that Herman and Brenda are madly in love with each other, but Colin Boxton will have none of it. Herman says Brenda and him have been secret lovers for the past ten years, can you believe that? Colin Boxton keeps setting up these meetings with his daughter to meet men he approves of, but Brenda refuses to co-operate. That is the reason she is in her mid-thirties and still a single woman. I know she is a bit on the heavy side but she is still a good-looking woman, it is not as though she has a face like the back end of a horse."

Richard instantly bucked up. "So Brenda is not expecting me to pay court to her?"

"I should think she feels exactly like you do and is dreading the meeting, poor girl."

"This is splendid news, best news I have had for the past two days. What a turn up. How are we are going to help them make it possible for them to marry. For help them we must." Richard declared.

"I don't know, but something will pop into my head, don't worry about that. After all, my happiness depends on it too. If you lose Lucy, May might want nothing more to do with me, for she will lay all this trouble at my door."

When they arrived at the entrance to the park, an attendant stood just inside the park gates directing the coaches and carriages and Lawrence's coachman was informed that Mr Boxton's box was the third one on the left, just around the bend. Mr Boxton was standing at the window watching out for the arrival of Richard, and he was more than pleased to see Lawrence Wedman alighting from the carriage along with the target he had in mind for his daughter.

"Come in, come in, out of the rain. Bad day for a regatta, pity the poor sods who will be rowing in the boat race, but that's life. You win some, you lose some," said Mr Boxton as he shook hands with Richard and Lawrence.

"This is my daughter, Brenda. Brenda, this is Richard Mellor and his cousin, Lawrence Wedman. No need for us to be introduced, Mr Wedman, you have been pointed out to me on more than one occasion."

Richard made a polite bow in Brenda's direction, but she did not make an effort to stand, she merely nodded her head, indicating to Richard that she was aware of his presence.

Mr Wedman on the other hand, walked straight up to Brenda and held out his hand. "I am pleased to make your acquaintance, Miss Boxton."

Brenda was taken by surprise by this sudden friendly gesture and no words came to mind for her reply, so she held out her hand and they shook hands.

Mr Boxton had had Richard in mind for his daughter but Lawrence Wedman was a much better option, and on seeing him shaking hands with his daughter, he took hold of Richard's arm and led him across to the other side of the box and started pointing out different aspects of the regatta, and also naming the people in neighbouring boxes, thus leaving Brenda and Lawrence to get better acquainted.

"I was talking to Herman the other day," Lawrence told her.

"You know Herman?"

"We have known each other many years, we frequent the same club."

"He has never mentioned you to me."

"No, he had never mentioned you to me either, apart from the other night of course."

Brenda's face turned white. "What did he say?"

"He said he was madly in love with you and had been for ten or so years, but you had to keep it secret in case your father found out."

Colour rushed to Brenda's checks and she whispered, "Please, don't let my father hear you or he will stop me going out."

"I think you should tell your father, Brenda, and if he refuses to let you marry Herman, you should elope with him."

"What! Elope? That would cause a scandal then my father would never let me marry Herman."

"If you were to elope and get married, your father would not be able to stop you, for the whole idea of eloping is to do it in secret. You could be over the border before your father realised you had gone. How long have you and Herman been seeing each other?"

"We met at a party some ten years ago. Herman came courting me to our house but my father said he was not good enough for me. Herman works as a clerk in a lawyer's office and although he is not flush to the gills, he has his own money and, if need be, he would be able to support me and any children we might be lucky enough to have. It would not be the luxurious living I am living now, but at least I would be happy, and I would dearly love children, and so would Herman, but time is running out, I am no spring chicken. I sneak out of the house twice a week, telling my father I am visiting my friend Linda, but I am not, I am going to Herman's house to spend a few hours a week with him. I just can't find the nerve to tell my father."

"So you are afraid of causing a scandal by eloping with Herman, but you are not afraid of causing a scandal if it is found out that you are visiting his house twice a week. That does not seem logical to me."

"I had not thought about it like that." Brenda cast a frightened glance in her father's direction. "What do you think I should do?" she asked.

"I think you should tell your father you want to marry Herman and be done with it."

"But what if he stops me from seeing him? I don't think I would bear it if I don't see Herman again."

"How old are you, Brenda?"

"Thirty-one."

"I think at thirty-one you should be able to make your own mind up. If your father refuses to let you marry Herman, head for Gretna Green. Take your own fate in your hands, think how thrilling it would be to be racing for the Scottish border with your lover and your father in hot pursuit."

Brenda looked from Lawrence to her father and in that split second, her mind was made up. She stood up and walked across the box and stood before her father. "Papa, I want you to know I am going to marry Herman Bammber."

"Over my dead body," shouted Mr Boxton.

"I am thirty-one years old and if I want to marry Herman then marry him I will. I am getting too old to be dithering over this subject, I want to have some children and time is passing me by. If you don't want to be a part of your grandchildren then that is for your conscience, not mine. Mr Wedman has shown me the error of my ways. He has offered to take me to see Herman tonight and I shall tell Herman that if he still wants to marry me, then I will willingly do so."

"What the devil have you been saying to her?" demanded an angry Mr Boxton.

"I only pointed out to her what she knew already. Brenda and Herman have been friends for the past ten years and their commitment to each other has not wavered. I think you should stop being a selfish old man, let your daughter marry who she wants and enjoy your grandchildren. After all, you are not getting any younger and Herman is a very nice chap. If you are looking for someone to help you out with your business, I think you could do much worse than Herman."

Mr Boxton looked at his daughter. "You mean to have this man no matter what?"

"I do."

"Then I will send a message to his house requesting an audience with me this evening. There will be no need for you, Mr Wedman, to take Brenda anywhere tonight, I will attend to it. Now if you don't mind, I will take my daughter home, we have things to discuss in private. This weather has put paid to the regatta anyway. The box is paid for, so if you wish to stay you are welcome to it. Come along, Brenda, we are going home."

Brenda needed no further encouragement. She followed her father meekly out of the box, mouthing, *'thank you,'* to Lawrence as she passed.

"I say, Lawrence, I did not see that coming." Richard stood open mouthed as the door closed behind them.

"I must admit it went better than I expected, I didn't take children into account. Thank God for children. Do you want to stay here for the rest of the day?"

"Hell no, let's get out of here as quick as we can in case Mr Boxton changes his mind."

Chapter Six

It had been a miserable journey home, the weather not helping to cheer the young ladies' spirits. But at the end of the journey both Lucy and May felt elated at the sight of the long winding drive leading up to Rollins Estate. The estate boasted thirty acres of the finest green pastures for miles around. The manor house was of low proportions but long in length and displayed two stories in height. Thus, the two long rows of neat, leaded, mullion windows. It was an impressive sight.

Mr Lingard was delighted to see his daughter again. "Lucy, my dear, welcome home." He held out his arms and she ran into them and gave him a big hug.

"Hello, Father, we have come home two days early. That is how much I have missed you."

"You make an old man very happy at the thought, but I will not push you into telling me the truth."

When Mr Lingard managed to catch May's eye when Lucy was out of earshot he asked, "Is Lucy all right?"

"Yes, of course she is. Why wouldn't she be?"

"Losing two days shopping in town is too big a temptation for two young ladies to be missing out on and returning home, something must have gone wrong."

"Let us just wait and see what happens in the next few weeks, shall we? Your plans to find a husband for Lucy might come to a satisfactory outcome after all. There has just been a slight hiccup, but nothing to worry about at present. If her young man does not follow her down in the next week or two, then we shall have to think of another ploy."

"Ah! I knew it. Playing fast and loose with affairs of the heart, May, can turn out to be disastrous you know. If Lucy is in love then I will see to it that she gets the young man she has fallen in love with, one way or another. I shall wait with baited breath for no more than two weeks, then I will take matters into my own hands. I will not see Lucy miserable. I shall make sure she gets what she wants."

"You can't make someone fall in love with someone else, sir, if they do not want to. If you force this young man to marry your daughter then the marriage is doomed before it starts. He has to come and find her, then she will know that he really does love her, that will make a strong bond between them. Have patience, he will come, I know he will."

"Very well, I will bide my time but this young man had better not be playing fast and loose with my girl."

"He is not that sort of young man. Now if we had been talking about his cousin, then that would be a different kettle of fish altogether. You will see what I mean when they appear on your doorstep."

"Two of them you say, are there two of them chasing my daughter's skirt?"

"I certainly hope not, I have other plans for his cousin."

"You don't mean to tell me you are now in the marriage market too? I would not have guessed that. He must be something special for him to take your eye, May. Never was one for having the opposite sex dallying after you."

"No, sir, I am not. But then again, I have never met a rake before and I am afraid I fell hopelessly in love with him. My grandpapa is very much against him. He was the one that told me he is a seducer of women, a libertine and a rake.

"There was no need for my grandpapa to inform me of that, I could tell for myself what he was, the moment I laid eyes on him. But I am the one that is doing the seducing, not Lawrence, and he does not know it. I think, sir, that I will never meet another man whom I like as much as I do him. I have to try and bring him about or I might easily end up a spinster, regretting not taking this opportunity now it has landed at my door."

"And what, pray, are the names of these two gentlemen who have influenced you and Lucy so much?"

"Richard Mellor is the young man who has taken Lucy's fancy, and Lawrence Wedman is the gentleman who I have taken a fancy to."

"Never heard of either of them. This Richard Mellor, he can, I hope, support Lucy. He had better not be expecting Lucy to support him."

"I think, sir, that Richard is well-heeled. We fleetingly met his mother and she was wearing a necklace with diamonds big enough to support England. Unless the stones were glass and not diamonds, which in that case, would complicate things. Although, sir, Lucy tells me they have not discussed finances or residences. Richard, I am led to believe, does not know where Lucy lives."

"So what you are saying is, you know nothing about either of the gentlemen you are talking about, except one of them is a seducer of women."

"Yes, sir, that is correct, but if it puts your mind at rest, Lucy has not fallen for the rake, I have. And they are both well-heeled, sir, I can assure you of that. Their appearance tells its own story."

"That does not put my mind at rest. Had I known this was going to happen I would never have sent you on this jaunt in the first place. You are as much a daughter to me as Lucy is, and since your father died, I have felt it my duty to keep an eye on you. You have never given me any reason to concern myself over your welfare before, but this is very disquieting, May.

"A libertine you say, no, May, I will not have it. What would your father think of me if I let you throw yourself at this scoundrel's feet?"

"There is no need for you to distress yourself, sir, over the matter. Once you meet him, you will understand why I am drawn to him. He is the very man for me. I have decided that it is him or no one. I am more than capable of dealing with his, shall we say, eccentricities."

"I will wait until I have met him before I decide what is the best way forward, but I warn you, May, I will not stand by and let you ruin your life."

"What are you two talking about?" Lucy wanted to know.

"Richard and Lawrence," replied May.

"In that case I will join in the conversation. Has May told you all about Richard, Papa? You will like him very much when you meet him," Lucy told her father.

"Will I indeed? I am keeping an open mind about the subject, especially about May's rogue."

Lucy burst out laughing. "May, what have you been saying about Lawrence? Have no fear, Papa, you will take to him too, as soon as you lay eyes on him. And you will have to agree, he is the very man for May."

"But neither of you know anything about these two cousins," her father stated.

"We know enough about them to really, really like them," his daughter told him.

"A happy marriage cannot be founded on really, really likes," snapped her father.

"It's better than marrying somebody that you really, really hate," May pointed out.

"You are splitting hairs. What I meant is you have to have stable ground to stand on to keep your balance. This means a home and money enough to live on, to support you and any family you might have. And I hope you do have a family because I want grandchildren, you know."

"You are trying to marry me off so you can get grandchildren! Really, Papa, shame on you. But have no fear, I was in the know as to why you sent me away for four months. And I must admit it was an excellent plan. Anyway, even if Richard has no money you have enough to give us a leg up, and you can donate all the money you want to your grandchildren, or even your daughter come to that," Lucy teased him.

"You are shameless, Lucy," her father snapped.

"Well, what about you, using your only daughter as a tool to acquire grandchildren? If that isn't shameless, I don't know what is."

"I will not stand by and let any young man take advantage of you, so this young man of yours had better be worth his salt."

"He is. May thinks so too. You will like him. Rest assured Papa, he is not after my money, or yours."

"In that case I will say no more about it until I have vetted this young man for myself."

"Good, now that is settled, we can all rest easy," replied May, smiling.

Mr Lingard didn't have to wait too long, for on the third day of his daughter's return, he was walking back to the house from the stables when he saw two young men riding up his drive.

He waited at the front door to greet them, and watched as the two gentlemen dismounted from their horses.

Mr Wedman was the first to reach the ground and he held out his hand to Mr Lingard and said, "Lawrence Wedman, sir."

Richard followed his friend's lead and held out his hand. "Richard Mellor, sir."

"Good morning to you both. David Lingard, Lucy's father. I am assuming that you are here because of my daughter?" Mr Lingard spoke to Richard.

"Yes, sir, I am."

Mr Lingard looked his two visitors up and down and he was in no doubt which one was the rake, one glance was all it had taken and Mr Lingard had marked Mr Wedman's card. He was more than pleased with how the two gentlemen were dressed. He turned his attention to Richard once more and said, "You had better come in then, and we will have a chat in comfort, you must both be ready for something to drink."

"Yes, sir, we are," confessed Richard.

"You must be May's rake?" It was a question Mr Lingard could not resist asking of Lawrence as he led them inside.

"I see my reputation has gone before me. What has May been saying about me?" Lawrence asked.

"Nothing you don't deserve, I would say," came the reply. "There is no need for you to bring reinforcements with you, young man." Mr Lingard looked at Richard. "*My* reputation is not that bad, surely?"

This made Richard laugh. "No, sir, in fact quite the opposite, Lucy told me nothing whatsoever about you. But I did not bring Lawrence as reinforcement, sir, he is here entirely on a mission of his own."

"Likewise, young man, Lucy has not told me much about you either, but I understand that you are Lucy's young man."

"Well, not quite that far yet, sir. I am hoping to become Lucy's young man. Lucy and I have not yet come to an understanding."

The entrance hall was spacious and stylishly decorated, bright and welcoming as they made their way across it. "There will be two extra mouths to feed at lunch if you could tell cook," Mr Lingard addressed his butler as he led the way into his library.

"Now then, sit yourselves down and I will attend to a brandy for us all before lunch. What has my Lucy been up to now?"

"Your daughter has not been up to anything, sir, I am afraid it was my mother that acted insensitively and I have come to apologise to her for it," Richard said as he took possession of his brandy.

"A mother's curse is it. Well, we all have to deal with our mothers overprotecting us and trying to pair us off with someone quite unsuitable. It is a trifling matter if we men handle it correctly.

"Tell me the story from the beginning and let me decide for myself if the situation was handled correctly or if I shall have to interfere. But I must warn you, lad, it is one of my pet hates, interfering, nothing good ever comes of it."

Richard related his story including taking his mother home after the fateful ball and their quarrelling until well after midnight. He also included how he came to be in the company of Colin Boxton's daughter at the regatta and the part they, or at least, the part Lawrence played in manoeuvring Brenda into the arms of her long-time lover.

His mother had agreed to apologise to Lucy when next she saw her for Richard had told her that Lucy was the only woman he intended to marry, so she had better get used to the idea.

"I can see how you got your reputation. I know we live out in the middle of nowhere, but I have heard of Colin Boxton's reputation, he is a hard man to outmanoeuvre." Mr Lingard said to Lawrence.

"Not where his daughter is concerned, sir. She held the high card, not me. Colin Boxton wants grandchildren."

"And May? I must warn you; I feel responsible for her since her father died."

"I am afraid the first time I met May, I poured oil onto burning waters, sir. I descended on May and made a fool of myself over a matter I knew nothing about. Richard's mother is my aunt and she came to me and told me Lucy was a gold-digger and asked me if I could put a stop to it.

"Needless to say, when I came upon May, I was like a tongue-tied schoolboy and said all the wrong things, and she has these eyes, sir, they are full of fun and I am afraid the damn woman has imprinted them in my head and I cannot rid myself of them."

"Yes, I am afraid women make us men quivering wrecks. But you two seem to have a handle on things so finish off your bandy and go and find the girls. You will find them at May's. Lucy went over to May's just after breakfast. Back down the drive and turn right when you exit the gates. About half a mile further on you will come across Trees Court. You can't miss it. I will have your horses taken to the stables and instruct them to be fed and watered.

"Lucy left on foot this morning and, as the weather is showing no signs of rain, they will be strolling back, enjoying the sunshine. Be back for one o'clock, as you heard, I have already booked you both a seat at my table. I expect you to be accompanied by Lucy and May on your return. Be off with you now, and let me finish my brandy in peace."

Chapter Seven

Autumn was fast closing in on the summer months but the weather was warm and pleasant and the two young ladies were walking in the garden, oblivious of the two gentlemen descending on them across the lawn.

Lucy said to May, "I think we had better be setting off for home now, Father is expecting us for lunch and you know he doesn't like to be kept waiting."

They were startled by a voice behind them asking, "May we escort you ladies home?"

Both ladies turned around and saw the two gentlemen standing side by side behind them.

Words failed all four of them and an uncomfortable silence fell over the little group.

Lawrence was the first to break the silence. "Oh, for heaven's sake, come here." He grabbed May around the waist, pulled her into him and his lips found hers.

Richard, not to be outdone, followed his friend's actions and the silence continued.

As they walked towards Lucy's home, Richard said, "Lucy, I can only apologise to you for my mother's shocking behaviour at the party and she will apologise herself when she next meets you."

"She thought I was after your money."

"Yes, I know."

"I have money of my own."

"Yes, I know that as well. Lawrence and I have been to your home and we have met your father. He has invited us to lunch and we are under instructions to bring you both back with us."

"What was the reason you cancelled our date at the regatta?" Lucy asked.

"It is a long story and I will tell you when we have more time. I guarantee that you will enjoy hearing about the embarrassing situation I found myself in. And even more pleased at the outcome. It involved the threat of elopement, very exciting it was too."

"Was it you that was going to elope?" Lucy asked.

"Good Lord, no, it was a couple who had been secretly engaged for the past ten years. Lawrence sorted it out in the blinking of an eye," Richard told her.

"That being the case, I shall look forward to hearing about it," Lucy replied. "How did you find us? I was not aware that you knew where we lived."

"Lawrence and I went to Tarrington Square the evening of the regatta but found it all locked up. Lawrence told me he knew May's grandfather so we descended upon him the next morning.

"Lawrence explained the situation and the old gentleman told us where to find you. When we left his house, we could hear him howling with laughter. I was keen to go back into the house and ask what was so amusing but Lawrence said, *'better leave well alone'*, so we did."

Lawrence looked down at May, and she was the picture of innocence. He was a very happy man.

"You will like my father once you get to know him," Lucy told Richard.

"I have already met him, and I can confirm that I like him."

"Good."

"You will like my mother, you know, once you get to know her."

"I will take your word for that. But will she like me?"

"How can anyone not like you, Lucy, my darling? You are adorable."

"I am pleased you think so."

Lawrence said to May, "I have no mother or father for you to like."

"Nor have I a mother or a father for you to like," May replied.

"In that case, we shall have to settle, for liking each other."

"I can live with that," confirmed May.

The End

Four Hours

Chapter One

Georgina looked at her reflection in the long floor standing mirror and was pleased with what she saw. It was the seventh of June in the year 1812, and two years since Georgina had lived in Degrey. Degrey was once the location of her family home until her father had been taken ill and they had to retire to the country.

He had sold the family home and bought a rather large house called Dropping Leaves in the country. But the house had run away with the money. After two years of neglect the house was no longer the impressive sight it once was.

Her father's health had much improved in the past two years and although he was not fully recovered, the doctor had said he had to take things easy from now on, and if he heeded the doctor's words, he still had a few more years left.

Her father had insisted on her spending a season with his father, Colonel Foulds, who still resided in Degrey. He said she must go and enjoy herself at least for one more season, she needed to mix with people of her own age instead of spending all her time in the country looking after him.

To begin with, Georgina had refused to go. Her argument was they could not afford it. But her father pointed out to her that it would not cost him anything because she would be staying with his father. Although money was tight, he could still afford to buy her the odd new gown. So she compromised by saying she had all the ball gowns she needed. They may be a couple of years old, but she would take a needle and thread to them, to bring them into fashion, and agreed to spend a week or so with her grandfather. The very thought of going back to Degrey filled her with dread, but also excitement. Memories of Lord Hanwell came flooding back and her eyes filled with tears. She wiped them quickly away with the back of her hand.

To her shame, Georgina had been glad her father had been taken ill for it gave her a good excuse to run away from all the gossip that was going around Degrey about her broken engagement with Lord Hanwell.

On the other hand, she was looking forward to meeting her best friend, Jane Fern, and going to parties and window shopping in town. Jane and Georgina had had some good times together, but Jane was now happily married with a child of her own, and Georgina did not expect to be spending as much time with Jane as she used to. They had stayed in touch by writing to each other and Jane had told her Walter had left the country and no one knew where he had gone.

When Georgina had finally made up her mind to go to Degrey, she had written to Jane and arrangements were made to meet and catch up with all their news.

Georgina let her mind wander back to the last few days before she had retired to Dropping Leaves with her father. Georgina and Lord Hanwell had been betrothed, but the week that her father became ill, the tittle tattlers were out in force. The rumour was, Lord Hanwell had a secret love. The gossip had reached Georgina's ears, and so she went in search of her fiancé to confirm the rumours.

Lord Hanwell's house in Degrey was of regal proportions and located in a quiet cul-de-sac in the more elite part of the town. Georgina had been announced and shown into the dining room, to find her betrothed sitting down to lunch. Also present at the dining table was Lady Hanwell, Lord Hanwell's mother, and Raymond Hanwell, Lord Hanwell's brother.

The two gentlemen stood up as Georgina entered the room and the atmosphere, along with the guilty look in Lord Hanwell's eyes, told Georgina all she wished to know. "So, the rumour is true?" she asked.

"If you are referring to the rumour that I had, and I stress had, a secret love, then yes, the rumour is true. I am so sorry, Georgina. I did not want you to find out this way. I should have had the courage to confront you with it, but I did not. Please come into the sitting room with me and let us talk things through." Lord Hanwell made to leave the dining table.

"No, thank you. Have no fear, I shall not make a scene. You have answered my question honestly and I shall of course put a notice in the Morning News that our engagement is over. I am sorry I interrupted your lunch. Please sit down and enjoy your meal, there is no need to show me out. I know the way."

Georgina made eye contact with Lord Hanwell and gave him a sad smile before turning on her heels and heading out of the dining room. She closed the door quietly behind her and hurried across the hall and out of the front door before she allowed the tears to flow.

Lord Hanwell looked down at his brother who was now seated, and he saw he had a satisfied smile on his face.

"You seem to be enjoying the outcome of that little scene," Lord Hanwell said to his brother.

"Oh yes. I could not be happier," Raymond confirmed.

Without a word Lord Hanwell took Raymond by the lapels of his jacket and dragged him to his feet. "You and that whore conspired together to get rid of Georgina. Didn't you?"

"It's your own fault, Walter. You are an easy target, you are easily flattered and it was easy for Lisa to seduce you. You fell for her wiles like the rain falls from the sky. Georgina is not good enough for you. She does not have enough money for a start," Raymond said, trying to remove Walter's hands from his lapels.

"Did you pay Lisa to seduce me?" Walter asked, still gripping Raymond's coat.

"Of course. Don't flatter yourself that she offered to seduce you for nothing, because you think you are irresistible to all women. Lisa has been the downfall of better men than you. You must make an advantageous marriage to keep this family living in this house," Raymond said. "Our father left us practically penniless and as you inherited this pile of stones, it is up to you to keep our mother and me in the manner to which we are accustomed."

With surprising speed, Lord Hanwell let go of Raymond's lapels and sent him a loaded right hook to the jaw and Raymond found himself in a heap on the floor.

"Were you in this conspiracy too?" Lord Hanwell turned to his mother.

"Of course, I knew. Raymond is right, we need money. Lots of money and Georgina doesn't have any. We knew you would not break your engagement to Georgina, so we set about contriving to make it happen. Now you are no longer betrothed to her, there is that very quiet, timid little creature, Miss Whitehead. She has plenty of money and I am sure her mother and father will be more than eager for you two to meet. She is one of the richest, single young women in Degrey, and her mother and father are out to get her a title. Yours will do very well, I think," his mother informed him.

"I don't believe this. You two conspired to get rid of the love of my life so you could feed me to the first woman you find with plenty of money to her name? Some family you are. Well it will not work. If you two want money to come into this house, then let Raymond marry your richest woman in Degrey, for I will not. I am leaving Degrey and the country.

"You are both welcome to stay in this house, but you will not get another penny from me. You had better find yourself a job and work some of the debt off that you have accumulated over the years. This house is mine but you may stay here as long as you pay the mortgage and any other debts that you run up from now on. There is nothing left to keep me here now." And with that, Lord Hanwell stormed out of the room.

The first day Georgina had arrived at her grandfather's was just before noon on a Friday. During lunch her grandfather told her that they had been invited to a ball that was being held by Lady Vestry, and he had accepted the invitation on her behalf. It was tomorrow night so he hoped she had brought something appropriate to wear.

She assured him she had.

After lunch with her grandfather, Georgina made her way over to her friend, Jane Fern's house. Jane was delighted to see her and wasted no time in showing off her offspring.

They had an enjoyable hour playing with the infant before she was put in her perambulator and rocked to sleep. When the baby was finally asleep, Jane tucked her hand through Georgina's arm and led her to a comfortable dark brown leather sofa and they both sat down.

"John is out at work so we can have a cosy little chat and I will bring you up to scratch with the latest gossip. I am so pleased to see you, Georgina, two years is far too long for us not be have been in touch with each other. I know how devastated you were when you broke off your engagement to Walter. But Walter was a broken man too, you know. On the same day you broke off your engagement with him, he walked out of his house and he wasn't seen again until about three weeks ago. John met Walter at the club and they got talking. Walter told John that he had left town and headed for the docks. The first boat departing from the dock was bound for India, and so he bought a ticket and boarded the ship.

"His mother and Raymond had contrived the seduction of Walter with the sole purpose of disposing of you. And it worked. They knew Walter idolised you and would never have taken up with the young woman called Lisa, who Raymond had paid to seduce him, unless his hand was forced. Then they spread the rumour and waited until you heard about it. You walked straight into their trap and you broke off the engagement, just as it had been intended.

"Walter told John he had had a fallout with his mother and brother over it and had left them to fend for themselves. Walter's brother, Raymond, instead of finding work, married a young woman who went by the name of Miss Whitehead. Apparently, she is as rich as a bank and she was the intended bride for Walter. Walter had not known about any of the scheming that had gone off, in fact he had never heard of Miss Whitehead, and had been in ignorance of her existence.

"Walter had been taking a turn around the park one day and he accidentally bumped into a young girl that was also out for a stroll. Her name was Lisa and she made eyes at him and it turned his head. Unbeknown to Walter, it had all been contrived for the sole purpose of getting rid of you. Their association didn't last long, only two weeks, but that was enough for the gossips to do their worst.

"Walter had made a big mistake, but he has paid a huge price. John thinks he is still in love with you. Anyway, Walter is back home and he has apparently amassed great wealth whilst he was in India. He is now living back in Degrey in his family home, but very much on his own. Raymond and his mother moved out of Walter's house and went to live with the Whiteheads. Do you think you can forgive him for his indiscretion?" Jane wanted to know.

"I have never wanted any other man, Jane. Walter is always on my mind. I have tried to make myself like other men but Walter always gets in the way. There's nothing I can do about it, so I am resigned to a life of spinsterhood."

"Are you going to Lady Vestry's ball tomorrow night?"

"Yes, my grandfather is taking me."

"Then chances are you will encounter Walter there. Lord Vestry and Walter are good friends and I am sure he will have had an invitation to attend."

"Really? Oh my! I don't think I can face him and all the other guests. They will all be agog to see what happens. I don't think I can do it, Jane."

"Nonsense, you are an idiot if you don't take this opportunity to grasp the happiness that was denied to you, two years ago. Don't let it happen again. You have to fight for what you want, Georgina, to hell with the tittle tattlers, if you want Walter, you must do something about it, and running away is not an option."

Georgina looked at her friend and she thought about what she had said. "Yes, you are right, Jane, to hell with the tattlers, Walter is worth fighting for. Thank you for your good advice, I am going to take it."

"Good girl, go get him, and don't lose him this time."

"I won't."

Chapter Two

A gentle tap on Georgina's bedroom door brought her out of her daydream and, with her heart pounding in her chest, she picked up her cloak and receptacle from off the bed and went to open the door.

"Begging your pardon, Miss Georgina, but your grandfather has asked me to come and tell you the carriage is waiting outside." The maid gave a small curtsey.

"Thank you, Susan, I am on my way down."

Susan, Georgina's maid, was the only luxury her father could afford, and although Georgina had protested that she did not need a maid, her father had insisted.

The colonel, waiting in the hall, looked up and watched as his granddaughter walked down the staircase and his heart was filled with pride. Her jet-black hair hung in shinning ringlets over her left shoulder and her pale lilac gown hung straight down from under her bust to her feet. From her bust up to her neck, the fitted bodice was encased in lace and the small puff sleeves left her arms bare. The neck line was V-shaped and showing just a hint of cleavage.

The only piece of jewellery Georgina wore was a gold chain around her throat and hanging from that chain was a gold ring with a single diamond that caught the light whenever she moved. It was her engagement ring that Lord Hanwell had given her. She had not given it back to him, nor had he asked for it. It was her most treasured possession. This was the first time the engagement ring had been seen in public since their breakup.

Unbeknown to Georgina, a week prior to her journey to Degrey, the colonel was sitting in his smoking jacket reading his newspaper when his front door was knocked upon. Putting his newspaper on the floor, Colonel Foulds went to open his door and, to his utter amazement, Lord Hanwell was standing upon his doorstep.

"You had better come in, my boy, before the curtain-twitchers' see you standing there. We have had enough of the tittle tattlers' mischief to last us a life time, have we not?"

"Thank you, sir. We have indeed, the tittle tatters have not been kind to me, but you are never going to stop gossip, no matter how clever you are," Lord Hanwell replied as the door closed behind him.

"Unfortunately, you are right. Rumours can start wars. We will have to live with them and try to sort out the truth from the lies."

Colonel Foulds led the way back into his sitting room and pointed to an old black leather armchair.

"My account does not run to servants, I am afraid, but I am lucky to have my batman stopping with me. I keep a roof over his head and he keeps me fed and watered. It is my old friend's day off today, but never mind about that, sit yourself down, my boy, and I will sort us out a drop of brandy. What say you to that?"

"That would be very nice, sir, thank you. I must admit I was expecting a certain amount of animosity at this meeting. Being offered a brandy comes as a pleasant surprise," Lord Hanwell told the colonel and accepted the glass filled with dark brown liquid.

"If I told you Roy Whitehead was a captain in my platoon, would that help explain things?" the colonel asked.

"It would go some way towards an explanation, Colonel, yes. If Roy Whitehead is the father of the young woman my mother and brother had plans for me to marry."

"He is, and to cut a long story short, Roy Whitehead found out about his wife, Lady Hanwell and your brother plotting to disgrace you and then force you into marrying his daughter. Roy Whitehead is a very brave man, he had to be to come to me with this information, you can imagine the atmosphere in that house when his wife found out that he had been to see me. Give me the battlefield any day. His wife was not best pleased about it. He and I have become good friends over the years. He knew that Georgina was my granddaughter and that she was engaged to you, so he came to see me and informed me of the situation.

"Georgina was very distressed at the time but two days after she broke off her engagement to you, my son was taken ill and they had to retire to the country. Which was a good thing at the time. It took the girl out of herself if you know what I mean. She had to nurse her father so there was not much time for her to wallow in self-pity.

"I did call at your house to see you and tell you Mr Whitehead had been to see me, but I was informed that you had left the country and nobody knew where you had gone, so there was no more for me to do," explained the colonel.

"I went to India, and have only just returned," stated Walter. "The first thing I did when I landed on dry land here in England was to go home of course. To be truthful I was dreading going home for I did not know what I would encounter when I got there, but after all, the house does belong to me. I had told my brother that he could reside at the house but he must find a job and pay the mortgage.

"I was informed that Raymond decided it would be better if he married Roy Whitehead's daughter, rather than seek employment. Both my mother and Raymond wanted an easy life and agreed it would be a more comfortable life if they left my house, and installed themselves with my brother's in-laws.

"When I arrived back home, my house had not been lived in for the past eighteen months. Because I know my brother so well, and I knew he would not keep up the payments on the mortgage, before I left for India, I went to the bank and made arrangements for the mortgage to be taken out of my bank account until I returned home. I did not want to lose my home as well as Georgina.

"I had left all the money I had in the bank to cover the mortgage payments, so when I arrived in India, I was in desperate need of money. I had to find myself a job. This was not a very hard task, for I soon found out that anyone who had any form of education could walk into any job he liked.

"When we disembarked, there were natives milling around the waterfront handing out pieces of paper with very illiterate writing on them. The writing was in a loose form of English and one of the papers I was handed told of a tobacco plantation wanting someone to manage the estate, so off I went in search of this plantation.

"The owner of the plantation was a very fat, very rich and uncouth man. I defer from calling him a gentleman because his manners were appalling. He had a servant that spoke a little English and between us we managed to come to an understanding.

"Not that I cared a fig that I could not understand a word the plantation owner said, he had offered me a very handsome wage to go and work for him, and that was all I wanted. Not only did he pay me for working the plantation, he also asked me if I would teach him and his children how to speak English. As he had ten children, I had my work cut out, but that did not worry me. There was nowhere to go and nothing else to do, and besides that, he was also paying me very well for teaching them English, and it kept me occupied. Every time one of his sons mastered a few words of English, he would hand me a trinket, a jewel or a piece of porcelain. He was a very uncouth man but very generous.

"He did not take much interest in learning English, but I have to admit his children were most enthusiastic. When I say his children, only the sons were allowed in the school room. Neither his wife or daughters were given the opportunity to further their education, which was a shame, for what I saw of them, they were every bit as intelligent as the sons. I know that his wife would have loved to attend the classes and she would also have liked her daughters to attend too. But it was not my place to say anything.

"The difference in India between the rich and the poor is vast and sometimes, when I saw people begging, I felt guilty at taking the money that was paid to me. But I was working ten-hour shifts on the plantation and two hours on an evening in the classroom and no one else seemed willing to do the job. I accepted the payment but I had to work very long hours for it, and in the end, I felt no guilt. None of the money I earned was spent, there was nothing to spend it on. The manager's job included free board and lodgings, it had to because it was miles from anywhere and if the job had not provided living accommodation, I doubt that anybody would have been prepared to stay. It suited me down to the ground.

"At the end of two years, I was an extremely wealthy man, not just in money but jewels and ornaments soon mounted up, they alone are worth a king's ransom. But I was also extremely homesick. I decided to come home. My mother had heard I was back and she called to see me and informed me that Georgina was not yet married, so I have come to you, sir, hoping to find news of her. You will never know the relief and excitement I felt when I heard she was still single. I loved her then, and I love her now.

"I was too ashamed to face her over my indiscretion, so I took the coward's way out and ran away. In hindsight, it all happened for the best because I made a fortune out in India, and have come home a much richer man than I ever would have been had I stayed in England. Do you think I would stand a second chance with her, sir, now you know the full story? Do you think she could see her way to forgiving me if I get the opportunity to explain to her how stupid I have been?"

"Yes, I do think she might forgive you, if you set about it in the right way. I know for a fact she has never had a romantic thought towards any of the other young men that dally after her. I think if you tell her the truth she will understand. Georgina is coming to stay with me next week for a couple of weeks and will be leaving for home the following Monday week. She is welcome to stay here as long as she likes, but she insists she will only stay for a week or two, she wants to get back home to make sure that her father is all right. He is of course, thankfully he has made an excellent recovery but, Georgina insists on returning as soon as possible.

"There is a ball being held at Lady Vestry's next weekend and both Georgina and I have been invited. It might be advisable for you to obtain an invitation to the ball from Lady Vestry, that way you will be sure to encounter Georgina. Then the wall building will be up to you. I know Lady Vestry very well, and if you would like me to ask her to send you an invitation to the ball, I will be more than happy to do so."

"I have set the ball rolling, sir, by trying to let Georgina know how things stood at the time of our engagement. I am aware that Jane Fern is Georgina's best friend and John Fern, her husband, is a fellow member at my club. I met John last week and told him the story, so, for once, I hope the gossip will spread and Jane will find out from John, and in turn, Jane will tell Georgina. A good example of the workings of tittle tattle, wouldn't you say?

"As for obtaining an invitation to Lady Vestry's ball, I have already received one. When you are flush in the pocket, sir, invitations flow. But that is not a fair statement for me to make. Lord Vestry is a friend of mine, that is why I got the invite, not because of the money.

"I am at my leisure at the moment. As for Georgina wanting to go straight home after the ball, that does not deter me. I have no objection to accompanying her back to her father if she will allow me to do so. Do you know if Georgina is aware of what happened between my mother, brother and me? Do you know if Jane has been in touch with Georgina and told her what I told John?" asked Lord Hanwell.

"I have not told her, she was too upset at the time and I thought if I told her what had happened, it might upset her even more. If Jane has told her, then Georgina has not informed me of it. I will leave it up to you to find that out, or to explain things to her."

"I am not trying to make excuses for what I did because there are no excuses. But I intend to explain the best way I can and hope she can forgive me. What a bloody fool I was." Lord Hanwell leaned forward and placed his elbows on his thighs and his head in his hands.

"Well, lad, all I can say is you are not the first man to make a fool of yourself over a woman and I'm damn sure you won't be the last. This ball of Lady Vestry's will last around four hours, so make the best of them. You will have a lot of competition to fight your way through, for Georgina is a very popular young lady. Four hours is not a long time in which to win a battle," Colonel Foulds chuckled.

Chapter Three

To her surprise, Georgina felt elated when she had heard the news that Walter was back in England. She hadn't expected to feel excited at the thought of seeing Walter again, but she did, and if she was truthful to herself, she couldn't wait to see him. To further her excitement, Jane also told her that he was still single. Thrilling news indeed.

Furthermore, he was to attend the ball, therefore their paths were bound to cross. If the story Jane had told her was true, then with a bit of luck she might be wearing her engagement ring once more after tonight. She was going to give it her best shot anyway, she had nothing to lose and everything to gain.

What would happen when she saw him? What did he look like now? Had he changed? These were all the questions going around and around in her head. She was soon going to find out.

The day of the ball had finally arrived and as Georgina descended the staircase, her grandfather smiled up at her. "You look good enough to eat, my dear."

"And you, sir, look splendid in your uniform. I shall be proud to walk into the ballroom upon your arm."

The ballroom was crowded and there were no spare seats to sit upon, so the colonel escorted his granddaughter to the side of the room as near to the open French windows as he could, and left her standing at the back, by the wall, whilst he went to get them both a drink.

Georgina was standing with her back to the wall, looking around the ballroom while she waited for the return of her grandfather, when a commotion grabbed her interest.

There he was, Lord Walter Hanwell, looking as handsome as ever, but with a rather tanned complexion. Georgina's heart skipped a beat as Walter turned to look at her and their eyes met.

Facing Walter, was a young man not long out of short trousers displaying a tendency to use his mouth to attract attention. Strutting his stuff for all and sundry to see and hear and causing much discomfort for Lord Hanwell.

"Well, well, look who we have here," the youth said, following Lord Hanwell's eyes.

Georgina saw the look of anger appear upon Walter's face and, fearing the worst, made her way over to the little group that was now gathering around the young man with the loud voice. They were all expecting to see some good sport. There wasn't anyone in that ballroom that didn't know Georgina and Walter's story, and all waited with baited breath to see what was going to happen next.

"Hello, Walter," Georgina said, smiling up at him as she held out her hand.

Walter took her hand and kissed the back of it, his eyes never leaving hers. "Georgina," was all Walter could manage to say.

Then still holding her hand, his eyes dropped down to the engagement ring hanging from a delicate gold chain around her neck. He raised his eyes to meet hers and he read in them all he needed to know, and the smile that accompanied the reply in his eyes, gave Georgina the confidence she needed to deal with this uncouth young man.

The young man with the loud mouth spouted, "You are most gracious to acknowledge someone who has done you such an injustice as to prefer another woman over you."

All the guests that were present in the ballroom fell silent.

"You have me at a disadvantage, young man. May I know who is addressing me without us being formally introduced?" Georgina asked.

"Lord Drummand at your service, Miss Foulds." And the young man made a low bow from his waist.

"I am surprised that a young man with a title to his name should be making such a cake of himself in this crowded ballroom," Georgina told him.

"It is not I who is making a cake of himself." He looked pointed at Walter. "I offer you my arm for the night, Miss Foulds. It will spare you the embarrassment of having to turn down Lord Hanwell once again. I saw the way he looked at you just now, there was no mistaking his intentions. I am sure you would much prefer to be seen in my company than his," Georgina was told.

"That is a most generous offer you hand out, Lord Drummand. I would like to point out that Lord Hanwell has not offered me his arm for the night, so there is no embarrassment for either party. But neither do I seek your attention, or your arm. Thank you for the offer, which I respectfully decline," Georgina told him.

"Are you saying you would prefer Lord Hanwell's company over mine? I find that hard to believe after the way he has treated you," the young lord spouted.

"You may choose to believe anything you like, sir. Lord Hanwell has never made a public spectacle of me. He has always conducted himself with propriety in public. The quarrel between us, if there was a quarrel, sir, is none of your business or anyone else's," Georgina told him.

"I am sure this is all bravado on your part, Miss Foulds. You are putting on a brave face instead of showing the shame you must feel. We all know why you broke off your engagement to Lord Hanwell, and I am sure you would much rather be escorted by me tonight than be seen in your ex-lover's company." Still the young man goaded Georgina.

"You should get your facts right, young man, before you go spouting your mouth off. Walter was my fiancé, he was never my lover, not in the way you are inferring. He made a mistake and he has paid the price for it. Much the way you are going to pay the price for the mistake you are making right now," Georgina told him.

"And what, pray, do you mean by that?" she was asked.

"You are making a big mistake in thinking that Lord Hanwell will forget this disgraceful show of bad manners. Were he to hold a ball of his own, I don't think you would be on his guest list, do you?"

"You think I care a fig about that?" he asked her.

"You may not think so at this moment, you seem to have all the guests in the ballroom agog with curiosity and you are basking in it. But when the invites to other balls do not land on your doorstep, just in case you cause such a disturbance at their ball, you may have a change of heart. But time will tell and I think you will have to pay the price."

Georgina could feel, rather than see, the anger building up in the gentleman standing by her side, and she knew Walter well enough to know that he was at breaking point. She glanced around the ballroom which was as hushed as a grave, and all eyes were trained on the three of them.

"Let me see, do I wish to be seen with a young man who has been short of a good spanking when he was in short trousers, and needs teaching some manners, or on the arm of a loved and respected gentleman?"

Georgina put her index finger to her lips and first she looked the young man up and down as she walked around him with a look of pretend consideration on her face. Then, Georgina turned and looked Lord Hanwell in the eye, and everyone in that ballroom was in no doubt as to whom she was going to choose.

"I think I would like to be seen with Walter." She placed her arms around Lord Hanwell's waist and was rewarded by a strong pair of arms encircling her and warm passionate lips covering hers. And still the ballroom was silent.

The colonel, coming back into the ballroom carrying two glasses of wine, stopped dead in his tracks at the sight of his granddaughter in a passionate embrace with Lord Hanwell.

'It would seem four hours was much too long. It hadn't taken him ten minutes to achieve his goal. I should have had him in my platoon. Or did Georgina know what she was about?' The colonel decided on the latter, and he proceeded to drink his wine. *'The tittle tattlers will have their day once more. But this time the gossips are going to tell a different story. This story is going to have a happy ending,'* the old gentleman thought to himself and he had a mischievous twinkle in his eye.

Lord Hanwell let go of Georgina and taking hold of her shoulders, he turned her so her back was facing him. He took hold of the gold chain around her throat and unfastened the clasp before removing the necklace from her neck. He slipped the diamond ring from the chain, and turned Georgina back round to face him. Lifting up her left hand he proceeded to place the ring on her engagement finger and said so that everyone in the ballroom could hear him, "That is where that belongs, and that is where it is going to stay."

Chapter Four

All eyes were riveted to the couple as they witnessed Walter placing the engagement ring back on Georgina's finger, and when this was accomplished, someone started clapping, then one by one others joined in and soon everybody in the room had joined in. Walter was clapped on the back by more than one gentleman and Georgina found herself being embraced by the ladies.

Her grandfather finally made his way to join them and handed Georgina a glass of punch remarking, "A fine spectacle you have made of yourself, I thought better of you, Georgina."

"I got carried away, Grandpapa, I didn't realise there were other people in the room."

"In that case, you are forgiven, here's to you both. Good job, well done, lad." The old man grinned at Walter.

"It had nothing to do with me, sir. I just stood there like an idiot, Georgina took control of the situation and in the end, I could not help myself from taking her in my arms, to hell with anyone else. We have both suffered at the hands of the gossips, let them do their best with this. You are going to have me in the family, sir, like it or not. Georgina is not getting away from me a second time, so you had better get used to the idea," Walter told him.

"You might be determined to keep Georgina to yourself, young man, but I will have things done correctly from now on. I will not let you push her into doing something she does not want to do," Walter was told.

"I expect nothing less from you, sir. Although I have not had time to discuss the future with Georgina, I was thinking of what you said about her wanting to go back to the country to be with her father. I will have to go and see him, so we can make plans to get married. If it is all right with Georgina, I will take her back home and I thought, sir, you might like to accompany us. Go and visit your son and take part in the wedding arrangements," Walter said.

"My, you have thought this through. I like the idea of going to see my son and I accept the invitation to travel into the country with you. I can act as Georgina's chaperon, but count me out of any wedding arrangements, to the devil with all that. Just let me know the when and where and I will be there to see her take her vows," the colonel replied.

Next day saw Georgina being shown into Jane Fern's living room, her friend was sitting on the floor playing with her daughter. "Jane, forgive this intrusion but I just had to come and see you."

Jane looked up and saw a radiant Georgina crossing the floor to greet her. "You don't have to apologise to me for calling to see me, you are welcome any time, day or night," her friend replied jumping up and embracing her.

"Jane, it is done." Georgina held out her left hand to her friend to show off her engagement ring.

"I am so pleased for you, Georgina, come and sit down and tell me all about it."

The two friends spent the next couple of hours discussing the new engagement and Georgina told Jane that, the day after tomorrow, Walter was taking her home and that her grandpapa was to accompany them. It was agreed between them that they would still keep in touch with each other by letter and if ever Jane and her family wanted to have a trip into the country there would always be a room for them to sleep in.

Lord Hanwell pulled his horses to a halt in front of Colonel Foulds' house and went inside. Walter had not had time to sort out a coachman, in fact he had only just bought the coach the day before. Colonel Foulds had told Walter that money was tight for his son, and he only had the one coach, so when the coachman had dropped Georgina off at his house, their coach had to return back to Dropping Leaves, where Georgina and her father resided, as it was his only means of transport.

Walter had not employed any servants since he had returned to Degrey, for until he had seen Georgina and found out how things lay in that quarter, he was undecided as to his plans for his future.

It was all hands on deck to take the luggage out of the house and stow it on the coach and when this was completed, they were ready for the off. The colonel sat up top with Walter, and Georgina and her maid were encased inside the coach and they were soon heading in the direction of Dropping Leaves. The colonel's old valet was left behind to take care of things until the colonel returned home.

The journey was soon accomplished and Mr Foulds Jr. was delighted not only to see his daughter, but to see his father too. Walter approached Georgina's father later that evening and told him of his intentions towards his daughter.

Mr Foulds said to Walter, "If you are expecting to make an advantageous marriage, Walter, I must disappoint you, for all my money is nearly spent. When you are not able to work and earn your keep then money becomes a huge problem. Georgina is not aware of the dire straits that we are in. She knows there isn't much money to go around, but she is not aware of the extent of the problem, so I thought it only fair to warn you."

"I am not offering marriage to Georgina for her money, sir, I love her and always have. I did a foolish thing when I let myself be seduced, but I make no excuses, I did wrong. By some miracle, she has forgiven me and we are once more engaged. I saw from the rundown condition of this property that things were, shall I say, less than affluent."

"Yes, you can put it that way if you like, no matter which way it is phrased, I am financially embarrassed, and that's the truth. But this house is a wonderful old house and with the right person in charge of it, it could be magnificent once more. The grounds are also utterly neglected and I shall have to sell it and find a smaller place for Georgina and I to live in before much longer. So, if you were expecting to come into money, my boy, you had better make yourself scarce before you break my daughter's heart again."

"If Georgina and I had to live in a tree house in the grounds, sir, it would not deter me. My time in India was well spent and I came home with my bank account much swelled. If it is all right with you, sir, I shall sell my house in Degrey and come to Dropping Leaves to live once Georgina and I are married, and work on this house and the grounds. So long as Georgina is by my side, I can turn this place into something the king could live in. I learned a lot whilst I was manager of the plantation out in India and it will take a lot of hard work, but I am not afraid of that."

"Does Georgina know of this?"

"She does not, sir. I did not know of it myself until we have just spoken of it. I am at this moment in time, without employment but not in any hurry to find any. If things did not work out with Georgina, I thought about leaving England for good and going abroad again, but I missed my home terribly and I would much rather find a purposeful form of employment here in England than have to leave it again. Like you said, sir, it is a beautiful house and once all the overgrown grass and weeds are taken care of we can build on that. Buy some cattle or sheep or both. I think it would make an excellent farm if done in the right way, don't you?"

"Then we had better have a family meeting, especially now my father is here, and see what we can achieve."

"I think, sir, we are going to achieve a lot," Walter told him.

"What are you two whispering about?" Georgina wanted to know.

"Walter was just saying, if he has to live in a tree house with you, then he would be content," her father told her.

Georgina smiled and replied, "I hope that was figuratively speaking, for I have no desire to live in a tree house."

"I lived in a tree house once," chipped in the colonel, "it was quite cosy once you got used to climbing the tree to go to bed."

"I was telling your father I am going to sell my house in Degrey and put all the money into this place, make it into a working farm. It should provide us all with a good living and it will be a good place to bring children up in if we are lucky enough to have any. Let the children play in the tree house."

"You are taking things a bit too much for granted, aren't you?" Georgina asked.

"No, it is all settled between us. You and I are getting married and coming to live here with your father and I will brook no opposition to it. I have been a fool for too long, things are going to change around here, and I am determined on that."

"In that case, you had better give me some money to buy my wedding dress for my father has none," Georgina told him.

"You shall have it," Walter replied.

The End

THE BIG BLACK CAR

Chapter One

Celia was driving her little yellow car down the narrow country lane, on her way to the cottage she had just bought. Her car was filled with boxes and cases and she had to take it steady, for the lane was prone to potholes.

Her reputation as a freelance typist had developed over the years and Celia was now working from home. The flat she had in Brookworth had become too noisy during the day, people clomping along the corridor, banging doors, loud music and voices. It broke her concentration, so she had made the decision to move.

She had found a little cottage in a village called Edgely, which was situated about fifty miles to the west of Brookworth. She had fallen in love with the little cottage and it was by far the most remote of any of the properties she had been to view. Also, a deciding factor was that the cottage had been up for sale for two years and she was able to acquire it at a knockdown price. The owners wanted to move it on. It was ideal.

After turning off the main road, she had to travel about a mile down a narrow country lane before she came to the cottage. There were no other properties on either side of the lane. She had a lovely garden to the front and a rather large garden to the rear, just what she'd had in mind when the search had started. True, the front and rear gardens were completely overgrown, and there were more weeds than grass, but she looked forward to attacking them. Would she be the winner, or would the weeds win? Only time would tell.

It was Friday evening, the traffic had been heavy along the motorway, but once she turned off the motorway, she had made good time. She could hardly wait to reach her destination. There was no turning back now, she had given the landlord of her flat a month's notice, and handed the keys back just after lunch.

The cottage, having been empty for the past two years, was in need of a bit of tender loving care and Celia had spent the last month while working off the month's notice, cleaning, scrubbing and hanging curtains. Today she was moving in. The garden would have to wait.

Celia came to an abrupt halt when turning the last corner, because walking slowly across the lane, was a hedgehog.

The honking of a car horn made Celia jump. She had been too busy watching out for potholes to glance in her rear-view mirror to see if is she was holding any other vehicle up. When she did glance in her rear-view mirror, all she could see were boxes. She glanced in her wing mirror, but her car was at an angle and all she could see was the hedgerow. She opened the car door and got out, and looking behind her, she saw a big black car had pulled to a halt behind her. The driver of the car was making threatening gestures to her from behind his steering wheel.

Celia, used to having irate men drivers gesticulating at her, chose to ignore him and slowly opened the passenger side door. Reaching into the rear of the car, she produced a scarf, closed the side door and turning to the front of the car, proceeded past it and into the lane. She approached the hedgehog and, gently wrapping the scarf over the hedgehog's spines, she gingerly picked the hedgehog up and carried it to the other side of the lane, where she let it waddle off into the undergrowth.

Through the now open window of the big black car, the driver poked his head out and shouted at her, "What the devil do you think you're doing, stopping on a bend on a lane this narrow? I nearly ran into you. A typical woman driver, not a brain in your head."

"And you, sir, are a typical chauvinistic male pig, who thinks he owns the road and knows everything there is to know about driving. That is one of the reasons there are so many hedgehogs splattered on our roads. If it's a choice between saving the life of a hedgehog, or having to hear you berating me for doing so, the life of a hedgehog wins every time. I hear and see the fast, impatient driving of men every day of the week, but it is not often I get the chance to save a little hedgehog's life." She got in her car and drove off.

At the age of forty-one, Celia was a spinster and with her experience of men, she intended to stay that way. The encounter with the driver of the big black car added another nail to the coffin.

Celia had been living at the cottage for two weeks. On one of her daily walks, she had discovered the only other dwelling in the proximity of her cottage. It was around the next bend, further up the lane. It was another cottage, but bigger than the one Celia had bought, and the front garden must have been twice the size of hers. Not only was it twice as big, but there wasn't a weed to be seen. Not even a blade of grass longer than the rest in the immaculately cut lawn.

To her dismay, there was a car parked in the drive, and it was a big black car. Celia, recognising it, decided not to walk that way again. One encounter with the driver of that car was enough for any woman. She had been engaged twice in the past, but neither time did the engagement ring turn into a wedding ring.

The postman was kept busy, bringing Celia lots of A4 envelopes full of work, and between working and attacking the overgrown garden, there had not been much time for anything else. Not that she minded, she loved living in the cottage and, bit by bit, the front garden was becoming well kept. But the weeds were still winning.

In the two weeks she had lived in the little cottage, she had not seen or heard anything of her neighbour or even seen his big black car roaming up and down the lane. But her peace and quiet was about to change.

It was ten o'clock on Monday morning and Celia had been sitting at her computer for the past two hours. The quietness of the cottage was disrupted by a scratching noise at the front door. Opening the door, she found a little white and brown Jack Russell dog sitting on her doorstep. Its tail started wagging as soon as Celia appeared. The dog barked, turned and ran down her drive, stopping at the gate, it turned to look at her. He wanted her to follow him.

She grabbed her mobile phone off the little table at the side of the door then went outside, locking the door behind her. She set off in pursuit, following the dog up the lane and onto the drive of the cottage boasting a big black car. The dog went to the rear of the cottage and Celia followed. There, laying on the grass at the side of a fallen ladder, was the driver of the big black car.

Celia got out her mobile phone and made the call while she watched the antics of the little dog.

The dog ran over to the prone man and started licking his face.

"Good boy, Goliath," the man on the lawn said. "Did you bring help."

Goliath looked across the lawn and the prostrate man turned his head and saw Celia. "Don't just stand there, help me up," the man ordered.

"Are you talking to me?" asked Celia.

"Well, I'm not talking to the dog," came the reply.

"I don't think you are in a position to order me about, and a please would not go amiss," Celia told him.

"Just give me a hand up and help me into the house, then you can go back to where you came from," she was told.

"Why can't you help yourself up?" Celia asked.

"Because I think I have broken my leg. I need a helping hand to get back into the cottage so I can telephone for an ambulance," he replied.

"Well, in the opinion of this woman without a brain in her head, if you have broken your leg, you must stay where you are until the ambulance arrives," she told him.

"And how am I supposed to telephone for an ambulance when I am out here and the telephone is in the cottage?"

"In this day and age, and with a car as big as a boat, I would have thought that you would carry a mobile phone with you. That way your problem is solved."

"My mobile phone is on charge in the cottage."

"Hard lines then."

"All right, *please*, help me into the cottage. Does that satisfy your petty demands?"

"Oh, yes." Celia smiled but did not move.

"Well, don't just stand there smirking."

"I happen to have my mobile phone on me, so I was able to phone for an ambulance five minutes ago, while your dog was washing your face," she told him smugly, "Best if you stay where you are until help arrives."

"You are enjoying this, aren't you?"

"Oh, yes," Celia had to admit.

"Look, I know we got off on the wrong foot, but could you look after Goliath for me until I get back from the hospital. He will need feeding around four o'clock and I usually take him for an evening walk around six. Could you do that if I don't get back in time?"

"I don't have any dog food at my cottage, no need for any," she replied.

"You will find dog food under the kitchen sink, and could you lock up for me too? The key is in the door. You had better go and get me my mobile phone and give me your number so I can call you and let you know when I will be back so you can come and let me in."

"You certainly know how to give a girl a good time. Is there anything else you would like me to do before they cart you off to hospital?" This was said with only a hint of sarcasm.

"This situation I have landed myself in is most inconvenient, now I won't be able to drive my car for at least six weeks, and although I work from home, it is going to be damned frustrating. It has put me in a very bad temper and I am taking it out on you. Surely you can understand that? I might even have to ask you to give me the odd lift. But you will have to drive my car, I wouldn't be seen dead in that yellow bug you drive around in."

"No, I can't understand why you are so rude. And don't upset yourself over having to sit in my little yellow bug. My little yellow bug would refuse to open her doors to you. You should be most grateful to me for stepping in and doing your bidding, there is no excuse for bad manners. I will go and find your mobile phone. Which room is it in?"

"It's in the kitchen, turn right when you enter the front door, you will see it on one of the worktops."

Celia found the mobile phone and, glancing at the screen, she saw it was 73% charged. *Well, it will have to do*, she thought and took the phone back outside and held it down to the irate patient.

"It's only 73% charged, so if I were you, I would turn it off until you need to use it."

"Put your name and telephone number in, will you? And you had better tell me your name so I can look you up on my contact list when I want to call you."

Celia hesitated, looked down at the patient and said, "What did your last slave die of?"

"Hurry up, I can hear the ambulance coming up the lane. It can only be the ambulance, not many vehicles come this way."

Celia listened and could hear the sound of an engine getting closer, so she said, "My name is Celia Taylor." She proceeded to enter her name and telephone number into the mobile phone then handed it to him.

"Thank you, I do appreciate it, sorry if I appeared bossy, this is most inconvenient, most inconvenient."

"You certainly appear bossy, it's not my fault you have fallen from the ladder, and you are lucky that I didn't walk away and leave you to get back into the cottage yourself."

The sound of the engine died away and Celia turned and went to the front of the cottage to tell the ambulance men that their patient was to the rear. To Celia's delight, the two ambulance men turned out to be two ambulance women.

"Can the patient walk?" one of the women asked.

"I don't think so, it looks like he has broken his leg," they were told.

A stretcher on wheels was taken from the back of the ambulance and they made their way to the rear of the cottage.

Without further ado, one of the paramedics asked, "What's your name?"

"Jack Firth," he replied.

"Right, Jack, I am going to strap your legs together, then roll you over onto your side and my colleague is going to push the stretcher under your back then I am going to roll you onto it. Are you all right with that?" the same lady asked whilst they were collapsing the stretcher.

"Yes, just do what you have to do, and get me to the hospital," he replied.

"I am trying to teach him the words please and thank you, but I am not having much success. Make sure you don't miss a gear whilst you have Jack in the ambulance or he will be taking the steering wheel from you, broken leg or no broken leg. Jack doesn't like women drivers," Celia told them.

"It's all right, pain makes people grumpy, we are used to it," one of the paramedics smiling at Celia.

"I think we all agree on that, he is certainly grumpy," Celia replied.

She watched as Jack Firth was driven away, and Celia was left looking down at a little Jack Russell.

Chapter Two

"Well, young man, it looks like you are landed with me for goodness knows how long. Come on, Goliath, show me where these ladders are kept. Better not leave them lying around, if the place gets burgled, no doubt I will get the blame."

Celia could see no other building with the exception of a large wooden garden shed at the bottom of the back garden, so she went to investigate. The door was open so she looked inside and saw gardening tools galore. She placed the ladders in the shed, closed and clicked the padlock shut, hoping Jack had the key in his pocket, then headed for the kitchen and the dog food.

Looking around the kitchen, she spotted a dog leash hanging behind the kitchen door. She put it with the dog food. Now she wanted a bag to put the dog food in, but none were visible. She took a towel that was hanging on a rail at the side of the sink, placed it on the table and proceeded to place the tins of dog food and biscuits, onto the towel. She did not know how long she would be in charge of the little dog, so she was preparing for the worst. She folded two of the corners over and tied them together and she did the same with the other two corners. She put the leash on the dog, picked up her bundle and went out. She locked the door and put the key in her pocket.

Goliath trotted happily alongside of her as she made her way back down the lane towards her own cottage.

Celia was behind with her work but it would have to wait, she had a dog to feed. She opened a tin of dog meat, found an old dish she didn't use anymore, but had kept for emergencies, tipped in the dog meat, sprinkled in some dog biscuits and placed it on the floor. Next, she found a second bowl, filled it with water and placed it next to the dog food.

"There, that should keep you satisfied while I get on with my work, this has thrown me back a couple of hours. You behave yourself and go and sit in a corner or something, whatever dogs do."

Goliath sat looking up at her and listened to what she had to say, his little white tail waving from side to side. But when Celia left the kitchen and went into a small spare bedroom she had converted into her office, Goliath ignored the food she had placed on the floor for him and was close on her heels.

Celia, not used to animals, chose to ignore him and sitting down at her little desk, she proceeded to continue typing where she had left off.

Thirty minutes later found Celia and Goliath treading the lane, the occasional bark and expectant stare Goliath had given her, won the day. Goliath was happy he was out on his morning walk. He had accepted long ago the fact that while walking at the side of the road, the dog leash was a must, but as soon as they reached open countryside and the leash came off, he shot off on his sniffing adventure, but he kept an eye on Celia all the same, he wasn't going to let her get away.

By the time Celia and Goliath reached home, it was lunch time. She gave a resigned sigh and put the kettle on, took out some bread and butter and made herself a sandwich. While Celia sat at the kitchen table, Goliath made short work of his dog meat.

Lunch over and Celia had just sat down at her desk when a knocking at her front door made her jump with fright. *'What now,'* she thought and, getting up from her desk she went to answer her door. Goliath followed.

Opening her door, Celia was amazed to see a glamorous young woman standing on her doorstep. She was wearing a shocking pink coat and fawn trousers. They eyed each other up, and Goliath began to growl.

The visitor said, "I'm looking for Jack Firth, he lives further up the road. Is he here? I see the mongrel is, so I'm guessing he is too. Tell him Kelly is here to see him," shocking pink coat said, ignoring Goliath.

"It must be something to do with the country air around here, manners seem to be a thing of the past. Mr Firth's mongrel, as you call him, is here, but Mr Firth is not. He has been taken to hospital with a suspected broken leg. You will find him at the cottage hospital," Celia informed her.

"What the devil is he doing breaking his leg?" Kelly snapped.

"That is a question you will have to ask him," replied Celia and she closed her door.

Goliath gave another growl as the door closed. "I'm with you on that Goliath," she told the dog.

Goliath finally decided it was nap time and he curled up on an armchair near the window and Celia finally got around to sitting at her computer again and began to type. But not for long, her peace and quiet was once again disturbed when Goliath jumped down from his chair and ran to the door barking.

The knocking soon started so she went to see who Goliath was barking at. As soon as the door was opened, Goliath shot out and she heard a male voice saying, "Hello, Goliath, is your dad here?"

Celia poked her head round the door frame to see a postman patting an excited Goliath. "If you mean by Goliath's dad, Mr Firth, I am sorry to disappoint you. Mr Firth is in the cottage hospital with a suspected broken leg."

"Had too much pop, has he?" grinned the postman.

"If you mean had he had too much to drink, I don't think so, he fell off a ladder."

"I have a parcel for him, I saw your car parked in the drive when I passed on my way to Jack's. When he didn't answer my knock, I thought I would come here and ask if you would sign for the parcel for him. I was going to leave a note telling him to come and collect it, but if he has a broken leg, that puts a different slant to the problem altogether," the postman said.

"I have a key to his cottage, if you want to go back there, I will get the key and meet you there, it will give Goliath a little run out at the same time," Celia told the postman.

The parcel was signed for and left in Mr Firth's cottage. Celia decided to take the long way home to give Goliath another run out before she returned to her cottage. Glancing at the clock on the mantlepiece when she got home, she was amazed to see it was five o'clock, and she was ravenously hungry.

"What shall we have for dinner, Goliath? Fancy a couple of sausages?"

Goliath waged his tail and Celia smiled. This was a turn up for the books, she never thought she would enjoy talking to a dog, but he was adorable and he seemed to know what she was saying to him. She knew he couldn't understand her, but she decided she wanted him to. So it was agreed between them, she would talk to him, and he would listen.

Dinner was over and Goliath couldn't believe his luck, he had watched Celia devour her dinner and not even a scrap was thrown his way, but after Celia had washed and put away her dirty plate and cup, she went over to the table and felt at some sausage on a plate that she had cut up into little pieces for Goliath. They were now cold, so he watched as she emptied the contents of the plate into his bowl, and he didn't even bother smelling at it. A treat indeed, he didn't get this at home.

Celia attacked her computer again but it was not long before she was interrupted by her mobile phone ringing. "Hello."

"Hello, Celia. This is Jack Firth,"

"Thank goodness for that, are you all right? When are you coming home?" Celia wanted to know.

"I am waiting for the ambulance to pick me up and bring me home, so I should be home within the hour. Is Goliath all right?"

"Goliath is fine, thanks for asking after me."

"Why, what's wrong with you?"

"Oh, I give up. Ring me when you get home and I will bring Goliath back," she told him.

"Ok, got to go, the ambulance is here."

Celia glanced at Goliath, he was curled up in the armchair, he'd had a couple of walks, his dog food and some sausage. Fed, watered and content. What a life. *'I could do with a bit of that myself'* she thought, and went back to work, but not for long. Someone knocking on the door brought her to her feet and she was once more heading in the direction of the front door. This time Goliath stayed where he was, he recognised the footsteps.

The glamorous woman in the shocking pink coat and fawn trousers was back. "Jack tells me you have the key to his cottage," she told Celia.

"Does he?"

"May I have it?"

"No."

"He rang me and told me to come and get it from you."

"He has just rung me to tell me that he is on his way home. He did not tell me to give you his key."

"Nevertheless, he told me to come and get it. I have been to do Jack a bit of shopping this afternoon, and now I need the toilet."

"I would like nothing better than to give you the key and wash my hands of the whole affair and get all of you out of my hair. But I can't give a complete stranger the key to someone else's house, so you might as well go back and wait in your car for the ambulance, and let me get back to work. As for needing the toilet, do what Goliath does, use the nearest tree, there's nobody around to see you." And Celia closed the door on the shocking pink coat.

Goliath opened one eye and seeing Celia entering the office gave a half-hearted wag of his tail and closed his eye.

"Some guard dog you are," she commented, but he chose to ignore her.

She sat at her computer but concentration had deserted her. She had left the comfort of her noisy flat in Brookworth for the peace and quiet of the countryside. Today there had been none. She decided not to wait for the phone call from Jack to tell her he was back.

Standing up, she went into the kitchen, took a plastic bag and filled it with the dog food and Jack's towel, and picked up the leash. Goliath, hearing the familiar sound of the beloved dog leash, was out of the armchair and at Celia's feet before she could turn around.

Bending down she attached the leash to Goliath's collar, picked up the plastic bag and proceeded down her drive. Before she reached the lane, she saw the ambulance creeping passed, trying to avoid the potholes. It failed to achieve its goal.

Waiting until the ambulance had passed the end of her drive, she followed it up the lane with Goliath happily trotting beside her.

When Celia arrived at the bottom of Mr Firth's drive, the ambulance men were just climbing back into the ambulance, so she waited until they had driven back down the drive and out onto the lane. *'No woman ambulance driver this time, bet Jack was pleased about that,'* thought Celia.

The door was closed when she got there, so she gave it three sharp raps with the door knocker. Shocking pink coat opened it, and Celia handed her the dog leash and plastic bag and, without a word, she turned and went home.

Shocking pink coat watched with some amusement, the retreating back of her brother's next-door neighbour. When Celia had vanished into the lane, she closed the door.

"Looks like you've met your match, Jack," she laughed holding up the plastic bag in one hand and the dog leash in the other. "It's a good job you remembered about the key you left under the plant pot, because the dragon lady neglected to give me your front door key."

"She'll be back with it, unless you want to nip round and get it for me."

"Er, thanks for the offer, but no thanks."

"Sometimes, Kelly, I wonder about you," her brother said.

"Sometimes you wonder about me! You can sit there and say you wonder about me."

"What's wrong with that?"

"You are forty-two years old, you live like a hermit, you have a Jack Russell for a dog, for Christ's sake, and Mother's given up on you finding a wife. She is pestering me to get married so she can see her grandchildren before she dies, she's no spring chicken, you know. She blames me for not being born sooner, would you believe, she is always onto me because I am twenty years your junior, as if that is my fault. You are very selfish not to have married and left me to deal with Mother."

"No more selfish than our father, dying on me like that, and leaving me with two women. Am I forty-two? I don't feel it," Jack told her.

Kelly burst out laughing. "I came down to tell you Charlie and I are getting married. I thought it would be better to keep you and Charlie apart, that's why I left him at home, less arguments to deal with."

"Getting married are you, I hope he isn't expecting me to be his best man."

"No, Jack, I can categorically say Charlie does not expect you to be his best man. In fact, he said he would be surprised if you even turn up at the wedding."

"Can't be coming to any wedding with my leg in a plaster cast."

"Don't worry, your leg will be out of the plaster cast by the time our wedding day arrives, and I will expect you to be there, even if it is only to look after Mother."

"Why does our mother need to be looked after, what's wrong with her?"

"There is nothing wrong with her, she is very fit for her age, but it would be nice for her to have someone by her side, a companion, a friend or even her son."

"My leg is beginning to throb."

"Well, throw that damn dog on the floor."

Jack looked down at Goliath who, as soon as he had been taken off the leash, had jumped up onto Jack's lap and that's where he was going to stay.

"Missed me, old fella?" Jack asked the dog, giving him a big hug.

"It's a dog, Jack."

"Yes, well, when I talk to him, he doesn't answer me back, nor does he push me into going to weddings and chaperoning my mother."

"It's about time you got married," Kelly told him.

"Why the devil should I get married?"

"Because you need somebody to look after you, that's why."

"I've managed by myself all these years, I don't want to get married. Anyway, I have tried living with a woman and it didn't work. They want complimenting all the time, forever wanting new shoes or that sort of thing, too much hassle."

"I have to get back home, I am working in the morning, I would have been home by now if I hadn't had to wait and see if you are all right. How are you going to manage, getting your meals, getting dressed, to say nothing about having a bath? But more important than you, who is going to take your mutt out for his daily walks?" Kelly asked with amusement.

"I'll get Celia to look after us."

"Celia being?"

"Her next door."

"The dragon lady. Good luck with that."

"Goliath will be all right, he likes her. At least he doesn't growl at her when he sees her. She might even cook me the odd meal if I ask her nicely."

"Oh well, in that case, I will love you and leave you. Just so long as I know Goliath is going to be all right. As for asking the dragon lady nicely, you don't know how to ask nicely, Jack. So if, by some miracle, the dragon lady does take up your offer to let her make you the odd meal, before you eat it, make sure there's no arsenic in it. I'd like to be a fly on the wall when you ask her to give you a bath."

"Now that should be interesting, very interesting. Good idea Kelly, glad you thought of it," remarked Jack.

Kelly decided to ignore the remark, not wanting to conjure up that image of her brother in the bath with the dragon lady wielding the sponge so she went to get her coat, but Jack could hear her laughter echoing in the hall. Coming back into the living room, she said to Jack as she buttoned up her coat, "Are you sure there is nothing I can do for you before I leave?"

Jack looked across at her and asked, "Where the hell did you get that coat from?"

"Why, what's wrong with it?" asked Kelly, looking down at her coat.

"Are you colour blind? You need sunglasses on when you look at it."

"You have no taste, Jack. This is all the rage."

"It doesn't send me into a rage."

"What does it send you into?"

"Despair."

Kelly laughed and bent down and kissed him, "Oh, what it is to be old. Bye Jack, see you at the wedding."

"Not if I can help it," she heard him say as she went out.

Chapter Three

Celia had just finished typing the last document and was in the process of emailing it to her client when her mobile phone went off. She read the display: Jack.

"What?" she asked.

"Goliath wants his walk."

"Well, get shocking pink coat to take him."

"She's gone home, because she has to be at work in the morning, and I will be laid up for a couple of days until I get used to this damn plaster cast."

"I've got news for you, shocking pink coat is not the only one who has to work, so do I. And as far as I can remember, I don't work for you, or Goliath."

"Even if Kelly was still here, Goliath would not have gone with her, he doesn't like her. He likes you though, I could tell that when he brought you here, when I was on my back on the lawn. When I was being carted off on the stretcher, I looked over at you and Goliath and he was sitting happily at your feet, it set my mind at rest seeing that. So, you are the natural choice."

"You've got a bloody nerve. I have only seen you once before today and you called me a brainless woman. Now you think you have the right to order me around as though I have been put on this earth to make your life more comfortable. Well I have news for you — I haven't. Get shocking pink coat to do your bidding, she seemed to have taken a fancy to you."

"There is no need for that language, I wouldn't have thought you were a swearer."

"You are enough to make a saint swear."

"What about Goliath? He's looking at me like that."

"Like what?"

"Like he wants to go out, you know. If he does have an accident in the cottage, someone will have to come and clean it up."

"And that someone is me?"

"Well, you are my nearest neighbour, and that's what neighbours do, help each other out."

"Ring shocking pink coat, I'm sure she won't mind coming back and getting her hands dirty. Anyway, are you sure you want someone without a brain in her head to be in charge of your precious Goliath?"

"It's only when you women get behind the wheel you seem to change, I don't think your brains are equipped for the technology and all that. You should be all right with Goliath; he'll look after you. He's got brains you know; look how he came to get you. When I walk him past your cottage, I would say to him, *'There it is Goliath, the little yellow bug',* so when I fell off the ladder, I said to him, *'little yellow bug, Goliath',* and off he went to get you. I was dead proud of him for doing that.

"Why do you keep bringing Kelly into it, are you jealous of her? You have no need to be. She's my sister. I know appearances are misleading, and I don't look my age, but Kelly is twenty years my junior. Very embarrassing it was when I was in my twenties and my mother told me she was pregnant. And then, to cap it all, she goes and has a daughter of all things, twenty years old, and I have a baby sister. My mates had a good time at my expense I can tell you. By the way, how are you fixed for going to a wedding and looking after my mother?"

Celia listened to Jack and she was speechless.

After a short silence, Jack wanted to know. "I say, are you still there?"

All she could think of to say was, "Jack, you are unique. I'll come and get Goliath."

The End